BAREBACK

by

D.Jackson Leigh

2008

BAREBACK
© 2008 By D.Jackson Leigh. All Rights Reserved.

ISBN 13: 978-1-60282-071-5

This Aeros Ebook Is Published By
Bold Strokes Books, Inc.
P.O. Box 249
Valley Falls, NY 12185

First Edition: December 2008

Credits
Production Design: Stacia Seaman
Cover Design By Bold Strokes Books Graphics

Acknowledgments

I owe so much of *Bareback* to my friend and equine expert Dr. Cindy Kimbrell, for clearing out the passenger seat in her veterinary truck and letting me ride along on her client calls. While riding in that truck, we solved the problems of the world and puzzled over the complexities of women while she also answered millions of technical questions about horses and eventing.

I also must pay tribute to Radclyffe and all of the people who work so hard at Bold Strokes Books. You are the wind beneath the wings of so many writers.

Finally, I owe the publication of *Bareback* to my wonderful, sexy partner. Her blue eyes commanded me from the moment we met. I finally listened when hers was the voice that said, "Finish it."

Dedication

For Angie, my heart, and the late Cody.
When I was astride him bareback,
he made me feel as strong and handsome as he was.

GLOSSARY

Chevrons: a series of V-shaped jumps.

Coggins test: detects equine infectious anemia in a blood sample. EIA is transmitted to horses by insects such as deerflies and horseflies, so infected horses must be quarantined for the remainder of their life. There is no known cure, and the disease is ultimately fatal. An annual negative Coggins is required for horses to be transported.

Cross-country course: a rugged course through the natural terrain, filled with obstacles the horse must jump.

Double ski jump: two jumps at the end of earthen ramps with a downhill drop on the other side of each.

Flying lead change: a lead change in which a horse changes leads at the canter while in the air between two strides.

Lead: Refers to which front hoof a horse steps out on first—left or right—when taking a stride.

Oxer: a jump with two elements that create a spread, forcing the horse to move both vertically and horizontally.

Quirt: a short limber whip made of braided rawhide.

Steeplechase: a level racing track that has artificial jumps the horse must jump.

The wall: a jump of solid appearance such as a stone or board fence.

The combination: a series of three fences placed only one or two strides apart.

The water jump: a fence with a shallow pool of water on the other side that the horse must land in but retain his footing.

CHAPTER ONE

Skyler Reese poured some glistening oil into her palm and rubbed her hands together to warm the lubricant. She smiled as she began a loving massage.

Her long fingers danced softly over the gentle curves of the shoulders and stroked the perfect arch of the backbone. She was mesmerized by her sure, strong hands as she watched them in the dim light, dipping into the cup of oil at her side, then moving over the supple, tanned surface. They were the hands of a sculptor, smoothing and shaping a classic form.

Dip, stroke.

Her fingertips moved quickly to catch the excess liquid as it dripped down smooth flanks, gently spreading the droplets until they were absorbed.

Dip, stroke, stroke.

The object of her attentions yielded and grew warmer, more pliant under each brush of her fingers. The musky aroma coaxed forth by her touch filled the small room. The rhythm of her movements and the rich scent filling her senses brought calm to her restless soul. Skyler sighed and closed her eyes, reveling in the elusive peace that settled over her.

"I sure wish that was me you were rubbing oil all over."

The low, silky voice came from the doorway behind her, but Skyler didn't pause in her task. She'd heard the scuff of boots against the hard-packed clay of the Creek Barn's hallway before the curvaceous redhead appeared in the tack room. She could feel Alexandra Rourke's cool, hazel eyes moving over her, visually tasting. The bored socialite took in the dove gray riding breeches that hugged her long, lean thighs before disappearing into dusty, knee-high riding boots. The cool stare then lifted to sun-streaked locks that fell over Skyler's forehead. She kept her hair in a short, practical cut layered against her neck. The look was boyishly sexy, and she was used to second glances from women, and some men.

Alexandra sauntered forward, moving purposefully into her field of vision. She leaned against the wall, folding her arms across her ribs in a way that called attention to her ample breasts. The flirting had slowly escalated in recent weeks from small hints to blatant propositions. Skyler continued to work the leather of the jump saddle secured to a metal stand in front of her. Cleaning and oiling the saddles and bridles in her barn was her time for thinking. The wall full of soft, gleaming leather in front of her was a testament to many hours of reflection. That is, when she felt like thinking. Sometimes she just felt like polishing and not thinking at all. That's why the saddles in Creek Barn were the softest of any on the farm; she kept them well oiled after they were cleaned with saddle soap.

"What can I do for you?" she asked when her visitor showed no sign of leaving her to enjoy her solitude. "Isn't Clint keeping you busy enough?"

Alexandra pursed her lips in a practiced pout few men seemed able to resist. Perhaps she expected to wield the same power over a lesbian horse trainer. "That's why I came to see you," she purred. "Some trollop at Edward's law firm met Clint at a party and has been gossiping around the office about what a stud he is. Now, my idiot husband is insisting that I change trainers."

Skyler chuckled. Clint Hansen was the trainer at Cherokee Falls' West Barn and a good friend. "Well, he *is* a pretty fine specimen." She shrugged one broad shoulder upward to wipe the sweat that trickled past her temple onto the sleeve of her dark blue polo shirt. "So, did Eddie catch you getting more than a riding lesson?"

"Don't be crude, Skyler Reese. Of course not," Alexandra replied with an irritated toss of her shoulder-length curls.

Her pretense at indignation was wasted on Skyler. "Not that you haven't tried, I'm sure. You must be slipping, Alex. I've never known you to fail to snag whatever man you set your sights on."

Alexandra scowled. "Seems he has some rule about not touching married women."

That particular restriction wasn't in Skyler's rulebook. She looked up from her task and arched a "do tell" eyebrow.

Alexandra's pout slowly turned to a smirk. "But I know he wanted to," she purred. "There's always that certain part of the male anatomy that doesn't lie. I've had fun torturing him."

Skyler rolled her eyes. "That's my friend you've been torturing," she warned as she dipped her fingers in the oil again and continued rubbing it into the leather.

They were quiet for several moments as Alexandra's eyes followed the movement of her hands. Dip, stroke, stroke. Her fascination was almost amusing. Alexandra viewed other women as nothing more than competition, but, like quite a few straight women, she made an exception for Skyler, instead seeing her as a challenge.

She moved to the wall of saddle racks and pretended to study the equipment. Licking her lips, she lowered her voice to a husky Lauren Bacall timbre. "So, Sky, I thought my husband would be happier if I had a female trainer."

Skyler paused, lifting her gaze from the saddle to Alexandra's full red lips. "Did you?"

Alexandra sashayed over and ran a manicured nail along Skyler's tanned forearm. "I've never had a female trainer before. I've been thinking lately that maybe a woman might be an interesting change." She watched as Skyler resumed her swirling strokes across the gleaming leather. "So, I've talked to Kate about transferring my mare to Creek Barn. I'm betting the fact that I have a jealous husband doesn't bother you in the least."

Skyler took a deep breath and leaned back. She brazenly ran her eyes over Alexandra's voluptuous figure before returning her shameless gaze.

"No, I wouldn't have a problem with that, Alex. I feel sure you would prove to be an eager student."

They both smiled at the double meaning.

A cloudless, blue sky hung over the sandy driveways that tied the Cherokee Falls Equestrian Training Center compound together. At the center of the farm was a huge, white two-story house with a porch, which, true to its Southern heritage, wrapped three-quarters of the way around the structure. The long, main drive to the house was flanked on one side by a large outdoor riding ring and on the other by an indoor arena of equal size. Five twelve-stall barns and an indoor pool/gymnasium building were positioned on the perimeter of the compound like spokes on a wheel. Green enameled metal roofs gleamed atop each oak-sided building. Past the barns were a thousand acres of paddocks, pastures, and forest.

The grand matriarch of the Parker family had established the center two generations ago. Old money made from a once-booming tobacco operation on the Virginia property now rested in an endowment that provided for the equestrian center and its heiress, Katherine Leigh Parker—Kate to her many friends. Although the task of running the facility fit her perfectly, the role of rich heiress wasn't exactly descriptive. Her deep, sometimes booming, voice had loosened more than one rafter at the local country club in her wild, younger days, but time had softened her demeanor. Loose gray curls cut up over her ears were an attractive contrast to her tanned face and electric blue eyes. While she was still a formidable figure with an equestrian's grace and erect posture, the once muscular shoulders of her tall frame had softened and were now, like her waist, slightly more padded.

Sitting behind the steering wheel of her golf cart and staring across the Cherokee Falls compound, she paused to soak up the good weather and the tranquility of the moment. The smell of freshly mown pastures and the nickering of contented horses as they drowsed in the spring sun were as close to heaven as she could imagine. She sighed as her eyes settled on the Creek Barn, and her mind turned back to the task before her. So much for peace and quiet. She'd delayed this conversation but she couldn't wait any longer to spring her news on Skyler. Resigning herself to an uneasy discussion, she pressed on the accelerator and guided the cart toward the barn.

She found Skyler exactly where she'd expected. Skyler was the only horse trainer she knew who loved cleaning tack. It was the grunt work usually imposed on low-paid stable help.

"I don't know why you just don't delegate that to the barn help," Kate said.

Skyler flashed a smile that showed white against her tanned face. "It keeps me out of trouble."

"Then we need to haul a hell of a lot more tack down here for you to polish. I saw Alexandra leaving just now. If that's not trouble, I don't know what is."

The two women shared a grin of acknowledgment before Skyler returned her attention to her task. "I love the smell and feel of the leather."

Kate's shoulders shook with a deep chuckle. "I wouldn't spread that around. That would drive some of the women around here crazy."

Skyler's mouth curled in a slight smile as she stood to hang the saddle on its wall rack. She wiped her oily hands on a soft cloth. "Well, all done here. Want to saddle up and take a ride with me to the south pasture? One of the boarders said they saw a broken fence board near the oak grove."

"Not right now," Kate said. "I came down here to tell you that we've got a new horse coming in for your barn, and they should be here this afternoon. It's a stallion, so I want you around to help out in case he's a handful."

"Whose horse is it?"

"Jessica Black is the owner."

"Jessica Black?" Skyler frowned. The name was familiar, probably another spoiled debutante whose trust fund allowed her to play with horses rather than get a real job. Just what she needed. "Is she going to be training here or just putting her stallion in training?"

"You've got a problem with Jessica?" Kate's blue eyes narrowed. "Don't tell me you… Just how well do you know her, Sky?"

Whoa, where did that come from? Skyler raised her hands in surrender. "Not at all, Kate. I swear. I've never actually met her. I've just heard on the circuit that she's a real handful."

Kate's expression relaxed, but she still seemed wary. "Jess is just very intense, and something of a perfectionist, exactly like you, Sky. Her goal is to make the next Olympic team. And she was well on her way, too, until her horse slipped on the cross-country course."

"I think I heard about that. Her gelding was put down, wasn't he?" News of a horse being euthanized on the course traveled fast around the world of competitive eventing.

Kate nodded. "The fall broke his leg and hers, too. Pretty badly. She's had two surgeries and six months on crutches."

"That's rough."

"Yeah, well. This horse shipping in here today is her chance to get back on the circuit. He's been campaigned by another rider and is in good enough shape to make the trials. But Jess has to get herself into shape and get to know her new mount. I've promised to help her."

Skyler stared at the saddle, her hands completely still. There was nobody she would like to help more than Kate Parker. She owed her. But she knew what this meant. It meant going back to the circuit that had banished her as a professional rider several years ago. It meant probably running into Sarah again. "Kate, you know I'm not the right choice for this."

But Kate's tone left no room for argument. "I'm putting her in your barn because I want her to have the best trainer available. You've been there, Sky. You know how to get there again."

Yeah, she remembered the hard work, seven days a week. The relentless push for perfection. The egos. The politics. She shook her head. "Plenty of trainers know how to get there."

Kate held her gaze. "You can't hide here at Cherokee Falls forever. One day, you'll have to go back, and this is the best reason you'll ever have. Trust me, please."

Skyler released a drawn-out breath. Each trainer who supervised a Cherokee Falls barn was given full authority over the horses and riders assigned to that barn. But the Parker Foundation owned the training center, and Skyler realized that Kate's insistence was a gentle reminder of that. "All right. I'll give them a look."

Kate smiled her relief, then waggled a stern finger in Skyler's direction. "And...I love you, old friend, but I'm here to warn you that this one won't be another notch on your bedpost."

"She's that cute, huh?" Skyler grinned, glad for the move back to a lighter subject.

"Beautiful, just like her mother." Kate grew serious again. "Really, Jess is like a daughter to me, and she's coming here to recover." After a brief pause, she said, "Her mother means a lot to me. I promised Laura I would take care of our kid."

Our kid? Skyler was surprised. It was the first time she had ever heard Kate mention her only serious relationship. She knew there had been someone in Kate's life, but during those years Skyler had been a rider for hire, traveling the eventing circuit to make a name for herself. By the time she returned to Cherokee Falls, Kate was a confirmed bachelorette again and never spoke of what had happened.

Keeping private thoughts private was something Skyler understood and she had no desire to pry further, so she smiled and executed a mock bow. "Enough said. I'll be a perfect lady."

Kate laughed. "That I've got to see."

CHAPTER TWO

S kyler leaned against the barn door frame as a big pickup truck drew close pulling a sleek aluminum gooseneck trailer. After a sloppy parking maneuver, the driver climbed out of the vehicle and surveyed the paddocks while Kate looked over the paperwork he'd handed her. Powerful hooves drummed an angry message from inside the trailer.

"Son of a bitch!" the driver cursed. "I'll be glad to be rid of that devil spawn." He rubbed a fresh bandage on his forearm. "I'd watch him when you unload him. He bites and means business when he does."

Skyler made no move to approach the trailer. "It's your job to unload him. He's not my insurance responsibility until he crosses the threshold of this barn."

The driver mumbled something under his breath and motioned to a blond man waiting in the truck. "Come on, let's get rid of him."

Hooves slammed against the side of the trailer again as the two men cautiously opened the back door and stepped inside. The trailer rocked violently, and the blond man backed down the ramp in a hurry as a large Hanoverian charged headfirst after him, teeth bared. The driver yanked on the horse's lead line as the stallion dragged him across the yard, oblivious to the stud chain digging into the top of his nose.

"He's well-named," Skyler said.

"Rampage...yes. Jess said he was spirited." Kate turned around as a white Ford Explorer hurtled down the driveway.

The vehicle had barely skidded to a stop when the driver's door opened and a booted foot hit the ground hard, followed by the end of a cane. The young woman who sprang out quickly assessed the situation, then flung her cane down to hurry over and grab the lead line from the struggling man. Elbowing him out of the way, she spoke to the frantic horse in quiet, soothing tones that didn't match her quick movements and angry ice blue eyes. She turned the big bay in tight circles until he calmed and finally stood still, lathered with sweat and snorting his displeasure.

The driver spat on the ground and waved his arm in a good-riddance gesture.

The horse squealed, bared his teeth, and aimed for the nearest flesh—the young woman's arm. But she dodged his open mouth and grabbed his nose, rubbing it hard. The surprised stallion rolled wide eyes at her and withdrew his head.

"Still playing that game, huh?" she said firmly. "I've got your number, tough guy, and I'm not intimidated." She turned back to the driver. "I thought I told you to wait until I got here to unload him."

"I wanted him out before he hurt himself and tore up my trailer. You've got your work cut out for you there, lady," the man said before heading back to his truck. "Good luck," he threw back over his shoulder.

"What does he know, big boy? Dumb jerk got you all worked up," she muttered as she walked the big horse, watching his legs for any signs of lameness.

"Jess, Jess, Jess." Kate smiled. "You never have been one to take the easy way."

"Kate, it's so great to see you." Jessica moved away from the restless stallion to give her a lingering hug. As she stepped back, Rampage tried once more for a nip at her arm, but she dodged him without turning her head, grabbed his nose again and rubbed hard.

"I hope he's a quick study or you're going to rub all the hair off his nose before he quits biting." Kate laughed.

"He'll learn." Jessica's eyes danced. "You should see him move, Kate. I'll admit he's more high strung than I would usually take on, and I prefer geldings. But he's got more potential than I've ever seen in a horse." Her excited words tumbled out. "He's been trained for advanced dressage, but the people who owned him ignored the fact that he loves to jump. That was their first mistake. Their second mistake was the guy who was riding him didn't understand him and tried to muscle him. They racked up some good points on the circuit this year, but I think I can get more out of this horse with a different approach."

"Whoa, we'll see." Kate chuckled. "How about you, kid? How's that leg coming?"

Jessica rubbed her thigh. "It's okay. The therapists keep telling me to slow down, but I'm going to be ready for the trials. You'll help me, won't you, Kate?"

The pleading look was one Kate had never been able to resist, not when she saw it on Jessica's face, or, as she had many times, on the face of Laura, Jessica's mother. "I'll do everything I can, honey, but I won't help you hurt yourself if your body just isn't physically ready."

Jessica glanced around the riding center complex. It hadn't changed much since she was here last. Still felt like home. She gave Kate another hug, this time closing her eyes and pressing her cheek into the strong shoulder. Kate felt like home, too. "I'm so glad to be here," she said with a sigh. "Don't worry. I've made arrangements for a physical therapist to visit me out here twice a week to help strengthen this leg."

"That's fine." Kate laid her cheek against the top of Jessica's head. "Oh, honey, I've missed you so much." She was about to ask about Laura when a hideous scream erupted from the Explorer. "Lord! What in the world do you have in your truck?"

"Oh, that's Peach. He comes with Rampage. How about grabbing the pet carrier and bring it in the barn. I'll get Rampage settled."

"Second stall on the left," Kate said. She slid the carrier from the back of the vehicle and hefted it with some effort. "Are you sure you only have one animal in this box?"

"Yeah, just one. He's a really big cat."

Jessica turned the stallion toward the barn where a lean figure stood slouched against the door frame. The image of muscular thighs, slim hips, and broad shoulders burned instantly into Jessica's mind. Who the hell was that? Kate had mentioned a trainer she thought would be ideal. She hadn't included the word "hot" in her description.

As she led Rampage past the woman, he wheeled and snapped large teeth in the tall stranger's direction. One second of hesitation and the instinctive sidestep would not have saved her skin from the sharp incisors. But the woman was quick. Rampage threw his front foot out at her and squealed his anger. Jessica yanked his lead line hard to the side, spinning him around and through the open stall door. Hooves rained against the oak boards of the stall.

"Quick, bring Peach," she called to Kate.

Kate pulled a huge orange, battle-scarred tom with one tattered ear from the pet carrier. She slid the stall door aside just enough to shove the cat in with the agitated horse.

"He's going to kill that cat."

The low, sultry voice sounded very close to Jessica's ear. Goose bumps raced along her arms and she turned to find herself staring into velvet brown eyes. "No, he won't."

Skyler had to force herself not to hold that stare. Kate hadn't exaggerated. Jessica Black was certainly a head-turner. Skyler couldn't help but notice the way the gray riding breeches and short-sleeved polo hugged Jessica's firm, but feminine frame. Raven-black hair was held back in a loose French braid. Jessica's eyes seemed even bluer by contrast with her coloring, and something in her stare made Skyler feel a little off balance. It irritated her that the young woman's gentle, but commanding presence had the cranky stallion, and Kate, instantly eating out her hand. Worse still, Skyler wanted to like her, too, for the same reason. And she hadn't missed the quick, assessing glance as Jessica approached.

Skyler frowned. She wanted to gaze into the unusually pale blue eyes once more. That also bothered her. She moved her attention to the stall as the cat yowled like his tail was being trampled. The stallion stopped in mid-tantrum to sniff the demanding feline. The cat rubbed against the horse's legs and Rampage shifted carefully so he could rub his nose against the cat's fur.

"Well, I'll be!" Kate exclaimed. "I've never seen a horse quiet down so quick. Peach? That cat looks more like he should be named Killer."

She and Jessica grinned at each other.

"I don't want that horse in my barn," Skyler said, ignoring Jessica's challenging stare. *I don't want you here either. I don't need complications in my life.* "He's dangerous. Besides, it's a waste of time. You can't take the cat in the ring with you."

"*Your* barn?" Those disturbing blue eyes swept her up and down. "Geez. All this time I thought the center was owned by the Parker family."

Kate moved hastily between them. "Oh, allow me to make the introductions. Jessica Black, this is Skyler Reese, your trainer."

Skyler Reese. Jessica turned the name over in her mind. She'd sometimes wondered what had happened to the notorious Ms. Reese after the scandal that made her name taboo around the circuit. "Your reputation precedes you," she said pointedly.

Kate shot her a warning look.

As if to clarify her earlier statement, Jessica added, "You and Con Man were an awesome pair." Now why did she say that? To spare this woman's feelings?

"Your reputation precedes you, also," Skyler returned stiffly. Her face was unreadable, and, apparently, she wasn't going to elaborate.

Jessica turned back to the stall and watched Rampage snuffle his food trough. Anyone who hadn't been there five minutes earlier would think he was gentle as a lamb. "He's not dangerous," she insisted, in full defense mode. "He's just worked up because of those idiots who trailered him here today."

Skyler stared hard at her. Then, with a disgusted snort, she told Kate, "This horse *is* dangerous, and I've got too many of the kids working in this barn. Get one of the other trainers to take him."

She turned away abruptly and left the barn. End of discussion.

Jessica stared after her in shock. It had been a long drive, her leg ached, and she had only months to prepare for the trials. She didn't need a hassle. Who was this arrogant woman? Had someone finally taken her mother's place in Kate's life? Fuming, she muttered, "What a bitch."

"Whoa, now," Kate soothed. "I'll talk to her. She'll come around."

Jessica wasn't sure if she wanted a trainer who had to be talked into accepting her. "Maybe you should put me with someone else. I've got enough obstacles to deal with. I don't need a trainer I have to fight every step of the way."

"Skyler Reese is the best there is," Kate insisted. "She's the best trainer, you're the best rider, and you say Rampage has the potential to be the best horse on the circuit. She's been there, Jess. She's stood on that podium and had a gold medal hung round her neck. She can take you there, too. We'll find a way for you to work together." She gave Jessica's shoulder a little squeeze. "Trust me?"

Jessica did trust Kate. She'd trusted those merry blue eyes and bearlike hug since she was small child. She had her doubts, but she could see that Kate was determined to help and she respected her views. If Kate thought Skyler was the best, Jessica believed her. "Of course. You've never let me down before."

"And I won't this time. You'll see."

❖

Skyler helped a twelve-year-old girl mount a Welsh pony and sent her to join the three other kids posting around the outdoor training ring. "I'm serious about that stallion," she told Kate. "What would happen if he bit a plug out of one of them and a parent sued the center?"

"Skyler, every day these kids ride, we risk an accident. I know you'll take every precaution to warn them about the stallion. And if one of them doesn't listen and gets hurt, the center is well insured."

"Damn it, Kate. You know I have a hard time saying no to you."

Kate paid her trainers well and provided them with state of the art equipment. The only thing she, and the center, demanded was that, in addition to the top equestrians they coached and horses they were paid to train, each accepted several youngsters to teach from beginning riding to advanced technique. The program was funded by the center's endowment and children were chosen through an application process. Some had minor juvenile records and most came with troubled histories at home and at school. The program was free, but the kids were expected to work around the barns, mucking stalls, feeding horses, and cleaning tack to build their character as well as their equestrian skills. It was the same program that had been a refuge for Skyler once.

"Good. Then I'll play that card if I must to get my way on this," Kate said. "I want to help Jessica, Sky. She's been my heart since Laura and I lived together. I had to pretty much walk out of their lives back then, and I'll never forgive myself for letting Laura push me away. I can never get those years back that I didn't spend with Jess, but I want to be there for her this time. Do this for me, please?"

"I'll think about it," Skyler conceded. She rolled her eyes as a final act of rebellion.

"I'll count on it." Kate had never in any way insinuated that Skyler owed the Parkers for anything they had done for her or her twin brother, Douglas, but her tone left no doubt she was calling in that marker now.

Skyler rubbed the toe of her boot in the dirt. She could imagine what she was condemning herself to. Jessica was a distraction, the kind she didn't need. Cute. Smart. Great with horses. *I bet she gets her way a lot.*

"Looks like this group is coming along fine," Kate said, changing the topic before Skyler could invent another reason to refuse her. "You're great with the kids, even though I thought I'd have to hog-tie you to get you to do this."

"I wasn't too sure about working with them in the beginning," Skyler admitted. "But I guess too many of them remind me of myself at that age. Besides, you can never have enough little grunts around to muck stalls."

"Right, tough stuff. And that's why all the kids love you," Kate teased.

"Hey, I don't need you spreading rumors about how nice I am. It will ruin my reputation."

The easy banter between friends was their way of communicating "no hard feelings" from the earlier confrontation. But Kate wasn't going to let Skyler completely off the hook. "Well, you did a pretty good job upholding your reputation as a hard-ass with Jessica."

"That must have been quite a novel experience for her," Skyler said dryly.

Kate gave her a long look.

With a shrug of resignation, Skyler said, "Okay. I'll do it. But if there's trouble—"

"There won't be," Kate said cheerfully. "Jess is a professional. And so are you."

Skyler stifled the reply she wanted to make, instead calling to a tow-headed girl, "You look like a piston bouncing up and down, Jamie. This is a ballet, a dance. Let the horse's movement move you. Relax."

The girl's shoulders visibly relaxed and she closed her eyes to shut out everything but the movement of the sorrel Thoroughbred mare she was riding. Skyler smiled. She loved working with the kids. It was the only time she could drop her guard. They didn't judge her.

CHAPTER THREE

Jessica put the last of her clothes away and shoved the suitcase into the closet. Her leg ached and she reached for the pain pills she had been trying to avoid all day. *I'll just take one,* she thought. Better go see what was up with Rampage. By now, Ms. Reese might have moved him to another barn. She hesitated and then dropped a second pain pill into her pocket. She limped badly as she headed for the door where she stopped again. Letting out a deep sigh, she turned around and picked up the cane that was propped next to her bed. Her pride didn't want Skyler to see her using it, but her more practical half told her that she should pamper the knee as much as possible when she wasn't riding.

She leaned heavily on the cane, hoping the pain pill would kick in quickly as she trudged down the long drive to the barn. When she entered the cool, cavernous building, her eyes took a moment to adjust from the bright sunlight to the dim interior. A neatly raked dirt hallway was lined on both sides with roomy, twelve-by-twelve stalls that had eight-foot-tall walls, four feet of rough-cut oak at the bottom and four feet of vertical iron bars at the top. The wide hallway was empty except for a young girl pushing a wheelbarrow that contained a muck rake and manure droppings she was cleaning from the stalls. With her back to Jessica, she began to slide back the door on Rampage's stall.

"No!" Jessica yelled as the horse squealed and charged toward the opening. She flung herself forward using her cane to push the door shut. The girl instantly dropped to a crouch and threw her hands up to shield her face. At the same time, Rampage whirled and drummed his hooves against the stall door.

Heart pounding, Jessica stood frozen as a voice yelled, "What did you do?"

A hand seized her wrist. Ripping the cane from her hand, Skyler Reese shoved her roughly against the stall. The fury in her face was startling. Pain seared up Jessica's thigh. Her mouth worked, but no words emerged as she hunched against the rough boards.

"Did you hit her?" Skyler demanded. She was shaking.

Jessica glanced down at the trembling girl, puzzled by her defensive reaction. "No, I couldn't get to the stall door quick enough, so I used my cane to push it shut."

Skyler's dark eyes burned into her for another long minute before she turned to the girl. "It's okay, Jamie." Her face and voice softened as she pulled the girl to her feet. "You didn't do anything wrong. I should have told you not to go in that stall." She shot another withering look at Jessica. "This lady will clean that stall herself. It's her ill-mannered horse."

Jessica watched, speechless, as Skyler guided the girl into the barn's office and pulled the door firmly shut behind them. Jessica rubbed her aching leg and took a few slow breaths to gather herself. What just happened here? *Well, I guess it was just too much trouble to thank me for saving her butt because she didn't tell the kids to leave that stall alone.*

She pulled a chair into Rampage's stall, and placed it in the corner before sliding the stall door shut again and carefully lowering herself onto the seat. She wedged the cane against the chair to use as a prop on which to straighten and rest her painful leg. The big stallion shifted nervously and snorted at the human in his stall. Her confidence obviously puzzled him. He pinned his ears and shook his head. Jessica showed no sign that she'd noticed the display. Shifting to try to find a comfortable position, she reached into her pocket and found the second pain pill. After swallowing it, she worked to push the incident to the back of her mind. She didn't need the stallion to pick up on her agitation.

"You're not so tough, big guy," she told him once she had her temper under control.

The stallion's ears relaxed a little. He lowered his head and nudged his feline friend, but Peach only batted at the big nose. He seemed more interested in snuggling down into the hay and returning to his catnap. The Hanoverian shifted his white-stockinged feet and stared at her curiously with large liquid brown eyes that flanked a blaze of white.

"How's it going, handsome?" Jessica pulled a paperback book from her back pocket. "This is where we get to know each other better, boy. I hope you like *Black Beauty.*" She flipped through the opening pages, and settled back. "Chapter one…"

The horse's ears flicked back and forth as he listened to the melodious inflections of her voice.

Jamie's sobs slowed to hiccups as Skyler swabbed her injury and taped a Band-Aid across it. The elbow scrape wasn't that bad, not enough to cause the fear and pain Skyler had witnessed. Jamie was one of her favorites. She wasn't aggressive and belligerent, as Skyler had been at that age. But, like Skyler, she was a natural around the horses and quietly private about her life outside Cherokee Falls.

"Tell me what happened," Skyler asked. "Did she hit you or just scare you?"

"She didn't hit me." Jamie's voice hitched. Shame-faced, she looked down at her hands. "I didn't see her coming, that's all. It's no big deal. I'll just go finish my work."

Kids didn't just fall apart like that from being startled. Giving Jamie's new bandage a finishing pat, Skyler requested softly, "Jamie, turn around for a second. I want to make sure you didn't scrape your back when you fell."

Terrified eyes glanced toward the door, calculating the distance to escape.

"Come on, James," she said, using Jamie's favorite nickname to coax her. "You know I won't hurt you."

Jamie hesitated, then let Skyler draw her closer. She lifted Jamie's shirt just enough to expose her back and swore when she saw the old bruises crisscrossing the flesh. Jesus Christ. She should have realized it earlier.

Jamie shrank away. "I just fell down. It's nothing."

"No, it's something. Jamie, my teachers thought I was the most accident-prone child around because I always had bruises." Jamie stared at the floor, unable to meet her eyes. Skyler knew she needed to be gentle, but she struggled with the anger she felt, knowing someone had beaten this child. "When I was ten, my father twisted my arm so hard he broke my wrist. That's when the social work people stepped in, and I ended up here with Kate's mom. I know what it feels like to be too embarrassed to tell anyone."

"Please don't tell anyone." Jamie's voice grew plaintive. "Dad isn't home much. He drives a truck and goes away weeks at a time. Mom gets lonely, and when she starts drinking...I do stuff that makes her mad."

Skyler was shocked. "Your mom does this to you? Does your dad know what goes on when he's not around?"

"No, Mom and Dad love each other. She's good when he's at home. I swear she is."

Skyler wanted, instantly, to rescue and protect this child from further harm. But she knew firsthand the pain of a family breaking up. No matter how dysfunctional they were, the loss was a permanent sorrow. She took Jamie's hand gently.

"I know what it feels like to blame yourself, like it really could be your fault that an adult is using you for a punching bag. But it's not." She moved to the desk, scribbled a number on a small piece of paper, and tucked it in the girl's pocket. "This is my cell phone number, and I don't give this number to many people. Promise me that you'll call me if you ever need help, or even just to talk. You call me any time, day or night. You understand?"

Jamie nodded and wiped her nose on her sleeve. Skyler offered a box of tissues and a tentative smile crossed Jamie's face as she took a few. But the smile was fleeting, and she shifted her feet nervously. "My mom's not really a bad person. It's just hard for her when Dad's not around."

Skyler's heart ached at Jamie's plea on her mother's behalf. It never failed to amaze her the capacity some children had for forgiveness. Somewhere along the way, she'd lost that herself. "Sure, James. That goes for what I told you about my dad hitting me. This is just between you and me."

Jamie looked relieved, as though the sharing of secrets reassured her that Skyler understood. "I better get the rest of my work done."

"Stay away from that bay stallion," Skyler warned sternly.

"I will." Jamie paused at the door. "I guess that lady did save me from getting run over by that horse. You really yelled at her."

Skyler cocked an eyebrow at the gentle admonishment. "Yeah, I guess I did. I'll make it right with her. Don't you worry about it."

After the door closed behind Jamie, Skyler sat in her office for a while, contemplating her discovery. She absently rubbed her left wrist as visions of her drunk and angry father surfaced in her mind. She'd worked hard to lock those images away and she didn't feel like revisiting them now. She considered telling Kate about Jamie's home situation, but she didn't want to lose the girl's trust. Undecided, she left her office and strode down the wide hallway. Ahead of her several kids scrambled up from where they were squatting beside the oak door of Rampage's stall, and darted out of the barn. The little scamps were supposed to be doing barn chores, but Skyler didn't yell after them. She could hear a muted voice coming from the stall, and realized they'd been eavesdropping.

Jessica was reading to Rampage.

Skyler smiled to herself and turned back to avoid disturbing her, but the stallion's head jerked up and he snorted a challenge.

Jessica peered through the iron bars. "Oh, it's you." She sounded irritated. "I guess you've come to move us to another barn."

"You guess wrong." Skyler looked into the palest blue eyes she'd ever seen. They were more like white clouds swirling in a blue sky. "I shouldn't have yelled at you," she said at last. This was harder than she thought. But she'd promised Jamie. And Kate. "I hope I didn't hurt you, shoving you like that."

Jessica stared at her but did not reply. It was unsettling, the way those eyes seemed to probe her innermost thoughts.

"I guess I'm just a little overprotective of the kids around here." Skyler shifted from one foot to the other. She could see the suspicion in Jessica's eyes. She didn't want to betray a confidence. "You just scared Jamie, that's all."

Jessica frowned. So, the gruff trainer had a soft spot after all. The fact that Skyler averted her eyes and shifted her feet told her there was more she wasn't saying.

Skyler cleared her throat. "So, it was really my fault for not already posting a warning against entering that stall."

An apology and an admission of guilt? "I'm just glad nobody was hurt," Jessica said.

"Well, you'll still have to clean his stall," Skyler said. "I can't trust him around the kids."

There was that annoying arrogance again. "I always insist on taking care of my own horse," Jessica replied brusquely.

Skyler nodded and started to leave. Painful as it was, the apology had lifted a little weight from her shoulders. They had almost connected there for a few seconds. But now, the moment was gone. She looked back, tempted to say something else, and caught Jessica staring. *She's checking out my ass! And Kate was worried about* me *jumping* her!

Jessica quickly looked away. "Was there something else?"

Skyler studied her defensive stance and knew Jessica was trying to hide her need to lean on the cane. What she saw was a lot of pain, and a lot of heart. She'd seen that kind of courage in a few horses, but seldom so clearly in a rider. Maybe she'd been hasty in her initial evaluation of Rampage and Jessica.

"Oh, yeah," she said softly. "Con's favorite book was *Misty of Chincoteague*. I read it to him many times."

Jessica stared after the retreating figure. She must have meant Con Man, the gray gelding she rode to a gold medal. She remembered watching from the stands as Skyler Reese bent her head to accept the gold medal after her spectacular ride seven years ago. One day, she vowed, Skyler could sit in the stands and watch that gold being hung around *her* neck. She looked over at Rampage. The big bay stared back as he munched his hay.

Man, have we got a lot of work to do in the next few months.

❖

"Hey, Skyler. I hope you're hungry." Kate waved her spatula over the full grill. "Jess and Charlie have made enough hamburgers here to feed an army. We may have to send a couple out to West Barn."

"Yeah, well, Clint certainly can put away a few," Skyler said, pulling a chair up and settling into it.

She smiled as Jessica handed over an opened beer with a slice of lime stuffed in the narrow neck. Her dark hair was loose, softly framing her face and draping just past her collar. Skyler could not tear her eyes away as Jessica helped Charlie unwrap cheese slices to pass to Kate. They could have been brother and sister, both dark haired with blue eyes.

The eight-year-old did not hide his curiosity about the new arrival. "Are you alone, too?" he asked Jessica.

She looked uncertain for a split second, then seemed to realize he was wondering about her reason for staying with Kate. Jessica gave him a warm smile. "Oh, no, Charlie. I'm not alone. My mom lives in Atlanta. But since I never had a daddy, Kate has been a sort of second mom for me."

Charlie sighed like he carried the world on his small shoulders. "My mom is gone. She had cancer. She died and Kate let me come stay with her until they decide what to do with me. I don't have a daddy, either."

"Then I guess we're both sort of strays that have ended up on her doorstep," Jessica said. "So maybe we could be friends. That doesn't sound so lonely, does it?"

The boy brightened immediately. "Kate said Trekker could be my horse while I'm here, and nobody but me could ride him."

Skyler almost laughed at the abrupt change of topic. Charlie's mood sometimes seemed to shift by the minute.

"That's great," Jessica said. "Maybe we could take a trail ride together while we're both here."

"That would be cool. I can show you the trails." Charlie grinned up at her.

His awed expression made Skyler a little jealous, but she wasn't sure of whom. Was she jealous that her shadow was suddenly enchanted by Jessica? Or was she wishing it was her cheese slice Jessica was helping unwrap?

"Hello, Earth to Skyler." Kate waved a hand in front of her face.

Skyler blinked. "Uh, just trying to remember if I closed the feed room door," she lied, relieved that Kate didn't seem to notice the faint blush she could feel creeping up her neck and warming her ears.

"Well, make yourself useful and light the torches to keep the bugs away." Kate gazed around. "It's a really nice night. I think we'll just eat on the patio."

Dinner went quickly. Kate skillfully introduced conversation subjects she knew were common ground between Jessica and Skyler. They all laughed at Skyler's compulsion to build her burger always exactly the same way each time—mustard on the bottom, mayo on the top with tomato, then pickles. Jessica's habit of using a French fry to draw designs in her ketchup was the object of teasing until everyone began competing to see who could draw the best ketchup picture. Kate pressed Charlie into service as the ketchup art judge. She then hustled him off to get ready for bed as dusk had turned to dark, leaving Jessica and Skyler on the patio.

The still-burning torches cast a flickering light across Jessica's face. With her elbows resting on the table, she leaned forward and said, "I was there the day you won the gold medal. I remember thinking that you seemed so calm and confident. You and that big gray made those jumps look like it was just the same walk in the park you took every day."

Relaxed by the three beers she'd consumed, Skyler closed her eyes and was instantly back in that indoor arena. She felt Con Man rise powerfully over each jump. The sound of his hooves against the dirt flooring thundered in her ears. Her mind constantly ran ahead to the next jump before they touched the ground from the one they were clearing. Shorten his stride, line it up, find her balance, push forward.

"Tell me what it felt like," Jessica's soft voice urged.

Skyler opened her eyes. She'd been asked many questions about that day. *Were you nervous? Did you worry about the last jump? What are your plans now?* No one had ever asked her to put them in that saddle and tell them what it felt like to conquer. The experience was a treasure she'd kept to herself. But at this moment, it was a piece of her that she wanted to share with this woman whose eyes were filled with so much vision, so much want.

There was barely a foot between them. Her eyes never left Jessica's. "When we entered the arena and the crowd went silent, the quiet sounded louder than a million drums beating in my ears," she said softly. "It was one of those perfect moments, you know, when you feel yourself slipping into the zone…when you feel like you and the horse are one animal. The jumps seemed so small and Con felt so powerful. He seemed to know what I wanted before I even thought it. It was almost like we could fly if we really tried. I didn't really have to look at the clock when we hit the home stretch. I knew we had done it."

Skyler's eyes glowed as she relived the memory, and Jessica's heart soared with her over that last jump. "I want to be in that same place," she said fervently. "Rampage and I can do it. I know in my heart this is our time."

For a few seconds, Skyler simply stared at her, then she said, "Well, it *was* a 'walk in the park,' as you called it. We'd practiced it over and over until we could have run any course blindfolded. Reaching that pinnacle takes hard grueling training with few days off. I was healthy, and it still was hard for me."

"How did you do it?" The question sounded lame. Jessica explained, "I don't mean physically. I mean…"

"I know what you're asking," Skyler said softly. "It has to be the total focus of your life. There's no time for personal issues or downtime to rest. Not just for days, weeks, or even months. If we get you a spot on the Olympic team, the rest of your life goes on hold for *years* as you prepare. If you aren't absolutely sure you can make that kind of commitment, then it's best not to start at all."

"I have no personal life," Jessica said. "There aren't too many dates willing to take a backseat to a horse." She reached out impulsively and curled her fingers around Skyler's bare forearm. "I want this more than anything in my life."

Looking into those eyes, Skyler found herself believing just that.

CHAPTER FOUR

Rampage ran through flying lead changes with the abandon of a kid skipping along the sidewalk, his thick neck arched and chin tucked toward his broad chest. His gaits were smooth and flawless. It was hard not to be impressed. The power and presence of this horse drew Skyler back to the time when she first saw Con Man. She'd known then that she was watching the ride that would put a gold medal within her reach. Just like her gut was telling her now this big bay could be her next golden ticket.

"He's an incredible mover, isn't he?" Jessica's dark head was tilted in concentration, her eyes pinned to the stallion's every movement.

Champion, Skyler thought once again. But this time, she was looking at the gold medal hunger written on the younger woman's face. Maybe they could make this work. "He does seem to have what it takes," she conceded. "But, like I said last night, going for the gold takes a lot more than just talent. It takes a lot of discipline and hard work. Are the two of you mentally and physically ready for that?"

"I know he's ready. And I think I can be ready, too." Jessica could feel Skyler's hesitation. It was time for some real honesty. This would never work unless they learned to trust each other. "Look, I know coming into the trials just recovering from an injury like mine isn't ideal, but I've got this gut feeling that this is it. I know I can do this."

"The physical demands are a strain for a rider in peak fitness." Skyler glanced down at Jessica's injured leg. There was no mistaking the doubt in her eyes.

"Just give us a chance." Jessica needed Skyler to believe in her and Rampage. "God knows, you must know what it is like to have everybody saying, 'She can't do it.' Help me prove them wrong again, Skyler. I know Rampage and I can do it with your help."

Skyler looked out past the paddock and into the darkening woods. This woman knew nothing about her, she thought bitterly, or perhaps she wouldn't be so convinced she could be counted on. With a deep sigh, she said, "No sugar-coating. I want to see that leg. And I want to see how well you can ride with that injury."

The brilliant smile that lit Jessica's face nearly took her breath away. *Beautiful.* Skyler couldn't help but smile back at her.

"I'll show you my knee and give you a full medical report." This would be the real test, Jessica knew. She just hoped Skyler wouldn't back out once she saw fresh scars and the still-swollen joint. Besides breaking her femur in the accident, she had twisted her knee so severely that she'd torn most of the ligaments. The ACL, one of two ligaments that provide the stability to the knee, was so damaged that a new one had to be fashioned from her patellar tendon and grafted into her knee. The break in her femur had taken longer to heal, but was solid now. While the ligament had initially begun to heal quickly, it still remained painful as Jessica rushed her return to strenuous activity.

"Okay, we can meet back at the house and I'll have a look at your leg." Skyler held out Rampage's halter and lead rope, making it clear who would be tucking the stallion into his stall.

Jessica heaved an overly dramatic sigh. "I don't know why nobody wants to touch my pussycat of a horse." She whistled softly to Rampage, who trotted over.

Skyler grinned. She liked this more relaxed side of Jessica much better than the haughty debutante from the day before. She didn't want to be charmed by Kate's pet, but damn it all, Jessica was hard to resist.

❖

Jessica pulled a folder from the leather attaché that held her laptop and handed it to Skyler as they settled onto the couch in the living room. "These are the records I'm supposed to give to the physical therapist who will be working with me here."

Skyler opened the file and began to read. She did not have a medical background, but her years as an athlete and her experience working with horse athletes gave her enough knowledge of sports injuries to understand much of the report. After several minutes, she said, "This type of injury would be career ending for most athletes. If you were a horse, I would have immediately put you out to pasture."

Jessica had expected the sympathetic tone, and the fact that Skyler would pull no punches. She stared hard into Skyler's eyes. "When she first dreamed of the Olympics, Wilma Rudolph was a skinny girl recovering from polio. They said she would never walk again without braces. But she didn't give up. She limped until she could walk, then walked until she could run, and then ran until that gold medal was hanging around her neck."

"That was almost fifty years ago," Skyler said. "The competition is even tougher now."

Jessica was under no illusions about that. "Maybe my knee won't hold up. But maybe it will. Either way, I'm not going to spend the rest of my life wondering. I intend to find out for sure."

Skyler laid the medical records aside. "Let's see that knee, then."

Jessica stood and quickly dropped her jeans to expose her legs. A blush warmed her face. It wasn't just that Skyler's eyes were fixed on her string bikini panties rather than her knee; the disapproving scowl on her face made Jessica self-conscious.

"I'm hoping that isn't what you wear under your riding breeches," Skyler said.

"I…what should I be wearing?" Jessica felt exposed standing there in her skivvies, but Skyler's tone was all business.

"You should be wearing compression shorts."

"You mean like basketball players wear?"

"They'll support the major muscles that attach to your knee. Pick up five or six pairs at the sports shop in town."

Jessica nodded. "Okay, compression shorts."

"And an elastic support sleeve for that knee," Skyler instructed. "A huge part of training is working to ensure both you and your horse do not suffer injuries that will lessen your competitive chances. You wrap your horse's legs before you take him out to jump, don't you? Why shouldn't you take the same precaution for your legs?"

"I'll wrap the knee," Jessica repeated.

"Have a seat." Skyler waved a hand toward the couch before taking a seat herself on an ottoman next to it. "Prop your leg right here."

Jessica sat and plopped her good leg in Skyler's lap with a saucy smile. When Skyler rolled her eyes, she switched legs, warning, "It looks worse than it is."

Skyler probed, then carefully flexed the knee in all directions. "How much do you still use that cane?"

"Less and less often. If I've been sitting too long, it gets stiff and it still aches when I've worked it too much. I use the cane to give it a break when I'm not riding."

Skyler's long fingers slid down the angry-looking surgery scars on Jessica's shin. "You must have taken some spill to do this much damage."

It had been the worst moment of Jessica's life. She stared past Skyler, picturing the sky that day. Clouds were gathering and the wind was beginning to sway the trees on the cross-country course. She and her dappled gray Thoroughbred, Racer, were only a half point away from taking the lead in the competition. Racer was in top form and they'd sailed over the course, but the encroaching storm was beginning to distract him. The next jump was not one of the gelding's favorites. The approach was downhill and required that the competitor clear a fence and land in knee-deep water.

Jessica felt his tension as they neared the jump. "You can do this, boy," she'd urged.

Her sure hands relayed her confidence to the gelding and his ears pricked forward in anticipation. Just as they launched into the air, lightning split the darkening sky and thunder boomed. Racer twisted in midair, landing all of his weight on his right front leg. A sickening crack resonated in Jessica's ears and she felt them tumbling as Racer screamed. Pain shot up her leg. She struggled to breathe as many hands held her head and shoulders above the water. Was that her or Racer screaming?

"She's hung up in the saddle or something," someone yelled. "Cut her free. Hold that horse down until we can get her free."

Another voice, harsh with horror. "Oh God, look at his leg. Somebody get the vet here quick."

"Racer!" she heard herself scream.

Skyler felt Jessica shudder. The color had drained from her face and a fine sheen of sweat covered her brow. "Jessica?"

The vacant blue eyes refocused. "That spot is sensitive to touch because of the pins still in the bone." Jessica's voice was thin. "I'm still icing the knee occasionally, when it swells, and I'm scheduled to work with a therapist three days a week here on the farm."

Her tension stiffened the muscles beneath Skyler's hands. Sensing she'd entered sensitive territory, Skyler carefully moved upward, testing the tone of the calf muscle. "It's important that you tell me when it swells or gets too painful so I can adjust your training schedule appropriately. It doesn't mean we have to stop, it just means we may need to change the order in which we do some things, or find a way to compensate for any weakness in the joint."

Jessica tried hard to focus on what Skyler was saying, but it was getting difficult. She despaired at the heat she felt flush her cheeks as Skyler's hands moved higher up her thigh. But Skyler seemed oblivious, frowning as she resumed her probing back toward the knee, her manner exact and clinical.

"I'll also want to talk periodically with your physical therapist so I can coordinate what we're doing with what he is asking you to do. So, you need to let him know it is okay to discuss your case with me."

"Okay." Jessica was less than enthusiastic. She liked her privacy. "I've been riding on it for five weeks now, and jumping for about two weeks. It's been holding up fine."

Skyler was skeptical, but it wasn't her job to give a prognosis for Jessica's knee. Her job was to train her for the Olympic trials. If the leg didn't hold up, it wouldn't be because she hadn't given it her best as a trainer. "We'll start at seven tomorrow morning in the indoor ring. I want to see you warm him up and run him through the dressage moves."

"Thank you. I promise you won't be sorry." Jessica slid her leg off the firm length of Skyler's thigh and stood, not sure what else to say. She felt drained, but elated too.

As she pulled up her jeans, Skyler asked, "If you see Kate, would you mind telling her I want to talk to her about our last grain shipment before I leave?"

"Sure, I think she's upstairs. I'll send her down."

Skyler waited, staring uneasily out the window. She was crazy agreeing to this and she intended to say so, not that Kate would listen. Surely she knew deep down that Jessica had almost no chance. It seemed cruel to let her hope for the impossible.

"What's up, Sky?" Kate strolled across the room toward her.

Skyler dug an invoice out of her pocket. "That last shipment of grain you got from Emerson's has maggots in it. You need to call them to come back and get it."

Kate let out a disgusted snort. "That's the second time this year. I think it is time to take them off our vendor list."

"You won't get any argument from me."

"So?" Kate met her eyes. "What do you think?"

"About the maggots?"

"About Jess's chances."

Skyler took a deep breath and let it out slowly. "You don't want to know what I think."

"Yes, I do."

"Kate, you may be right about Jessica having the skill and the heart to do this, but she isn't being honest with herself. That knee isn't ready to hold up to the kind of training we'll need to do."

"We can't be certain about that," Kate said stubbornly. "Athletes come back from serious injuries all the time."

"It's not just the injury." Skyler let her frustration show a little. "This process was hard for me when I did it. Not only did I have two good knees, I was used to life being hard. I was mentally tough. Forget her leg, I think Jess is still too mentally fragile from the trauma of the accident. You should have seen her zone out on me when I mentioned it."

Kate rested a shoulder against the window frame. "My first instinct is to protect her from hurting herself more, but this is her decision, not ours. If we don't help her, she'll just go to someone else who won't care as much about her welfare."

"I'll put her through the training she'll need to win. Just don't blame me if she falls short. I'm not a miracle worker."

"I'm just asking you to give her your best, Sky." Kate's tone brooked no further argument. "Your best, and nothing short of it."

❖

Jessica sagged against the wall just outside the living room door. Skyler's words scalded her, rubbing every tender nerve raw. She retreated hastily down the hallway as she heard the two women approaching. Taking cover in the kitchen, she poured some juice. Her hand shook as she held the glass. Skyler didn't believe in her. *Arrogant son of a bitch. I'll show Her Royal Highness.* Even Kate sounded unconvinced.

She would show them both just how little they knew. She hadn't survived that day to spend the rest of her life mourning for all she'd lost. Her horse. Her strength. Her confidence. There was one thing she hadn't lost. Her dream.

CHAPTER FIVE

Sweat ran down her face with each leg extension. She used her anger to lift the weight around her ankle. She refused to acknowledge her anger was fueled by the fact that Skyler's assessment had given voice to her own nagging doubts. Next was twenty minutes in the hot tub beside the pool to loosen up the muscles she'd just worked, fifteen minutes icing the knee against swelling, and then down to the barn to saddle Rampage.

The Olympic-sized swimming pool sat under a glass dome adjacent to the fully equipped gym. Jessica hobbled out to the main room and dipped her fingers into the Jacuzzi to test the temperature, then looked around for her gym bag. Oh, crap. She was still half-asleep when she'd stumbled out of bed, and had forgotten to add her swimsuit to the rest of her workout gear. No way was she walking all the way to the house to get it.

She glanced around. The farm outside the pool's dome remained dark except for a few lights in the barns that probably were left on overnight. She turned off the overhead lights and left only the pool lights burning. The water in the hot tub was very warm and she felt the tension begin to leave her body as she floated in the silence. *Just relax. Think about Rampage. Don't think about Miss I've-Got-a-Gold-Medal.* She envisioned sailing over jumps, completing a perfect dressage routine. Collecting her own gold medal!

Grasping the side of the hot tub, she let her feet float out behind her and began the aquatic stretching exercises her physical therapist had prescribed. The splash of the water and the hum of the filtration system faded as she listened to her own breathing and saw that medal again, glinting as it was held aloft in front of her. Then the national anthem and the cheers.

"Uh, sorry to interrupt—"

Jessica froze at the closeness of the low, silky voice. She could hardly bring herself to look up. Skyler stood just a few feet away, with her arms folded across her chest and head cocked to the side. Her grin made Jessica's face burn. *Damn, damn, damn.*

"Sure is early in the morning for skinny-dipping." Skyler continued to stare down at her, obviously enjoying her embarrassment. "I do hope you're planning to wear clothes for dressage later."

Jessica clenched her teeth to stop the caustic remark on the tip of her tongue. She needed to get the upper hand on this woman just once. Collecting herself, she pulled herself up on the other side of the Jacuzzi and stood there naked, her unwavering gaze on Skyler. She waited for several seconds before sauntering toward her.

Skyler's heart beat wildly as the dark-haired vision approached. The image of a feminine, yet well-toned, frame burned into her brain. This was Kate's little girl. *You are her trainer. You will not look down.* The mantra her brain recited apparently wasn't reaching the part that controlled her eyes. For an ever-so-brief second they flicked downward.

Kate would kill her.

Skyler took a step back. Jessica was just trying to get under her skin. She stopped only inches away, her naked flesh almost brushing Skyler's shirt. Pale blue eyes looked deeply into hers. Skyler shifted her stance in a futile effort to relieve the building pressure between her legs. Her lips parted reflexively as she felt the warmth of Jessica's breath on her face. She reminded herself that she'd seen beautiful women before. They only played with her until it become inconvenient. Then they dumped her. *Remember?*

Skyler's clit twitched when Jessica's pink tongue flicked out to wet her full lips. A hot blush crept up her neck and burned her ears as she struggled to appear nonchalant.

"You said seven." Jessica lifted the towel hanging on the chair next to Skyler and stepped back to wrap it around her glistening body. "It's only a little after six."

Skyler sucked in a quick breath. "I...uh, I wanted to let you know I already fed Rampage a light breakfast." Her voice was hoarse. She let her gaze travel down the sculpted shoulders to where the soft swell of Jessica's breasts disappeared under the thick towel. "We probably should go over his training schedule in my office before we head to the ring."

Amused by the effect she was having, Jessica couldn't resist pushing it a little. She pulled the ends of the towel loose and brushed them across her erect nipples, wiping the droplets of water from them. Skyler's eyes followed her movements before snapping to safer territory.

Looking everywhere but at her, the trainer said, "I want to see you work the stallion on...dressage this morning and on the jumps after lunch."

"Yes, that's what you said yesterday. I'll be there as soon as I get dressed." Jessica strolled toward the locker room. "I just have to ice my knee for a bit first."

"Sure. See you there." Skyler didn't move. She stood staring down at the Jacuzzi.

Not so cocky now, are you? But you are lethally cute when you are flustered. Jessica paused at the locker room door. "I said I'll be right down," she repeated.

"Oh, right." Skyler gulped a deep breath to regain her composure, then turned on a booted heel and exited with long, smooth strides. Images of Jessica's pale, shapely hips filled her thoughts. Groaning, she muttered, "Yep, you are a big complication."

❖

Skyler's boots crunched in the sand as she headed for the refuge of Creek Barn's office. The more she thought about how easily Jessica had made her feel like a drooling idiot, the more her mood soured. She'd seen plenty of breasts before. She couldn't believe she'd stood there stuttering like a stupid teenager. Skyler liked being in control. She resented the way those moments by the hot tub felt…like free falling with nothing to stop her. The heat was still rising up from her collar, and the throbbing between her legs irritated her. She just needed to get laid, that's what. Too many nights in the barn lately.

Her eyes were drawn to the headlights traveling up the main drive. *Alexandra Rourke.* Coming in early to braid up Shoshanna's mane before her ride. Skyler quickened her pace as she drew closer to the barn. It was time to head back on to more familiar ground.

She entered the dim interior a few minutes after Alexandra had parked and disappeared inside. The full hips of the auburn-haired woman swayed as she pulled the comb through the mane of her sorrel Thoroughbred. Oh, yeah. Skyler licked her lips in anticipation and moved in on her prey.

Next to the smaller woman's ear, she asked softly, "Is it my imagination or have you been trying to seduce me?" Alexandra froze as Skyler pressed her against the horse she was grooming and massaged her buttocks. "Well?" Skyler prompted, reaching around her body to caress her breasts. "Tell me what you want."

Alexandra's chest heaved. "I want you to make me scream when I come."

Skyler chuckled. "I had such a hard-on when I woke up this morning, I was thinking of taking matters into my own hands.

But here you are, those luscious hips swaying back and forth, inviting—no, begging—for a good fucking."

She placed hot kisses down the back of Alexandra's neck. The redhead tried to turn to intercept them with her own, but Skyler held her firm, grinding her hips against Alexandra's fuller ones. God, she was turned on. She needed to feel in control, and she could sense Alexandra loved to be controlled. She was one of those women who wanted her to talk nasty. To take her.

"I know what you need, Alex, and you're just what I need right now."

Skyler began to free the buttons on Alexandra's jeans. She heard a whimper as she worked her fingers toward the wetness that soaked Alexandra's crotch. She found the growing clit and stroked it once, twice, then withdrew her fingers and leaned in so Alexandra could hear her licking the moisture from her hand.

"You taste so good."

Alexandra whimpered. "Oh God. Please, Sky."

"How can I resist when you ask so nice." Skyler ground hard against her quarry's buttocks.

"Why, Skyler, I didn't know you cared so much," Alexandra singsonged in low, silky tones. "Let's go up to your apartment."

But Skyler held her firmly, pulling her away from the horse. "No. Right here. I don't have much time." She took Alexandra's hands and placed them on the feed trough fastened in the corner of the stall. "Keep your hands there."

"Sky, God, you make me so hot."

Skyler pulled the tight jeans down to reveal Alexandra's milky white hips. Stroking her fingers through the wet heat, she commanded, "Tell me what you want. I want to hear you say it."

Alexandra moaned. "Please fuck me, baby. Fuck me hard."

Skyler slid her fingers quickly inside and began to thrust. She hated herself for needing this, for feeling she had to prove something to herself. She reached around to roughly massage Alexandra's clit. Alexandra stiffened and convulsed as she quickly peaked. On impulse, Skyler dropped to her knees and bit hard on the trembling haunch.

Alexandra whirled around to face her. "Jesus, Sky. Did you have to mark me? How am I going to explain that at home?"

Skyler's low chuckle echoed in the stall. "Tell Eddie the horse bit you. He won't know the difference."

"He's going to make me buy a new horse. Christ, you didn't even kiss me," Alexandra complained.

"You didn't ask to be kissed." Smiling, Skyler brushed a quick kiss across the other woman's pouting lips.

Alexandra pulled her face close. Her urgent hands tangled in Skyler's hair. "Oh, baby, you have a very talented mouth."

"Oh, you like this, huh?" Skyler kissed a path along the delicate jaw line and traced the outline of Alexandra's small ear.

"Please, Sky."

"Please what? Please stop?" Skyler traced her fingertips in a teasing dance down Alexandra's soft abdomen to glistening curls. She nudged the redhead's legs apart to insinuate her hard thigh between them and press against the hot apex that wantonly opened to her. Nipping at Alexandra's hard, pink nipples, she rolled her knuckle against her clit. Alexandra's red manicured fingernails raked down her back, drawing a low growl. She gasped as Skyler's strokes grew harder and faster.

"Oh, Sky! Sweet Jesus!"

"Come for me, Alex," Skyler demanded as the red nails dug into her narrow, muscled hips. She abandoned her stroking and plunged her fingers, two then three, deep inside. Using the thrust of her hips, she drove her fingers hard and fast as she bit down on the pulse that hammered along Alexandra's straining neck. Alexandra's body arched and Skyler felt the muscles tense around her ramming fingers as she reached the edge of her orgasm.

"Oh! Oh, Sky." She convulsed into a screaming orgasm.

"I love how wet you are." Skyler slowed, but continued the stroke of her hips and the thrust of her fingers until Alexandra fell limply against her, gasping for breath.

"Twice! I hardly ever have even one orgasm with Eddie." Alexandra's hot, hungry mouth found hers. After a greedy kiss, she pulled up her jeans and said, "I could get used to this."

"Yeah, well, I'm afraid I only give equestrian lessons. If your husband needs lessons in the bedroom, you'll have to find another instructor." Skyler straightened up and tucked her shirt in. "I'm going to take a quick shower. I've got horses to work and lessons to give. I don't need the stallions smelling sex all over me."

Alexandra pouted. "Well, you're not totally unlike my husband. That's it? Get your rocks off and you're done?"

"The difference between me and Eddie, my dear, is that you were the one who got your rocks off," Skyler said. "Sorry about that bite mark on your neck. You'll have to think of something to explain that to him."

Alexandra's hand flew to her throat. "Bitch!" she muttered.

Skyler grinned. "Seriously. Eddie doesn't deserve you. Thank you, Alex."

Alexandra ran her fingers through her auburn locks. "Any time, stud."

Would there be another time? Maybe, maybe not. The truth was, Skyler would really rather just take care of her needs herself. But she enjoyed being in control. She was empowered each time she passed the test to her satisfaction, taking everything offered to her and then being able walk away without a twinge of emotion or regret.

She would never be hurt again. Not as long as she could still pass the test.

❖

Skyler quickly washed up in her apartment, then hurried downstairs. She whistled softly to herself as she made her way down the center aisle of the barn, pausing to throw a wink at Alexandra as she passed Shoshanna's stall. Alexandra blew a kiss at her, and then went back to braiding the Thoroughbred's mane.

The office door was open, but Jessica leaned against the wall outside of the doorway, arms folded and a distant expression on her face. Skyler quickly shut out the image of the naked woman standing in front of her by the hot tub. She concentrated instead on the milky white buttocks from moments before. Yeah, that worked.

"Ready to plan out some training schedules?" Skyler asked.

"If it's not an inconvenient time for you," Jessica snapped.

Skyler raised an eyebrow, but before she could reply, she felt Alexandra's hand brush across the seat of her riding breeches.

"Just got to get some more rubbers, um, rubber bands for Shoshanna's mane," Alexandra purred as she gently insinuated herself between Skyler and Jessica. Directing an insincere smile at Jessica, she added, "And, honey, no time is inconvenient for Eveready here." She brushed a fleeting caress across Skyler's cheek before disappearing into the office.

Skyler glanced at Jessica, and then looked quickly away, unable to meet her eyes. She flushed with embarrassment. This was what she wanted, wasn't it, that Jessica would know she was bad news, like everybody said?

"See you later, sugar." Alexandra breezed back through the office door. Trailing a possessive hand across Skyler's belly as she passed, she headed for her horse's stall.

The look on Jessica's face said it all. She wouldn't flirt with Skyler again, not after this. Skyler stared at her boots. She felt sort of sick. For some reason, it mattered what this beautiful woman thought of her.

Jessica watched a myriad of emotions swirl in Skyler's dark eyes. A moment ago, she'd felt only disgust when she entered the barn. The moans she'd heard were loud enough to leave no doubt what was going on. Skyler hadn't noticed her, but Alexandra's gloating expression was like a slap in the face. Jessica had been almost breathless with anticipation walking down from the pool, looking forward to being alone with Skyler and having her complete attention. She felt foolish now, yet she saw something in Skyler's expression that surprised her almost as much the trainer's awkward stuttering by the Jacuzzi. She saw pain and self-loathing.

"Jess, I feel like I owe you an apology," Skyler said gruffly. "I thought you'd be a while in the gym." She rubbed at some dirt on her hand. "We had an appointment. I'm sorry I kept you waiting."

"No harm done," Jessica said. She reached out to still Skyler's fidgeting hands, but Skyler jerked away.

Jessica stared at her. Something just didn't fit. This woman was arrogant and insufferable, and obviously thought she was God's gift to women...and horses. But Kate had seen something in her, enough to entrust her with Jessica's career. And Jessica kept glimpsing someone entirely different from the player she'd heard about. This seesaw of bad girl versus noble trainer was enough to give her whiplash.

"Let's get to work," Skyler said, ducking into the office.

Jessica followed her, still angry over what she'd seen but determined not to show it. The next hour was all business. They evaluated Rampage's strengths and weaknesses. Then they charted his training schedule for the upcoming months, right up to the competition. The challenge of the competition ahead fed a need they shared, to test themselves and win. It was a comfortable common ground that allowed Skyler to relax and be herself.

While Jessica reviewed the chart they'd made for Rampage's training, Skyler studied her softly sculpted profile. She'd never seen a more beautiful woman. But Jessica Black was out of her reach, just like Sarah. To women like them, Skyler would always be a stray from a screwed-up blue-collar family. The really sad thing was, she didn't need Kate to tell her she wasn't good enough for Jessica. She already knew that herself. She'd known it from the moment she laid eyes on her.

"I think we're done here," she said, rising from behind the

desk. "See you at the indoor ring as soon as you get Rampage saddled."

"Okay." Jessica stood.

Skyler strode to the door, then paused. "My personal shortcomings have nothing to do with my abilities as a trainer," she said, dropping all pretense that they were talking about anything but the incident with Alexandra. "I'll make sure they won't be a problem in our professional arrangement."

❖

The dressage session at the indoor ring started smoothly enough. Rampage was initially nervous and danced impatiently. Jessica expertly quieted him and worked the reins until he yielded to the bit and settled down to work. Skyler called out advice from the sidelines and occasionally stopped them to demonstrate a specific technique that would improve their performance. It didn't take long to see that her advice was already making a difference. Jessica moved quickly to correct herself and the horse when they misread each other. The stallion slowly began to relax and his confidence in his handler grew. Skyler watched silently as they glided by. Jessica's lips were pressed together in concentration. Focus wasn't going to be a problem.

They worked on the dressage patterns for well over an hour before Skyler waved her in. "Let's give him a rest, then try him over the jumps in the outdoor ring after lunch. Not a bad workout," she allowed.

"Well, he's too tight in that end turn and tensing during the crossover."

"Stop right there," Skyler said sternly. "At the end of each session, I want him to pick up nothing but positive feelings from you. This horse wants to please you. He doesn't need to work hard for an hour, and be left with the feeling he just didn't measure up."

Jessica's knee had been screaming with pain for the last

half hour of the session and the abrupt lecture grated on her raw nerves. "Are we talking about the horse or your ego?"

Skyler ignored the question. "At the beginning of each session, we'll talk about the things that need improving and immediately work on them. We'll saddle back up at one. I've got a horse to ride myself right now." Skyler started to leave, but looked back at Jessica. This power struggle between them wasn't going to work. "If you don't want my advice, then I can't be your trainer. I promised Kate I'd do this, so you'll have to be the one to ask for someone else. You know…a trainer who lets you tell them how to do their job."

Jessica stared at the retreating back. Of all the egotistical, infuriating women. Right when she'd started thinking Skyler might just be okay. *You're not getting rid of me that easy. I'll show you, you arrogant horse's butt.* No, horse's butt was too good for her… Pig butt. Yes, that was it. She was a pig's butt.

Rampage tossed his head as he sensed her irritation.

"Whoa, boy. That's not directed at you. Okay, Ms. Reese, we're only thinking positive thoughts. Happy thoughts, Rampage. Good boy."

She stroked the strong neck and turned the steed toward the barn for a good rubdown. The afternoon would be their real test. She needed to ice her knee and grab a pain pill before tackling those jumps. Maybe that would take the edge off her anger.

Jessica hummed softly to herself as she entered the barn. What she saw made her stop dead. Skyler already had cross-tied Rampage in the aisle and was nearly finished saddling him. She checked her watch to see if she was late. No, ten minutes early.

"You didn't have to saddle him for me." She prepared herself for another lecture.

Instead, Skyler offered a tentative smile as she pulled the irons down the stirrup leathers. "Consider it a peace offering."

Jessica couldn't hide her surprise. "Does this mean you've changed your mind about trying to get rid of me?"

"Maybe we need to quit reacting to each other based on some preconceived ideas. I was wrong about Rampage. He's very impressive. And...you're an exceptional rider." Skyler paused. "But you have a tough road ahead."

Jessica chewed her lip, waiting for the whiplash again. But she was wrong this time, too. Skyler's tone was matter-of-fact.

"I could tell your leg was hurting you this morning, but you never complained or let up. You don't need to fight me and the pain at the same time."

Jessica sighed. She knew she needed Skyler if she was going to make this bid for the Olympic team her best effort. She also knew she could prove to Skyler that she had what it takes to be a winner. "You're right. And it was good advice...this morning. I guess I get grumpy when the pain gets too bad. But Rampage shouldn't suffer because of it. I know I snapped at you, but I do want you to call me on my mood again if you see it affecting our workout." She extended her hand. "Let's start over. Hi, I'm Jessica Black."

Skyler grinned broadly and returned a firm handshake. Rampage nodded his head and pawed at the dirt as if to punctuate the truce. Laughing, Jessica waited as Skyler unclipped the crossties, then followed her and the stallion toward the jumping ring.

If she had any worries about jumping Rampage, they quickly vanished. He approached the course with eager confidence and "jumped big," clearing the obstacles with inches to spare.

"He's impressive, all right," Skyler said as Jessica reined the prancing steed in and walked him over. "I find it hard to believe that he's only been training as a dressage competitor. He's got the power and timing of an exceptional jumper."

Jessica grinned down at her from the saddle, flushed from the success of their jumps. "He loves to jump. You just tell us what to do, and he can do it."

Christ, she was beautiful. The unbidden thought startled Skyler. She looked away and cursed herself for letting her attraction to this beauty seep into her conscious thoughts. A deep breath helped her refocus.

"We need to work toward three goals," Skyler said. "Condition him for the stamina he'll need for the three-day event competition. Condition your leg to hold up. And help the two of you get to know each other's cues."

Jessica listened carefully as Skyler described a couple of revisions to the training schedule they'd mapped out. The daily dressage would be shortened so he could get more jumping experience and conditioning. As a stallion, Rampage already had an advantage in the strength and stamina departments. But Skyler wanted them to work on his control over the jumps.

"The more he jumps, the more excited he gets and the less he listens to your cues," she explained. "We have to teach him to focus his entire attention on you."

Jessica patted the big horse's neck. "We're ready, aren't we, boy?"

Her enthusiasm was contagious. Skyler squinted against the sun and returned her smile. Just for a few brief moments, they both let down their defenses and shared an unguarded admiration for the big horse.

"Why don't you turn him out for the rest of the day and let him relax?" Skyler suggested. "But, don't forget. You get to clean his stall."

Jessica shrugged. "I don't know why everybody makes such a big deal over your stall, Rampage. You're just a big, misunderstood pussycat." She smiled down at Skyler as she turned the stallion toward the barn.

Pussycat? Skyler let out a breath she found herself holding. She meant the horse, right?

CHAPTER SIX

It wasn't even noon and already it was hot, unseasonably hot and humid for the end of May. A drenching rain the day before had kept them inside, so Jessica had taken Rampage out for his conditioning trots first thing. Now they were enjoying Rampage's cooling bath in the outdoor wash stall. She hummed softly to herself as she used a hard plastic wand to scrape the excess water from his gleaming coat.

"How's the next gold medalist doing this morning?" Kate's teasing voice sounded behind her.

"He's doing just fine," Jessica responded, knowing Kate was referring to her, not the horse. "We worked out early because of the heat."

"Excellent!" Kate grinned back. "I heard a couple of riders who might be at the trials are showing today near Richmond. It's only a little over an hour away, so I thought you and Skyler would want to go check out the competition."

Jessica cocked her head, running through her mind which riders may be there. Over the past few weeks, she and Skyler had settled into a comfortable training pattern. Rampage was an incredible horse and the three of them were quickly bonding into a championship team. She and Skyler had decided not to enter any of the intermediate shows leading up to the trials. Rampage had enough experience showing, and she and Skyler relished the thought of being the mystery team at the trials, rather than risking injury to show what they had all across the countryside beforehand.

"Have you asked Sky yet?"

"No, and I'm not traipsing all over Cherokee Falls to find out who she bedded last night," Kate said. "She never seems to sleep in her own bed anymore."

"Don't believe everything you hear," Jessica said stiffly. "She's always at the barn when I go looking for her." She didn't know why she felt she had to defend Skyler's honor. Her reputation was earned, but Jessica still didn't like the jokes and insinuations she heard about the woman she was quickly learning to respect and trust with the most important thing in her life, her quest for the gold.

"I've known her for a long time," Kate said.

Jessica knew she was being warned off, and that Kate meant well, but she wasn't willing to believe everything she heard. "I think half her reputation is just gossip. People expect her to be out somewhere and spread rumors no matter what the facts are."

"Whatever." Kate sounded resigned. "I'll go see who is right today. You go get cleaned up and ready to go."

The ride to the show went quickly. Kate drove and Jessica sat up front with her, while Skyler stretched her long legs out across the backseat of the truck. They started out talking over the competition, but the conversation between the three quickly turned light as Kate began to recall for Jessica some embarrassing moments from Skyler's early introduction into the horse world.

"Yeah, young Sky was pretty sure someone was pulling a joke on her when I first showed her that her job would be to muck stalls," Kate said. "She was such a city kid, she couldn't believe I wanted her to pick up huge piles of horse poop."

"Kate," Skyler warned.

Kate laughed. She'd known Skyler since a teacher-friend of the Parker family brought her and her twin brother to Cherokee Falls. The two ten-year-olds were being abused at home and stayed with the Parkers off and on for many years, arriving whenever their father came home from his construction job building large bridges. Except for near-identical features, the twins were night and day. The self-confident Skyler was aggressive, risk-taking, and volatile. The shy, awkward Douglas had a genius I.Q. and tutored his sister patiently through the more complicated subjects at school. She was his champion, protecting him from the teasing of other children and interceding with their father, taking beatings meant for Douglas.

Kate was in her early thirties then, and Skyler became her constant shadow at the farm. Horses were truly her calling. She was a natural rider and intuitive trainer. She seemed to find animals easier to relate to than people and the horses she schooled responded to her in the same way.

"You've got to know by now that Skyler always thinks there must be a better way to do almost everything," Kate continued with her story. "So, one day, I keep seeing her take the horses out of the barn and walk them around like they are dogs. Then I notice that when they finally poop, she puts them back in their stalls." Between howls of laughter, she explained, "After a while I realize she's trying to housebreak…or I guess barn-break them, to go to the bathroom outside."

Skyler folded her arms over her chest. "Very funny."

Kate wasn't done. "So I snuck in the barn and heard her telling this big chestnut mare what a good horse she was for going to the bathroom in the pasture, not her stall. But that mare would pee a bucketful the minute you put her in a stall with fresh, clean bedding. So there's Sky with a smug look on her face leading her into a clean stall…I can still see it." Tears began to roll down Kate's face, she was laughing so hard. "God, I wish I'd had a camera when it sounded like someone had turned on a fire hose behind her."

Jessica was wiping away her own tears of laughter and holding her sides. Skyler's embarrassed look, the brown eyes peeking from under the thick blond bangs the wind had whipped around her face, was just too precious. Jessica had never seen this playful side of the all-business trainer. She definitely wanted to see it more often. She could tell that, even being the brunt of the laughter, Skyler was enjoying the easy camaraderie.

"Hey, Kate. I just bet you know a story or two about Jessica, too," Skyler prompted.

Kate raised her eyebrows. "Hmm. Did I ever tell you what a hard time her mother and I had keeping clothes on her when she was little?"

"Do tell." Skyler grinned.

"Don't you dare." Jessica knew exactly where this was headed. Kate loved telling people about her exploits and Jessica had a feeling she would embellish them for Skyler. To spare herself, she decided to strike first. "Apparently I was an exhibitionist. I removed my clothing in restaurants and anywhere else likely to make Mom and Kate cringe. Enough said."

"Oh, no. You have to do better than that," Skyler teased. "I want an example."

Jessica was tempted to remind her about that morning several weeks ago, when they stood by the hot tub. But she didn't plan to relive that moment in front of Kate. She preferred to pretend it had never happened and had carefully maintained professional boundaries with Skyler ever since.

"I have a story," Kate said. "We were on a plane—"

Jessica covered her face with her hands. "No, please. Not the plane story."

"Turnabout is fair play," Skyler said.

Kate nodded agreement. "Sorry, Jess."

"Okay." Jessica raised her hands in mock-surrender. "But I get to choose the story. Tell Skyler about the dinner party Mom threw for Gram and her little group from the Daughters of the Confederacy."

Kate groaned. "I'm afraid that moment has been wiped from my memory banks."

"I'll bet." Jessica slapped her shoulder playfully before turning to Skyler. "Well, I was about four years old and I wanted to see what was going on that was so special."

Kate interrupted. "Laura and I were on pins and needles. It was the first time our mothers had met, and we were hoping they would like each other."

"I came downstairs," Jessica said. "But it was a warm evening—"

"So, she shows up in the dining room when we're in the middle of dessert," Kate interjected. "She's butt naked and telling these stuffy bluebloods that she wants ice cream."

Skyler smiled. "Kids run around naked sometimes. I don't know why anyone worries about it."

"Oh, the crime wasn't being naked. It was what I said when Gram asked me, 'Jessie, honey, where are your pajamas?'" Jessica lifted her chin in imitation of her four-year-old self. "I simply told the ladies that if Mom and Kate didn't have to wear pajamas, then I didn't either."

"No." Skyler guffawed. "You didn't!"

"Oh, she certainly did," Kate growled. "I could see my life flashing before my eyes. You could have heard a pin drop as Little Miss Jessica strutted her naked self over to me, climbed in my lap and took a big drink from my water glass, then waved good night over her shoulder as she skipped back down the hallway to her bedroom."

"Oh, my God. What did you do?"

"Well, we were stunned. We just sat there until we heard her bedroom door shut, then Laura said, 'That child has the most vivid imagination.'"

"Gram was horrified," Jessica said.

"My mom thought it was funny seeing me stuttering and trying to smooth things over," Kate added. "She was used to me not giving a damn what other people thought." She paused, and a soft note entered her voice. "I wanted to laugh, but Laura would have killed me later. She was trying to make everything so perfect."

Skyler chuckled, but Kate's wistful tone made her wonder again what had happened between her and Jessica's mother. They were lovers and she'd said something recently about Laura pushing her away. It sounded like Kate still cared, and she and Jessica had remained close. So, what went wrong?

❖

The sun had broken through a thick cloud cover only a bare hour before, so although the day was warm and the sun's glare strong, the parking area, little more than a commandeered pasture, was still slick with mud.

"Good thing this truck has four-wheel drive," Kate grumbled as she parked.

Skyler eyed the mud. "Jess, maybe you should grab your cane. This mud looks pretty slick."

Jessica frowned. She hated that cane. She saw it as a sign of weakness. Secretly, in the back of her mind, she'd been looking forward to showing up at this event with Kate and Skyler in tow. Cherokee Falls was well known for producing winners. She relished the thought of showing off a bit and making the competition uneasy.

"I'm fine, Sky. Don't worry about it. I don't even think I brought the damned thing."

Skyler fished around in the back of the vehicle and produced the cane. "There's no point in taking chances. You could rip that knee out again with one slip in this crud."

Jessica stood with her hands on her hips, refusing to accept the cane. She had a better idea. "That cane could get stuck in the mud and make things worse. Why don't you just carry it for me, and I'll hold on to you. I'm sure I'll be safe hanging on to your arm."

Kate snorted. Did she see Jessica just bat her eyes? When Skyler obediently offered her arm Kate's mouth dropped open. Jessica looked like the proverbial cat about to eat the canary and Skyler was blushing. Shit. Kate wanted them to be friends, but the chemistry between them felt like dangerously more than that.

Skyler helped Jessica navigate the bleachers to reach a good vantage point about midway up. There were a lot of Olympic wannabes on the roster but probably only one serious contender for the trials. That was Rachel Sorensen and her German bred Trakehner. Skyler didn't miss the fact that Rachel's husband and trainer, Joe, was sitting with several of Virginia's horse community bluebloods just a few rows from them. He watched with interest when she and her companions took their seats. *That's right,* Skyler thought, *check out the women who are going to steal that Olympic team slot right out from under you, buddy.*

Kate nudged her. "See that chestnut stallion over by the barn?"

Skyler followed the direction of Kate's nod. Her eyes traveled over the lean neck, tapered shoulder, and long legs. "Nice. Isn't that the stud over at Rolling Meadows?"

"That's him. I was thinking of breeding Summer to him next season."

"I thought you were going to retire her."

"I'd like to try her one more time. She's still young enough and never had any problems."

Skyler shrugged. "For my money, I'd wait and think about breeding her to Rampage if you are looking for just one more shot."

"What? And end up with a bad-tempered baby? Why, I'm shocked that you would suggest that."

Skyler knew she was being teased. "Yeah, well, he does have some redeemable qualities. He's a great jumper, very solid, and a good pedigree. You could do worse."

Kate shot Jessica a "you-go-girl" look.

"Besides," Skyler continued. "I figure Summer is so good

natured, maybe she could prevail and produce an offspring with at least a decent temperament, even with that demon horse."

Jessica swatted Skyler on the arm. "That's my boy you are bad-mouthing, and he's a sweetheart. A little misunderstood by most people, but a real sweetheart."

"Yeah, so is Skyler," Kate joked. "Misunderstood...by too many women."

It was routine for Kate to tease Skyler about her womanizing reputation, and Skyler's usual response was cocky and boastful. But she didn't play that game today. The teasing made her uncomfortable, perhaps because she sensed Jessica's disapproval. She covertly studied the smaller woman. She wanted this partnership to work. The tug-of-war between them had ended and training was progressing better than Skyler had anticipated. Training an Olympian could sort of fill out her resume, she told herself, but there was more at stake for her than improving her credentials. She had come to admire Jessica and wanted her to succeed. She liked the way she communicated with her horse. She liked the fact that she never mentioned her injury, even when it was obviously causing her a lot of pain. And she never quit until a training session was done, no matter how much she hurt. Skyler didn't want Kate's flippant banter to affect the way Jessica saw her; she'd already made more apologies to this one woman than she had to all the others in her life.

The thought of spending the afternoon with Kate and Jessica looking over the competition had sounded like a good idea to her. She thought it would motivate Jessica to see what she was up against. Also, Skyler hadn't been off the farm in a while. She shrugged off the question nagging at the back of her mind: Why had she stuck so close to the farm lately?

"Damn," Jessica complained. "I forgot to find the restroom before climbing all the way up here."

Skyler pulled the cane from where it rested between her feet. "Take this. You should use it to get back up these bleachers and save the wear and tear on your knee." As Jessica began to protest,

Skyler softly patted the muscled thigh next to hers, gentling her the way she would a skittish colt. Her eyes radiated her understanding. She knew the proud rider hated to show her weakness, temporary as it was. "There's a method to my madness," she said softly. "You see the guy sitting two rows back?"

Jessica's eyes flicked discreetly over Skyler's shoulder. "In the blue shirt?"

"Yes. That's Joe Sorensen, Rachel's husband. We are going to see him again at the trials. He's already checked us out. Obviously he knows who you are. I'd rather they saw you limping. Let them think you're not a threat."

Jessica looked doubtful, but the gentle stroking against the top of her thigh was distracting. She found herself mesmerized by the slow smile that creased Skyler's handsome face.

"We can surprise them in a few months when they find out you and Rampage are really their worst nightmare." Skyler held Jessica's gaze a moment longer. *God, those blue eyes are gorgeous,* she thought. She held out the cane again, and this time Jessica accepted it without protest.

Kate didn't like what she was seeing. The affection on Skyler's face was obvious as her eyes followed Jessica's descent down the bleachers. Kate loved Skyler like a younger sister, but she also knew her shortcomings. She loved Jessica in a different way, as a parent with a fierce protective urge that surpassed her regard for her close friend.

"Don't even think it," she growled in Skyler's ear.

Skyler flinched, then leaned back, resting her elbows on the vacant bench behind her. "I don't know what you're talking about."

"I can see what's developing between the two of you." Kate watched Skyler's gaze flick once again to Jessica's trim frame before settling down at her own feet. "The chemistry needs to be good between you two to be a successful threat in the show ring, but Jessica is young. She may not know how to draw the line to keep it professional, not personal. You need to draw that line."

Things never changed. Kate Parker had always treated her as an equal, but she was still a blueblood from the right side of the tracks. Apparently she didn't want a mutt like Skyler coming after someone in her family. "Good enough to be her trainer, but nothing else, huh, Kate?"

"Sky, it's got nothing to do with how worthy you are. You know I love you. You're a great trainer and a really good friend." Kate sighed. "But we both know you can't stick to one woman. If you need to scratch an itch, I'm asking you to do it with someone other than my Jess."

What she felt for Jessica wasn't an itch to be scratched. It was more, and that scared her. Truth was, Skyler herself was afraid she wouldn't be able to handle those feelings, and she *would* end up hurting Jessica. That mattered to her a whole lot more than Kate's concerns. Yet it hurt worse that her mentor didn't trust her, that she seemed to think Skyler would use Jessica. Skyler stared darkly into the crowded bleachers. She hated herself for not being worthy. And, at that moment, she hated Kate for pointing it out. And she resented Jessica for being so beautiful and talented and wonderful…and, hell, sexy, too.

"There's nothing going on between us but work," she told Kate. "But now that you mention it, maybe I do need to scratch an itch."

She'd spotted an old conquest she knew would be more than eager for a scratching session. She rubbed her sweaty palms on her jeans. The idea of chasing after a bed partner didn't seem all that appealing, but she started down the bleachers anyway. "Don't worry about me after the show. I see my ride home," she threw over her shoulder at Kate. Then she paused and turned, the old Skyler leer firmly in place. "Do me a favor and ask Clint to feed for me in the morning. I probably won't make it back to the farm until tomorrow afternoon."

"Sky, wait!"

But Skyler ignored Kate's call and stomped down the bleachers.

"Shit." Kate knew Skyler's choice to have only casual sexual experiences was a form of self-punishment, a way of reminding herself that she wasn't worthy of anything deeper and permanent. It was typical behavior, resulting from physical abuse as a child, but after years of careful nurturing from Kate's mom, she had seemed to overcome her low self-esteem. She'd fallen deeply in love with Sarah Berrington Tate, and her career as a rider took off. She was at last something other than the abused, belligerent waif the Parkers had rescued.

But Sarah's betrayal had crushed her, and Kate had doubts that Skyler could ever recover. It was a hard choice: protect Jessica or trust Skyler's fragile emotions. Jessica was the only daughter Kate would ever have. The only part of Laura, the woman who would always own Kate's heart, Kate still possessed. She would not allow Skyler to damage her.

❖

On her way back from the restrooms, Jessica took some time to watch the contestants in the warm-up ring. Rampage had it all over these horses, she gloated. Their workouts had been going really well, and the knee was still holding up. Skyler really had been able to sharpen their performance.

Skyler. Jessica smiled at the thought of her.

They were proving to be a good team. Kate was right. Skyler had been in that winner's circle and understood what it took to get there. She was steady and sure in her instructions. It made Jessica feel a confidence in herself that she hadn't felt before, and Rampage responded to the change.

A couple of times during the past weeks, Skyler had ridden him herself to see what kind of cues he was giving Jessica and recommend responses that could improve his performance. When Skyler took the saddle, she and her mount became one beast. Even the temperamental Rampage bowed to her commanding confidence and moved smoothly through his paces. The roguishly charming trainer atop twelve hundred pounds of equine muscle was the sexiest thing Jessica had ever seen.

Her pulse jumped at the thought and she stumbled slightly. She was eager to get back to the bleachers and take her place next to Skyler again. Maybe they could go to a nice restaurant before they headed home. Why she wanted to spend more time with Skyler outside their training arrangement wasn't something she wanted to analyze just yet. She was looking forward to the afternoon and didn't plan to spend it trying to second-guess herself.

Jessica took a shortcut through the barn next to the warm-up ring, and was surprised to spot Skyler leaning against the entrance talking to a very attractive, slender blonde. Not just talking. There was something else going on. The blonde was standing a little too close for casual conversation, and Skyler was gazing down at her.

Jessica forced a pleasant expression on her face as she approached the pair. "There you are, Sky. Rachel and her horse are warming up, so they must be on the program soon. We should get back to our seats."

But Skyler avoided looking at her. Waving a dismissive hand, she said, "You go ahead."

Jessica felt her hackles rise. "I thought we came here to evaluate horses and riders. To see who our competition is."

"I'm going to watch from down here," Skyler said.

"You'll miss Rachel's run through the jumps."

The blonde finally dragged her eyes away from Skyler to look Jessica up and down. "Do I know you?"

"Amy, this is Jessica Black," Skyler said with obvious reluctance. "I'm training her and her stallion. Jess, this is Amy Satterfield. She's…"

"An old playmate," Amy supplied. She trailed a slender finger along the outline of Skyler's deep-cut V-neck shirt.

"Are you coming or not?" Jessica asked Skyler.

The hesitation said it all. "I told Kate I'd meet you guys back at the farm."

"Fine." As Jessica turned on her heel, she heard a stifled giggle.

The blonde's smug words followed her. "Pity about the accident. She must have been quite attractive before it happened."

❖

"Let's get out of here," Jessica snapped, hovering over Kate.

"Now? Isn't Rachel coming up in the program soon?"

"Not much point in evaluating the competition without our trainer, is there?"

"Well, I'm here. What am I? Chopped liver?"

Jessica's shoulders slumped. She was tired. The sunny day was suddenly too warm, the glare too bright, and she wasn't in the mood for company anymore. "Do I have the only trainer who is terminally in heat? She draws every bitch in season like a magnet."

Kate didn't reply, but her eyes were apologetic. The gentle older woman was a steady, bright spot in Jessica's life, and had always been her confidante for issues she didn't want to discuss with her mother. But, Kate wasn't the person to talk to about her confusing feelings for Skyler.

"I must be PMSing or something," Jessica said. "I just want to go home, okay?"

"Sure, baby, whatever you want. I'll just go make sure Sky has a way home if she isn't coming with us."

"If the blond hussy I saw her with earlier has anything to say about it, Skyler may not be home for days," Jessica muttered.

"Yeah, well, that's our Skyler."

Jessica glared at her. "That's *your* Skyler."

Kate wrapped an arm around her shoulder. "Honey, you need to accept who Sky is. She's one of the best trainers I've ever worked with. And, she's not a bad person. In fact, she's the best friend you could ever have. She's just lousy in the love department. There are reasons for that, reasons that are too deep and too personal for me to share with you. That's up to her to share if you become good enough friends. But to get the good part of Sky, you have to allow for her flaw. When you accept that, you'll have a friend you can always rely on."

A friend. Jessica sighed. Trouble was, she seemed to want more from Skyler. Her mind ran wild, replaying images of Skyler. She couldn't stop thinking about the sexy trainer, seeing Skyler on Rampage or rubbing oil into a saddle. She constantly fought not to notice her body or wonder how her touch would feel. Common sense told her she needed to keep Skyler at a distance, but she wasn't sure if she could suppress her impulses indefinitely. She had to keep her mind on the prize, and most of the time she could, but seeing Skyler with that blonde made her want to cry.

"Jess, I'd have to be blind not to see the chemistry between you guys," Kate said. "But you shouldn't pressure Skyler for more. She has a lot of respect for you, and her leaving us today is her rather stumbling way of discouraging you. She knows her limits."

"And I know mine," Jessica said. God, if she started dreaming about her, too, what was she going to do?

Chapter Seven

Rampage made steady progress over the hot summer months that followed, but the pain in Jessica's leg never let up.

"I don't like the looks of this." Richard, her physical therapist, flexed the leg again. "That graft should have healed long ago."

"I'm too close to getting what I want," Jessica said. "I'm not going to let a little pain stop me."

"Pain is a message from your body that something isn't right. If you push this injury, you could rip that whole knee up again. Then you may not be able to ride at all, much less jump."

Jessica refused to meet his stern stare. "I'll take my chances."

"I'm telling you now that you are probably slowly shredding that ACL graft. You should get it scoped again to see what's going on."

"I can take a few months off to let it heal better after I make the Olympic team."

With an impatient snort, Richard lowered her leg. "Your knee probably won't last that long. I don't know how you are jumping horses with the kind of pain you are in now."

"It's got to last that long. What about another steroid injection to take down the inflammation?"

"You just had one four weeks ago. Those shots are supposed to last at least eight weeks."

Jessica stared out the window at the deepening shadows of late afternoon. "Can't we make an exception this time?"

Richard mumbled something beneath his breath, then said, "If you won't listen, I'll go talk to your trainer."

"You absolutely will not!"

Skyler had sat in on Jessica's first appointment with Richard, but Jessica had conveniently forgotten to sign and return the form for access to her medical records. There was nothing Richard could do but back down, and they both knew it.

"I'll keep quiet for now, but I can't believe Skyler can't see how much pain you are feeling," Richard grumbled. "She should know better. I guess she's only concerned about the horse's legs."

"That's all I pay her to concern herself with," Jessica shot back.

Richard fell silent, massaging and stretching her leg.

Jessica felt guilty about pressuring him to compromise his professional ethics. "I'm sorry," she said after a few minutes. "I shouldn't have asked for the extra shot, Richard. I know you are just looking out for me. Don't blame Skyler, though. I've done a pretty good job of hiding it, and she's been working Rampage herself on the cross-country course to give me a break."

"I'm just asking you to slow down," he said.

"Okay, I will." Jessica hopped down from the table, careful to land with most of her weight on her good leg. "See you next Thursday?"

Richard frowned. "Hey, use that cane when you can."

Jessica hobbled down to the barn a few hours later. Rampage was going to get only a short chapter tonight. After Richard's manipulation, her knee was painful and she needed to pop some more pills for relief. The sky had begun to dim as twilight approached. The kids and other equestrians in training had all gone for the day. The only sound was Clint Black's voice drifting softly from a barn radio and contented munching as the barn's equine residents dined on a supper of sweet feed and orchard grass hay.

Grabbing the paperback she'd been reading to Rampage, Jessica was headed for his stall when Charlie appeared at the other end of the barn. He motioned silently for her to join him, then pulled her toward the barn's rear opening, whispering, "Want to see Skyler dance with Con Air?"

In a green meadow sprinkled with yellow chickweed flowers, Skyler sat bareback astride her large dappled gray gelding, the brother to Con Man. She still wore her riding breeches, but soft moccasins had replaced her knee-length boots. The horse wore only a bridle and the reins lay across his withers rather than in Skyler's hands, which rested casually on her thighs.

Ghostlike in the dying light, horse and rider melded magically into one being as they executed a flawless crossover and passage. When they approached the center of the meadow, the gelding halted. A smile slid across Skyler's face as she closed her eyes and raised her arms in imitation of a ballerina. Taking an undetected cue, the big horse pivoted slowly on his hindquarters in a complete circle. He then pranced forward in a goose step, holding alternating forelegs an extra beat, each touching the ground as the other lifted to repeat the similar step. Skyler's eyes were still closed as she extended her arms out to her sides like a high-wire walker.

Jessica was mesmerized.

"It's beautiful, isn't it," Charlie said in a reverent whisper.

"Yes, it is," Jessica breathed. "How does she get him to do that?"

"She says to really be one, there has to be nothing between you. That's why she isn't using a saddle. She feels what he's thinking, and he feels what she's thinking," Charlie recited. "She showed it to us in class one day when she was trying to teach us how to use your legs to tell the horse what you want him to do."

Con Air wheeled and moved diagonally across the field in another crossover move.

"It *is* like a dance," Jessica said. "I can't imagine what it must take to teach a horse that."

"Sky's the best."

Jessica could understand his hero-worship. She would never have guessed Skyler would be a soft touch with the kids, but over the past few months she'd seen her amazing patience with them. She even helped with their homework, always insisting on seeing their finished assignments before she would let them take their saddles out of the tack room.

Jessica gave the boy a quick hug. "Thanks, Charlie. Thanks for showing me this. You better scoot now. I heard Kate say you were supposed to help her grill burgers tonight."

As he scampered away, she turned once again to watch Skyler for a few moments.

Your mystery deepens, Skyler Reese. And I love a good mystery.

❖

Jessica waited in the dusty parking lot of the honky-tonk with the Explorer's window wound down. She wasn't going in that place until Bruce arrived. She'd have every redneck around hitting on her. She must have been nuts to agree to meet him here on a payday weekend.

She was relieved when her friend's black Firebird pulled in next to her and his tinted window slid down. "Hey, beautiful." The driver grinned. "I sure was surprised to hear you needed old Bruce's services. Let's go inside and have a beer."

Jessica eyed the stocky, former pro football player. "Just show me how to use the stuff, Bruce. I don't want to go inside."

"Uh-uh. We'll fix you up, but then we need to go inside and test it. You do want to know it's going to work before you pay for it, don't you."

"Yeah, I guess I do." Jessica limped over to Bruce's car and got inside.

He patted his thigh. "Just lay that knee over here and relax. Think good thoughts." He pulled a small vial from his console and filled a slim syringe from the contents.

"What were you able to get?" she asked.

"Just lidocaine, the stuff the doc would use to deaden your skin to sew up a cut. We're injecting it right under the kneecap to deaden the inflamed tissue that's causing you so much pain. I'll try to get you some bupivacaine, but my contact for that wasn't around on such short notice. It lasts longer and is better for orthopedic stuff."

Jessica had worn loose jogging pants so her knee would be easily accessible. He prodded the swollen joint. "Damn, Jess. This doesn't look so good. You sure you want to do this?"

"Just do it, okay? Let me worry about my health," Jessica snapped.

"Hey, whatever you want, babe." Bruce showed her where the injection should go on each side before sliding the small needle into her skin. "You know, since you're around horses, vets normally use Carbocaine or mepivacaine. It lasts longer than lidocaine, too. You should check around the barn to see if there is any stuck in a cabinet somewhere. All this stuff is pretty cheap, so nobody keeps a close eye on inventories of it."

He shot half the syringe into one side of her kneecap and the rest on the opposite side. He rubbed his hand along her silky leg. "You always did have great legs, and now you have a very sexy scar on this one."

Grimacing from the sting of the shot, Jessica said, "That's where they put the pins in. And you run that hand any farther up my leg and I'll have to call up that bad-tempered redhead you live with and tell her you were hitting on me."

Bruce jerked his hands up and held them aloft in surrender. "Hey, just giving you a compliment. No need to threaten my manhood. Let's go see if this works."

They headed into the smoky bar and took a table away from the dance floor. They ordered two sandwiches and a couple of beers. Before they'd even gotten their food, Jessica's knee felt very numb.

"Okay, time for a little two-step to test it out." Bruce stood and offered a hand. Unlike a lot of former athletes, he kept himself in good shape. Jessica was surprised that she was able to move comfortably for the first time in months. The knee was nearly painless. She grinned up at Bruce and he twirled her around a few times in celebration.

Back out in the parking lot, he pulled two more vials from his car. "That's two hundred dollars, little lady."

"I thought you said this stuff was cheap."

"Risk mark-up. My contact takes a risk swiping it, and I take a risk selling it to you." He held the vials just out of her reach, and his eyes grew serious. "Be careful, Jess. Use it too much and you'll do permanent damage to your knee and never feel it. How do you think I screwed up my football career? Total knee replacement is no fun and a real career ender."

"I'll be careful," she said, handing over the money. She couldn't wait to ride Rampage free of pain.

Lantern-shaped lamps lined the main drive as cars pulled up to the house and deposited their guests. The cars were then parked near the gymnasium by valets. The yard was illuminated by string after string of lights, and the large brick patio served as a dance floor. A live country-western band cranked out Garth Brooks and Shania Twain tunes for the dancers while caterers pulled sizzling burgers and tangy barbecue ribs off a hot grill.

The dance was the biggest local fund-raiser put on by the Parker Foundation each year. This year's western theme promised to be a fun evening for both the upper crust who paid five hundred dollars a plate to attend and students of the youth equestrian program who, along with their families, were honored guests.

Skyler paused at the edge of the lights to wipe the pointed toes of her dusty western boots on the back of her jean-covered legs. Attendance was mandatory for center staff, but Skyler didn't mind. At least the party's theme allowed her to dress in something comfortable. Her tall frame fit well into the faded Levi's and dark blue V-neck knitted top that accentuated her broad shoulders.

"Hey, Sky. I've been waiting for you to get here. I need a dance partner." Clint Hansen's eyes glowed and he held out his hand as an invitation. "Come on, let's show these shufflers a step or two."

"I do declare, I just can't resist such a handsome devil," Skyler replied in her best Scarlett O'Hara voice.

"You have to let me lead," Clint warned.

"I guess you'll never get better if I don't let you practice. Lead on," she replied with a mock sigh.

She was teasing, of course. Clint was an excellent dancer. He was several inches taller than Skyler's six feet and was ruggedly good looking. He knew and accepted Skyler's sexual orientation, but her height and graceful athleticism made her the perfect dance partner. They appeared to be the perfect couple as they glided a fancy two-step across the dance floor, Clint twirling Skyler and her following with ease.

He had been one of the few people not influenced by Skyler's blacklisting from the circuit. As a trainer, he'd tried to throw a few rides her way, but the owners he worked for had sided with the other gentry and threatened to hire a new trainer if he continued to employ her. That was before they both came under Kate's protective arm. Only Kate had enough money and influence to stand firm against blacklisting. Her compromise was to employ Skyler as a trainer, not a rider. That had satisfied the angry gentry, since it meant she would be less visible.

The dance floor thinned as couples paused and stepped aside to watch Clint and Skyler. When the band wound up the tune, they were the only couple left on the floor, and the crowd clapped their appreciation. Clint bowed to the crowd, then to Skyler, and they both laughed when she grabbed him and gave him a smacking kiss on the mouth.

Thirsty, she headed to the bar and ordered a Crown Reserve and Coke.

"Don't forget the cherry, honey," a familiar throaty voice instructed the bartender, and Skyler turned to find herself nose-to-nose with Alexandra. "Been hiding from me, huh?"

"No, I've been right there at Creek Barn, doing what I do every day, working horses and training riders."

"That's not what I meant." Alexandra batted her eyes. "I could use another private lesson."

"Alex, you know me. I have a short attention span. But you sure were fun, sweetie." Skyler winked.

"Now, Sky." The socialite imitated Skyler's drawl. "I wouldn't want to have to tell my husband that you seduced me. He would be very upset."

Think again if you think you can control me, lady.

"Oh, you are so right, you know. You messing around with a lowly horse trainer, a female to boot, wouldn't impress his business clients. Why, I'll bet that would give him the ammunition he needs to cut off your shopping money and take up publicly with that secretary he's screwing."

Alexandra's face turned red with anger. "Fuck you, Skyler Reese."

Skyler raised her drink in salute. "I believe you already did," she muttered as Alexandra stormed off. Showing her empty glass to the bartender, she said, "How about another of these? A double this time."

If he'd heard their exchange, he showed no reaction. "Yes, ma'am. Coming right up."

Skyler leaned against the bar and scanned the crowd, searching for one woman only.

"So, you ride, you train, you dance. Is there anything you

can't do?" The silky voice sent a tingle through Skyler. Jessica's black hair, usually kept in French braid, fell loose around her shoulders. She wore snug black jeans and a cobalt silk shirt that complemented her iridescent eyes.

"Hey there." Skyler let her eyes linger on the tempting curves she was not allowed to touch. "Kate puts on quite a shindig, doesn't she? You having a good time?"

"Better every minute." Jessica gulped down the last of her drink and signaled the bartender for another. "I saw you dancing with Clint out there. You're pretty good."

"Thanks. I'd ask you to dance, but some of this crowd wouldn't appreciate it and I promised Kate I would be on my best behavior."

"Oh, that exchange with Alexandra was your best behavior?"

Skyler sighed. Why did Jessica always seem to be around to witness her at her worst?

"Maybe you should slow down on the alcohol a little," Jessica suggested.

"Don't worry, I always throw up before I get drunk enough to embarrass myself."

"Now that sounds attractive."

They laughed together at Skyler's sarcasm, but Jessica's irritation was tangible. Skyler was trying to come up with a smooth compliment when Kate came over and made an excuse to draw Jessica away. Skyler saw straight through the move. Whenever they were at a social event, she always made sure Jessica wasn't left alone with her for more than a few minutes. Skyler didn't know whether to feel insulted or flattered that Kate couldn't trust Jessica to resist her. Was she that irresistible?

She glanced down as a hand slipped into hers and Charlie looked up at her in tears. "What's wrong, buddy?" she asked

Charlie fought back a sniffle. "Scott punched me." Gingerly touching his nose, he choked out, "I'm okay."

There was a tiny amount of blood, but Skyler suspected his

tears were from shock and humiliation more than pain. "I know I'd be bawling if I got hit in the nose like that. How about if we go get some ice for it?"

She led him into the kitchen and wrapped an ice pack from the freezer in a dishtowel. She held it to his nose until it stopped bleeding then sat him on her lap and stroked his tear-stained cheek. Charlie leaned his head against her shoulder and let out a long sigh. "Jessica danced with me before. She sure is pretty, isn't she?"

Skyler chuckled deep in her chest. "She sure is, Charlie."

Skyler squinted in the sun as she watched Jessica take Rampage over the show jumps a couple of days after the fund-raiser. The big horse flew easily over the course, and Jessica's eyes shone when she pulled him up next to Skyler.

"He's really on today," she said, catching her breath.

"How's the knee?" Skyler asked.

"It's doing good. I've never felt better." It had been tough, earlier, to inject the knee herself for the first time, but she'd managed to do it without passing out and the results were well worth the trouble.

"He sure looks warmed up enough. Since your knee has improved so much, maybe you can take him on the cross-country course today. What do you think?"

"Definitely."

Skyler grinned at the excitement on Jessica's face. She reached over and squeezed her knee, partly as a show of support and partly to make sure Jessica wasn't covering real pain. Not a twitch. Skyler was amazed. That knee really had taken a sudden turn for the better. The physical therapy was obviously paying dividends.

"Let me saddle up so I can trail you and see how you guys do together," she said. "You know, if your knee keeps mending this way, you'll be in good shape for the trials."

"Well, that's the plan," Jessica said brightly.

Skyler saddled Con Air and they walked the horses toward the course. "Just take it slow. Don't let him get away from you. He really likes to fly and I don't want either of you injured."

She gave Jessica and Rampage the go ahead, and held Con Air back for a minute to give them a decent lead.

Jessica hunkered down on the big bay and relaxed. The two blazed over the jumps. Skyler had to push Con Air a little to keep up. It looked like it would be a perfect run until they approached the downhill water jump. Skyler saw Jessica's head lift and her body tense. Suddenly, she yanked on the reins as they approached the jump and the stallion skidded into rather than launching over the jump. The impact nearly unseated Jessica, but since she'd initiated the balk, she was prepared and managed to maintain her seat.

Skyler couldn't stop Con Air without crashing into Rampage, so they sailed past to clear the jump. She wheeled around and came charging back. "Good God, Jess. Are you all right?" Skyler jumped down from Con Air and ran to Jessica's side.

Jessica's face was white and she was shaking so hard her teeth chattered. "I fro—froze up," she choked out. Tears began to slide down her pale cheeks.

Rampage fretted and pawed the ground, irritated by the sudden stop. Skyler pulled Jessica off him and hugged her in a protective embrace.

Sobs choked Jessica's words as she fought for control. "What if he fell when he hit the water on the other side? I couldn't go through the whole hospital ordeal if I got hurt again. I only have to smell rubbing alcohol and I launch into an anxiety attack." She clutched Skyler's shirt in her fists and buried her face against the strong chest.

Skyler rubbed the tense muscles of Jessica's back. "Hey,

that's understandable," she said softly. "This is the first time you've been on a course since the accident?"

Jessica's shoulders shook with silent sobs. The tears flowed hard for a few minutes before she finally regained her voice. "I just keep seeing Racer lying there with the bone sticking out of his leg. I can hear him screaming. I can hear me screaming."

"It's okay," Skyler soothed her. "It takes time to get over a really bad experience like that. You should have told me it was your first time since the accident. We should have talked about this before we hit the course."

Jessica sniffled against Skyler's chest, her voice childlike. "I didn't want you to think I was a sissy."

"Honey, you are no sissy. Look at me," Skyler commanded. "We can fix this. Nothing is going to stop us."

Jessica wrapped her in a fierce hug and they stood there for several long moments while Skyler stroked her back. She didn't want to move, but they both seemed suddenly aware that they were standing with their arms around each other. Skyler's heart beat wildly against Jessica's ear and she felt a hot blush flood her cheeks. But it was quickly forgotten when she noticed dark spots of blood on the dusty ground. Where was the blood coming from? "Look," she pointed.

Skyler stepped back and checked her over frantically, demanding, "Are you hurt?

"No." Jessica stared down at the blood, then her eyes flew to Rampage.

At the same time as Skyler, she saw the long, thin splinter protruding from beneath the skin of his chest.

"Let's get him in the barn and call the vet," Skyler said grimly.

The moment they'd shared was quickly forgotten.

CHAPTER EIGHT

By the time Dr. Victoria Greyson arrived at Creek Barn, Kate had joined Skyler and Jessica at Rampage's stall. The tall veterinarian smiled at the worried group. Her dark blond hair was cut much like Skyler's, but while Skyler's eyes were a soft brown, this woman's were an unusually dark forest green. She gave Skyler a quick wink and reached to shake Kate's hand as her eyes lingered over Jessica.

"Jessica, this is Dr. Greyson," Kate said.

"That's Tory to my friends, Jessica. So, please, call me Tory. I've heard your name from Kate so many times."

Kate hadn't told Tory how stunning her young charge was. She'd said their Olympic hopes were pinned on this horse, but one look at the attractive rider ratcheted Tory's concern for the horse's injury even higher. The opportunity to be Jessica's white knight was too good to pass up. She studied the stallion. "So what's up with this guy?"

Jessica slid the stall door back. "He crashed into a jump and he has a splinter stuck in his chest. Oh, wait. You might want to keep one eye on him because he has a biting problem when he's around strangers."

"That's easy enough to fix with a little tranquilizer if needed." Tory eyed the horse's chest. "Hold his head to the side. Hmm. This actually looks fairly superficial because it went in sideways, but this is a really large splinter. Nearly six inches long. The best thing to do is to make an incision along the skin to remove it rather than pulling it out. I don't want to risk leaving some small pieces that could cause infection."

Tory worked extensively with performance horses, so she knew the next question would be from Skyler, about his workouts. Anticipating her, she said, "It will take a bit of stitching to close but since it will be a shallow incision, he should be able to resume dressage and gallops in just a few days. The skin will have had time to begin mending by then. I wouldn't jump him for a week."

Jessica was quiet, her eyes filled with worry. Tory smiled at her. "Hey, don't look so serious. He'll be fine. And…you've got the best vet in these four counties at your service." With her most dazzling smile, she asked, "How about coming out to my truck with me? You can help me carry back some of the stuff I'll need to take care of this."

Skyler rubbed her neck and frowned, her eyes following Tory and Jessica as they exited the barn. She wanted to be sure they were out of earshot before she told Kate what had happened. "Jess froze," she said.

"Damn." Kate looked worried.

"They came to the downhill water jump. She was almost able to stop him, but he still ran into the fence a bit." Skyler paused, knowing what Jessica's loss of confidence might mean for the future. "I don't think his injury is serious. I'm more concerned about Jess freezing. It could have been much worse."

"I'm wondering if she's not trying to do the impossible," Kate said. "She has to ice that knee down every night. I know it's hurting her. I had a talk with her physical therapist. He couldn't tell me anything specific that would violate Jess's privacy, but I could tell he's worried, too."

Skyler was surprised. "That's funny. The last few days, she doesn't appear to be in that much pain during our training sessions. I was under the impression the leg was getting much better."

Kate scratched her head. "Hell, I don't know. Jessica has always been a very private person, but she's really closed down since the accident. Maybe she needs some professional help."

Their conversation was cut short when Jessica and Tory returned. As Tory injected a numbing agent in the skin around the splinter, Jessica asked, "Is that the same thing they use on humans?"

"It's similar," Tory said. "Carbocaine lasts a bit longer than the lidocaine they use on people. Vets use it because you can't exactly lay an animal down on a table and have easy access to the wound. So, it sometimes takes longer to stitch them up."

Skyler frowned. Jessica seemed really interested in what Tory was explaining. She didn't want to think about why Jessica's attention to Tory pissed her off. Turning to Kate, she said, "Well, it doesn't take four people to take out a splinter."

The two women working on Rampage didn't seem to hear her. She stalked off toward the feed room, leaving Kate squinting quizzically at the vet and rider. It certainly looked like Tory and Jessica were hitting it off.

"Maybe I'll get Tory to stay for dinner," Kate said when she arrived in the doorway of the feed room a few seconds later. "A new friend could get Jessica to open up some."

Over dinner, Jessica found the attractive vet a wonderful conversationalist. The subject matter, of course, was centered on horses. With Kate and Charlie rounding out the group, the conversation was lively and the time went quickly. When the time came for Charlie to get off to bed he was reluctant to leave and shuffled toward the stairs only after a stern look from Kate. Pausing at the bottom of the stairway, he announced, "Hey, you know what? When I grow up, I'm going to be a vet, too."

The women laughed as he sprinted up the stairs.

"He's really cute," Tory said.

"Yeah, well, he wanted to be a trainer like Skyler until Jess arrived," Kate said. "Then he wanted to be a rider. So tonight's revelation doesn't surprise me." She sighed. "I would adopt him in a skinny minute, but he has an uncle coming to get him in about two weeks."

They cleared the dishes and Tory picked up her jacket. "I'd better be heading home. My own animals haven't been fed and I've got a few hours of paperwork waiting on me." She turned to Jessica. "Walk me out?"

"Sure." Jessica led the way. They paused on the porch and leaned against the railing.

"Kate says you haven't been out at all since you got here," Tory said.

"I guess I have been training pretty hard," Jessica admitted. "Tonight, though, was great. I think it was the first time I've forgotten about my leg and training for even a few hours."

"I have a problem myself putting work aside and just having fun. So, I thought maybe we could go to a movie or dinner sometime. I can always use another friend."

"That sounds good."

"Great. How about Friday night? I've been dying to try out that new Mexican restaurant in town."

Jessica smiled. "I'd like that."

"I'll have to call you to let you know what time. I never know how my schedule is working out until the last minute… what with emergencies and stuff."

"I can imagine." Jessica looked into Tory's beautiful eyes. "See you on Friday."

As the veterinarian's truck headed down the drive, her thoughts turned to Rampage. The anesthetic she'd injected into her knee that afternoon had long since worn off, but she needed to check on him before she turned in. She found her cane and hobbled wearily down the drive to the Creek Barn.

❖

The stallion was lying down when she peeked into the stall, but got to his feet when she slid the stall door back. Her throbbing leg, the long line of stitches across the stallion's chest, and the memory of freezing at the water jump suddenly weighed heavily and her eyes began to fill with hot tears.

"Hey, I thought I heard someone down here." Skyler's low, rich voice was the last straw. Jessica leaned against Rampage's shoulder and choked back a sob.

Skyler's face was tense with concern as she slipped into the stall. "Jess, hey, what's the matter? Rampage is going to be fine."

She drew Jessica into a firm embrace and held her close. Something deep inside rejoiced that it was still her shoulder Jessica preferred to cry on. The young rider's body fit perfectly against her own, and after a while, the sobs turned to sniffles. Skyler pulled a bandana from the pocket of her jeans and dabbed at Jessica's face.

Jessica took the cloth from her and blew her nose into it. "You must think I'm a real crybaby." She inspected Skyler's front. "I got your shirt wet…again."

"It's okay," Skyler said softly. "And I don't think you're a crybaby."

"I guess everything just closed in on me." Jessica snuggled into Skyler's strong embrace once more.

God, she felt good. Stroking the dark, silky head, Skyler repeated, "It's okay. Everything's going to be fine."

With her damp cheek pressed against Skyler's chest, Jessica realized the trainer was wearing nothing under her T-shirt. Her heart began pulsing harder as she felt the nipple underneath the thin material harden against her cheek. She tilted her head back. After only a split second of hesitation, she touched Skyler's cheek and looked into her eyes. They were soft with affection and yearning, and Skyler's breath was warm on her face. Their lips parted and barely brushed. It started as a soft thank-you kiss, but Jessica knew she had to have more. More of Skyler. More of the heat that tingled in her groin. More of the warmth that infused her soul and made her feel safe.

Skyler stiffened when the hand on the back of her neck beckoned her down again, then she closed her eyes and gently complied. She opened to the tentative tongue that requested entrance. Their tongues slowly danced together, feeling and tasting. Skyler shut out the alarms that were going off in her head and instead listened to this dark-haired, blue-eyed siren whose call was becoming too powerful to resist. Jessica's warm body melded to hers, and Skyler fell headlong into the abyss she'd been dancing around for months.

When Jessica pulled away at last, her smile was soft. "Thank you," she whispered, caressing Skyler's cheek again. Without another word, she turned and limped away to the house.

Dazed, Skyler put her fingers to her lips and stared at Rampage. Her mind raced. Did they just do that? Did she just let her do that? She couldn't stop the blazing grin that grew as her heart began to slow.

The big horse snorted at her.

"Hey, don't be so jealous." Skyler chuckled. "All I got were her lips. You get to feel those beautiful legs wrapped around you every day. Want to trade?"

When Jessica went looking for Skyler, she found Con Air's stall empty. Since Rampage had a few days off, she'd been helping Skyler with the youngsters under her charge. Jessica found she really liked working with the kids. Charlie was just starting to take small jumps, while Jamie was showing real promise on the short cross-country course. Scott, who preferred Western riding, was working on reining patterns, the Western version of dressage.

Skyler had the afternoon off, so there were no lessons today and Jessica was taking the kids trail riding. It was a perfect day, probably the last brief warm spell they would enjoy before fall set in and winter was on the way. A warm September sun shone down from a blue, cloudless sky. Tall pines shaded the trails as they wound up one hillside.

"Is Skyler out riding?" Jessica asked the kids.

"I'll bet I know where she is," Scott replied smugly. "I'll show you."

He took the lead and headed for a steep path up the mountain. When they neared the top, Jessica saw Con Air tethered under a shade tree.

Scott stopped and turned to them. "You have to get off your horses," he said with a conspiratorial smile. "And be quiet."

He led them to the cliff's edge and peered down. On a ledge below, Skyler was sprawled nude on a blanket. She lay dozing on her stomach, bathed in hot sunlight, and with a book open at her side. *I always wondered why she never had tan lines no matter what she wore,* Jessica thought.

"See that eagle's nest," Scott whispered, pointing out a large bed of twigs further along the cliff. "Skyler says the eagles come here every year. I started watching it for homework. Next thing, there she is, ripping off her clothes."

His grin made Jessica uneasy. Scott was thirteen and the first surges of testosterone had already begun to cloud his thinking. He obviously wanted to impress the group by sharing his discovery. Jamie and Charlie stared at him blankly before Jessica pushed them back from the ledge.

"It's not nice to invade someone's privacy," she scolded.

Scott scowled. "She shouldn't take her clothes off out here if she doesn't want someone to look. Besides, why should she care? The guys say she's not exactly a nun."

Charlie looked puzzled and Jamie stared at her shoes.

"That's enough, Scott," Jessica said firmly. "You three mount up and ride back to the barn right now."

"Yeah, what are you going to do?" Scott sneered.

Jessica grabbed the boy by his shirt and shoved him toward his horse. "Now, Scott. You *don't* want to see me really mad."

He shot her a sullen look, but mounted up and followed the other two down the trail. Jessica looked for the path that led down to Skyler's ledge. She left Summer tied to a tree at the top of the path, then crept around the last boulder that sheltered Skyler's sunny ledge from the path. She contemplated kicking a few stones to signal her presence. But her eyes settled on the broad shoulders that tapered down to a very muscled backside, and she just stood there staring.

When Skyler sighed and slowly turned over, Jessica ducked quickly behind the boulder. Her sharp intake of breath nearly gave her away as Skyler settled on her back and resumed her restful slumber. The warm sun kissed the small firm breasts and taut abdomen. Jessica's mouth went dry, and other parts grew wet, as her gaze lingered on the triangle of light brown curls that began Skyler's long, very sexy legs. It wasn't easy to ignore the little voice telling her to strip off her clothes and fling herself on that incredible body, but she made herself look away. For a few seconds, she considered sneaking back up the path but she remembered Skyler surprising her in the hot tub and her qualms vanished.

"Uh...sorry to interrupt." She gleefully repeated the same words Skyler had used that morning.

Skyler's body jerked in surprise, and then relaxed as she recognized the voice. A small smile emerged as she shielded her eyes against the glaring sun. "You *are* interrupting, but it's okay. How'd you know where I was?"

"I didn't. It seems that Scott knows about your sunning habit and his testosterone just wouldn't let him keep it secret."

"Ah, I see. Well, he would have learned about female anatomy sooner or later." Skyler looked toward the cliff top. "Where are they?"

"I sent them back to the barn."

Skyler casually crossed her ankles and raised up to rest on her elbows. "Want to join me?"

Jessica hesitated. She really hadn't planned what to do after she surprised Skyler. She'd expected Skyler to jump up and put her clothes on. "I don't know if that's wise."

Skyler read Jessica's uncertainty with satisfaction. It didn't normally bother her to be nude in front of other women, but she felt exposed in front of Jessica and needed to reclaim control of the situation. She'd already lost her struggle against the blush that flooded her chest and rose to her ears. Maybe Jessica would think it was sunburn.

"Wise?" She stood up and sauntered toward Jessica. "Do I seem like the *wise* type to you?"

Jessica's heart began to beat wildly as that tall, magnificently nude body approached. She remembered Skyler's soft lips, that tender kiss in Rampage's stall a few days before. Desire closed her throat and she held her breath as Skyler stopped only inches from her, then reached around her for the clothes lying on the rock behind. Skyler's slow smile made even her good knee feel weak.

"On second thought, we should be getting back," Skyler said. "We can't be sure Scott went back like you told him."

It was her intention to leave while Jessica was still off balance. She pulled her clothes on and started up the path toward Con Air, but she couldn't resist looking back. The helpless desire on Jessica's face matched the craving that burned hot in her. Skyler closed the distance between them in a few short strides and took Jessica in her arms. Her mouth was as hot and sweet as she remembered. Jessica's hands dropped down to pull Skyler's hips snug against her own. The kiss seemed to startle her at first, but she quickly recovered and her warm tongue asked entrance into Skyler's hungry mouth.

Skyler groaned. Ripples of heat ran through her. She struggled to slow her breathing. This wasn't the right place for all she yearned to do, for the hours she wanted to spend exploring the woman in her arms. Easing back, she met eyes glowing with passion. "Race you back to the barn," she invited hoarsely.

Jessica barely hesitated before scrambling up the trail to mount Summer while Skyler quickly tightened her saddle on Con Air. They raced down the trail, knowing it was more than the barn they were racing to. But as they emerged at a full gallop, Skyler recognized Tory's truck parked outside Creek Barn. Damn it. Her hormones were screaming with the anticipation of one hot, young rider, cool white sheets, and long, passionate kisses. She couldn't stand it any longer, spending her days with Jessica within touching distance and her nights with the beautiful rider invading her dreams. She and Tory had been friends since they were teens, and they'd dated a lot of the same girls, but this was different. Skyler didn't feel like sharing, this time.

Tory greeted them with a smile, oblivious to her intrusion. "Hi, Jess. I called a while ago to see if you were ready to go to dinner. When Kate said you were out riding, I just decided to head on over here. You want to change real quick and head to town?"

"Oh…I didn't realize how late it was."

"No problem. I can wait."

Jessica turned to Skyler. "I told Tory that I'd go with her to check out a new restaurant tonight," she said weakly.

Skyler's face was stony. Jessica dismounted and shifted from one foot to the other. There was really no way of getting out of this awkward situation. What could she say? *Uh, Tory, thanks for the invitation, but Skyler and I were headed to her apartment to finally tear each other's clothes off.*

Hoping they could reschedule, she said, "I still need to unsaddle Summer and rub her down. I haven't taken care of Rampage's stall either, or showered. Perhaps we should do this another time."

Tory swept a quick, perceptive glance from Jessica to Skyler and her smile grew tight. "That's all right," she said. "You go shower and change. I'll take care of Summer, and I'm sure Skyler wouldn't mind mucking Rampage's stall this one time. I'll pick you up at the house in about thirty minutes."

Jessica looked to Skyler for help. *Bail me out here, please.*

But Skyler turned away and began unsaddling Con Air. "I'll take care of Rampage."

Her voice was flat and devoid of emotion, but Jessica had seen the disappointment on her face. She liked Tory. She really didn't want to hurt her feelings. But she could sense Skyler distancing herself, and was suddenly afraid that if she let this chance slip away, she might not get another one. Maybe they would wake up tomorrow and decide they'd narrowly avoided making a big mistake. Training would resume, and life would return to normal.

She moved to Skyler's side and said very softly. "I don't have to go. Just say the word and I won't."

Skyler didn't look at her. "Go. I said it's fine."

Jessica turned away quickly, not wanting either woman to see the tears pooling in her eyes. Something had wounded Sky so deeply, she'd backed off. One day Jessica would ask her about that, but now was not the time. "Well, I guess I'll go get ready," she said with regret. "Thanks."

"So what's going on between you and Jessica?" Tory asked after they'd unsaddled the horses.

"I don't know what you mean," Skyler growled.

"I get the distinct feeling that I interrupted something."

Skyler leaned her head against Con Air's shoulder. "We were just out for a ride." *Shit, that didn't sound very convincing.* "I mean, I was out riding and she was out riding with some of the kids. We ran into each other and rode back together."

Tory stared at her. "Sky, I like her a lot. Kate told me everything she's been through this year. Jessica really needs something stable to hold on to."

"What are you saying?" Skyler was getting really tired of hearing what she knew was coming next.

"I'm saying that she's more than just a roll in the sheets. And as much as I love you, your track record speaks for itself. Jessica doesn't need her heart broken."

Skyler dug the toe of her boot into the dirt and fought the sick ache in her chest. What made her think she wouldn't want to walk away once she had Jessica in the sack? Tory spoke the truth. Jessica deserved better. "I'm just her trainer," she said miserably. "Go take her to dinner. She deserves a night out."

"Okay," Tory said softly.

After she left in her truck, Skyler turned Con Air out into the paddock and stomped up the stairs to her apartment.

Despite Jessica's frustration at Skyler's withdrawal, she found dinner a relaxed and enjoyable affair. Conversation with Tory was easy. They talked about horses at first, but later found they both enjoyed reading and women's college basketball.

After driving her home, Tory walked her to the door. "I had a really good time," she said softly. "I think we have a lot in common. Kate will tell you I'm a pretty decent person, and I think you should know right up front that I'm interested in more than just your friendship."

Jessica met her eyes. "Tory, I'm just concentrating on Rampage and getting my leg well right now. I don't know how much more I want to deal with on top of that."

Tory smiled. "I understand. I am a patient woman." She placed a soft, lingering kiss on Jessica's lips. "Good night," she said softly before turning to leave.

The house was dark except for the porch light Kate had left on. Jessica watched Tory's truck head down the drive, then her eyes wandered to the Creek Barn, a dark hulk under the light of a nearly full moon. She started down the steps but hesitated, wondering if she should wake Skyler up. Maybe she was still pissed. Or upset. Or whatever it was that she felt. Why was life so complicated?

Her throbbing knee ultimately made the decision for her and she went back up the steps and let herself into the house.

Over in the Creek Barn, Skyler stepped away from the window and took another long drink from the bottle of brandy that had been keeping her company most of the evening. The ache in her chest felt like it was burning a hole in her heart. *More like a hole in my stomach.* Her luck with women she actually cared about had never been good. When was she going to accept that?

She heard a faint scratching at her apartment door and opened it for a fat orange cat. He shot through the gap and headed right for Skyler's bed.

"Oh well, looks like the best offer I'm going to get tonight." Skyler stripped off her clothes and climbed into bed as the cat snuggled into the pillow on the other side of the bed. "I guess we're just two old toms past our prime, Peach."

She closed her eyes, but the darkness couldn't block out the visions of Jessica floating naked in the Jacuzzi. Her incredible pale blue eyes and soft lips would haunt Skyler's brandy-induced dreams, but she was powerless to think of anything else. The images taunted her. She could have had so much more.

CHAPTER NINE

The memory of Skyler's lips burned in Jessica's mind the next day and she was anxious to have the sexy trainer alone for a few minutes. She was frustrated and puzzled when Skyler appeared chipper but somewhat distant toward her. Skyler seemed to be making sure they were never alone. She suggested that Jessica run Rampage through some light dressage exercises, and then progress on to his Saturday gallops. But Skyler didn't take up her usual post to watch. Instead, she left Jessica alone with her task and spent the morning working with a new colt that was brought into her barn earlier in the week.

It was well into the afternoon when Jessica finally saw her head for her studio apartment in the loft of the barn. She waited a few minutes in case it was the bathroom that Skyler was headed for, then knocked on the door.

Skyler answered with a sandwich in one hand. "Everything okay with Rampage?" she asked, blocking the doorway.

"He's fine," Jessica replied. She could have guessed Skyler would ask about the horse first. She waited a heartbeat or two for an invitation, then asked, "May I come in?"

Skyler shrugged and stepped back, leaving Jessica to follow her to the kitchen bar where she resumed her lunch. The small apartment was neat and orderly. The bed was made. Two partially open doors next to it gave a glimpse of a bathroom and a walk-in closet. A tiny kitchen took up one corner, and in front of the bar where Skyler sat was a recliner and an end table angled in front of a television. Just enough space for one.

Jessica wanted to throw herself into Skyler's strong arms and take up where they had left off, but Skyler had erected a wall between them. "I want to talk about yesterday," she said.

Skyler made a show of chewing slowly, staring at her plate and refusing to look at her. "It's none of my business if you're dating Tory."

"I'm not dating Tory. We went out one time for dinner."

"Well you're not dating me either." Skyler shoved her plate away and stood. But instead of moving toward Jessica, she backed up to lean her back against the wall and stuff her hands in the pockets of her jeans. "You should date Tory. She's a really good person."

"You're a good person, too, Sky."

Skyler appeared to give that some thought. When she spoke, she sounded as if she was thinking out loud when asked to give her opinion of a horse. "No, I'm not all that good. I'm a good trainer. I'm a good rider." Her tone turned soft. "I can be a good friend, Jess. That's what we need to be. Friends."

"What about the rest?"

When Jessica took a step toward her, Skyler pulled her hands from her pockets and folded her arms across her chest, a clear signal for her to keep her distance. "Sexual attraction doesn't always last. Our friendship could."

Jessica stopped her advance, but her eyes bored into Skyler's. "What about the fact that I want to throw myself into your arms every time I hurt? What about the fact that we couldn't wait to get back here yesterday to tear each other's clothes off? You know that's where we were headed if Tory hadn't shown up." She softened her tone. "I can still feel your lips, Sky. I can still taste your mouth on mine. I still want to see where that was going."

Skyler stared at her boots, the flexing muscles in her smooth cheek giving away her turmoil. When she finally spoke, she didn't look up and her voice was low. "Well, you see now, that's where I'm not so good. I have a really short attention span when it comes to women. Don't know why, but that's just the way it is." Her eyes pleaded with Jessica. "We've got a good working relationship, Jess, and an important goal ahead of us. You are right about Rampage. You two are Olympic material. This is my career, hell, both of our careers at stake. I don't want to do anything to mess that up."

Jessica was stunned. It was obvious that she felt there was more between them than Skyler did. She was nothing but a career opportunity to her. An angry retort rose to her lips, but the sadness in Skyler's eyes confused her and kept her from lashing out. She composed herself before she spoke. "If that's the way you want it." She gave Skyler a weak smile. "I would like to think we're more than rider and trainer, Sky. I'd like to think we are friends, too."

Skyler looked relieved. "Definitely friends. You can never have enough friends."

Jessica left without another word. The door closing behind her opened up an emptiness inside, the like of which she hadn't felt since she woke up in that hospital more than a year ago with a cast on her leg and Racer gone.

Tory showed up in the late afternoon and invited Jessica to take in a movie with her in town. Still stinging from Skyler's rejection, she accepted the invitation.

The movie was a romantic comedy, but Jessica didn't laugh.

Afterward, Tory took her to a very upscale women's bar, the patrons white collar and a single performer playing tunes on a baby grand in the corner. Jessica sipped on the wine Tory placed before her and watched several women dancing.

"I didn't think the movie was that bad," Tory joked.

Jessica blushed. "I'm sorry. I guess I've just got something on my mind." *More like someone.*

Tory cocked a questioning eyebrow. "Care to talk about it?"

Skyler had said Tory was a friend. Would it be wrong to ask her some questions? Jessica needed to understand why Skyler was pushing her away. She knew if she didn't get answers she wouldn't be able to relax and enjoy the rest of the night.

"You may not want to talk about this, but I was wondering what the real story is on Skyler. What exactly happened that got her blacklisted from the circuit?"

Tory gave a deep sigh. She wished she could go out with just one woman who didn't ask the same question, but Jessica was more than just another Skyler groupie wanting to know her whole life story. Tory collected her thoughts. She didn't want to send Jessica rushing back to the Creek Barn to try to "save" Skyler from herself. She'd tried that once, herself, to no avail.

"Skyler was one of the first kids to go though the equestrian program at Cherokee Falls," she told Jessica. "She's an exceptional rider, and with the Parker family backing, she was working in no time as a professional. But she has a wild streak. Her downfall was rich, straight women. Seducing them was a conquest for her, these rich women throwing themselves at a kid from the wrong side of the street."

"Like Alexandra Rourke," Jessica said quietly.

"Yes, and dozens of her ilk. Skyler overplayed her hand, though, when she went after Sarah Berrington Tate. She made the mistake of falling in love. Sarah wasn't married, but they didn't hide their affair very well, and Sarah's father found out. He gave Sarah an ultimatum. Either she drop Skyler or he would cut off all her money."

"That's appalling." Jessica could imagine how effective that threat would be for many of the people she met on the circuit, who lived lives of privilege.

"Sarah wasn't anxious to share a barn apartment with Skyler

and have to work for her money. Skyler was crushed. Old man Tate went a step further. He managed to convince the rest of gentry that Skyler was a sexual predator and he got her blacklisted on the circuit. Nobody would hire her as a professional rider, so she had to wait tables, groom horses, muck stalls, or whatever else."

"That's when Kate came to her rescue?"

Tory nodded. "She gave Skyler a job training horses and equestrians. But Skyler was still devastated. She's never returned to the circuit and rarely goes to any of the shows. She hasn't seen Sarah since. At least, I don't think she has."

"That really sucks," Jessica said sadly.

"I've known Skyler since we were in high school." Tory took a sip of wine. "Sarah really, really hurt her. Since then, Skyler has stuck to one-night stands or married women who won't leave their husbands' money." Her eyes sought Jessica's. "Don't underestimate how damaged she is. It's more than a broken heart. Skyler's father was abusive. I think the first time she ever let herself open up to another person was with Sarah."

"Quite a betrayal," Jessica sighed. Now that she had a context for Skyler's behavior, she should feel optimistic. But she wasn't confident that Skyler was the kind of person who could just "get over it."

"I'm not sure she could trust someone enough to fall in love again. Some really good women have tried, but only been hurt. Skyler knows her limitations. She values your friendship too much to encourage anything more. You should respect that."

"I guess that was what Kate's been trying to tell me, too," Jessica said.

"However, *I* would love to cultivate more than a friendship with you." Tory smiled warmly and held out her hand to Jessica. "Would you like to dance?"

Jessica smiled and took her hand. Tory was an excellent dancer and they glided smoothly across the floor. Her arms were strong and Jessica felt safe and relaxed in her embrace. There was no denying that the veterinarian was very attractive. Many of the women in the bar had been eyeing both of them all evening. Tory pressed warm, soft lips against Jessica's forehead. Jessica smiled weakly and responded with a soft kiss to Tory's lips. The sensation was pleasant, but it did nothing to ease the pain or chase away the sad thoughts of her tall, blond trainer.

❖

Across town, Skyler stepped into a dimly lit bar not quite as upscale as the piano bar Tory had picked out for Jessica. The black walls and ceiling vibrated with the dance music spun by a disc jockey in a booth overlooking a strobe-lit dance floor. At one end of the bar, a pool of light illuminated denim-clad women gathered around four pool tables and leaned casually against the wall to watch the action and the dancers. Her faded Levi's and thin, sleeveless Lycra shirt accented Skyler's athletic physique, and many eyes followed her from the door to the bar.

"So, Skyler Reese is on the prowl tonight," teased the bartender as she poured the neat Bourbon Skyler asked for.

"Pickings are getting slim around the barn, Mindy."

The bartender ran her fingers through her short dark hair. "There's not much here you haven't already had or turned down." She laughed. "There is a really cute blonde I haven't seen in here before. Seems to be single, just hanging out with friends."

Skyler's eyes traveled to the table Mindy indicated with a subtle nod of her head. She shrugged her disinterest. "Not what I'm looking for."

"One day, you're going to reach a point where you have to go out of town to find what you're looking for."

Skyler's eyes settled on a short woman leaning uncertainly against the wall near the pool tables. "That's more my style tonight."

Mindy's eyes followed her stare. "Hold on, Ace. She's just here for the weekend, and Robbie is already working that one.

In fact, I think she's trying to impress the girl right now with her billiards expertise."

Skyler glanced toward the stocky woman bent over the pool table. Robbie sank a bank shot and tossed a grin at the short woman. The woman returned a weak smile.

"Give me another bourbon and one of what she's drinking, Mindy."

"Shit, Skyler. Don't go starting anything. We make all our money on the weekends. I don't need the cops hanging around here and scaring my customers off."

"No sweat. I'll whisk that girl right out from under Robbie before she notices." Skyler took the two drinks and made her way across the room. She leaned against the wall next to the woman. "Are you waiting a turn at the pool table?"

"No. I'm just watching," the woman said tentatively. She didn't have Jess's sexy voice, but she was cute enough. Her eyes were blue and they moved over Skyler with interest.

"Looks like you could use another drink." Skyler turned a brilliant smile on her new acquaintance and replaced her empty glass with the one Mindy had just filled. "The bartender told me what you were drinking."

The blue eyes softened with amusement. "Oh, you're smooth."

Skyler rewarded her with her cutest, crooked smile. "I'm Skyler Reese. And you are…"

"Kelly Thompson."

"Ah. What are you doing in Cherokee Falls, Kelly Thompson?"

"I install computer systems for a software company. I've been in town all week to install a new system at the Savings and Loan on Fifth Street. I'm heading back to Seattle soon. That's where I live."

Skyler smiled. Perfect. Short-term and no strings attached. Her maneuvers had not gone unnoticed, unfortunately. Robbie glowered at them as she missed a shot at the eight ball and proceeded to lose the game.

She threw her cue down and stalked over as the deejay began a new dance tune. Ignoring Skyler, she asked, "How about a dance, Kelly?"

Kelly handed her drink to Robbie, who took it, obviously thinking Kelly wanted her to put it somewhere safe for her. "Actually, I had just told Skyler here that I would dance with her. You seemed tied up shooting pool. Do you mind holding my drink for me?"

Robbie stuttered in surprise as Skyler took Kelly's hand and guided her expertly to the dance floor.

"You're pretty smooth yourself." Skyler chuckled.

Kelly turned out to also be a very good dancer, mimicking Skyler's timing. She watched Skyler through her thick eyelashes and moved her hips in perfect sync. They danced through two songs while Robbie still glowered from the edge of the dance floor, and then Skyler pulled her close when the third song slowed the tempo. Kelly's eyes were hungry, and Skyler kissed her deeply as she pressed their bodies together.

"Let's get out of here," Kelly suggested. "I'm staying at the Marriott."

Skyler smiled her agreement, and they headed for the door.

"Hey, Reese. Just where do you think you're going?" Robbie moved between them and the exit.

Skyler was nonchalant. "Well, Robbie. Kelly here has invited me up to her hotel room, and I accepted. So, if you'll excuse us."

The stocky woman held her ground. "I'm sick and tired of you waltzing into this bar like you own it and every woman in it."

"I'm not looking for trouble. We were just leaving." Skyler was navigating a path around Robbie when the woman's fist connected with her left eye.

Mindy was immediately at her side, restraining Robbie and

hustling her to a nearby chair. Another large woman who worked as the bar bouncer stood over Robbie, assuring she would remain seated.

"Tell me you don't want to press charges, Sky," Mindy pleaded.

Skyler touched her cheekbone to feel the swelling, but shook her head. "No. Just keep her in here until we can get out of the parking lot."

"You got it." Mindy sighed in relief. "You should put an ice pack on that eye. You'll probably have a pretty good shiner tomorrow."

"Great." Skyler nodded and nudged Kelly toward the door.

Skyler had forgotten about her eye until she crept home just before feeding time and looked in the mirror after climbing out of the shower. Damn. Robbie had sucker-punched her a good one. Lots of alcohol and a burning desire for the elusive raven-haired rider with pale blue eyes had fueled a sex-filled night. But the encounter hadn't quelled Skyler's need, and only left her feeling worse. There was no substitute for the woman who haunted her every thought.

Her bad mood lifted when she heard Jessica's voice downstairs near Rampage's stall, but sank again when she saw it was Tory, not Rampage, Jessica was talking to while she mucked the stallion's stall.

Tory grinned when she spotted Skyler. "Whoa! Who gave you that shiner?"

Jessica's head jerked around.

"That new colt head-butted me when I was working him in the round pen," Skyler lied.

Jessica walked over for a better look, grasping Skyler's chin to turn her face toward her. "Maybe you should have a doctor look at that."

Skyler looked away, afraid her eyes would reveal more than she wanted. She grasped Jessica's slender wrist, holding it for a moment before pulling her hand away. "I'm fine," she replied gruffly. "No reason to see a doctor for a simple black eye."

Jessica looked to Tory for help, but the vet only shrugged. They watched Skyler quickly tack up the colt she was breaking and head for the round pen.

CHAPTER TEN

Fall had begun to turn the center's hardwoods into an artist's palette of red, yellow, and gold before the mild winter put a nip in the air that energized both riders and steeds. Because Jessica's knee didn't seem to bother her as much anymore, Rampage's training sessions lengthened. Skyler would saddle Con Air to share their exercises, and both women relished the hours they spent riding and talking together. They didn't speak again about Skyler's black eye, and the tension between the women began to ease once Skyler seemed assured Jessica wouldn't press the bond that continued to grow between them into something more than friendship. It was Jessica's relationship with Tory that didn't seem to be going anywhere. While every day was a struggle not to fall into Skyler's arms and kiss her senseless, Jessica was content to keep her physical relationship with Tory limited to a few innocent kisses. She'd noticed that Skyler was keeping a low profile. She seemed to have lost her lust for one-night stands. Instead, she'd thrown herself into the youth equestrian program, spending additional hours training the kids and their horses, swimming with them in the center's pool, and helping them with their homework in the afternoons.

Jessica had followed her to a paddock behind Creek Barn an hour earlier, to watch a group of kids testing their mounts at barrel racing. The object of the contest was to run their ponies the length of the arena, loop tightly around first one then a second barrel, and race back across the arena in the shortest time.

Jessica's smile faded when she saw Scott showing a short whip made of braided rawhide to the other boys. He waved to the boy holding a stopwatch, mounted his horse and headed for the barrels. He whipped the pony with the rawhide quirt around the first barrel and aimed for the second. The pony was running hard, but slipped coming around the second barrel and struggled to recover. When he was back on his feet, Scott flogged him hard to make up the lost time.

"Skyler," Jessica began, but the woman next to her was already heading across the paddock, her face flooded with anger.

Scott quickly dismounted and, holding the colt by the reins, he whipped him repeatedly across the face. The young horse dragged him several feet, trying to escape his tormentor.

"Scott!" Skyler grabbed for the whip, but Scott was quicker. He brought the quirt across Skyler's face, its rawhide cutting into her cheek.

"Stupid bitch! Get out of my way!" he screamed. He was out of control.

He swung again at Skyler, but she was ready this time and ducked, grabbing the hand that held the whip. She twisted Scott's arm to force him to the ground on his stomach, and put a hard knee in his back.

"I had better never, ever see you raise a hand to one of our horses again. Never, never, ever," Skyler growled through clenched teeth. Her face was scarlet as she held the boy's face in the sand.

Scott struggled underneath her strong grasp. "Get off me, dyke! You just let me up and I'll take care of you. No woman is going to tell me what to do."

Worried for both of them, Jessica was about to intervene when Charlie came running from West Barn with Clint in tow. "Skyler," Clint called. "Let him up. I'll take care of him."

She stared up at Clint for a long minute before recognition began to register in her glazed eyes and she relaxed her grip.

Clint grabbed the boy by the collar and snatched the whip from his hand. "That's it, Scott. Let's go find Kate. It's time we talked about whether you should be here at the center."

Jessica followed as a dejected Skyler led the colt to the barn and cross-tied him in the wash stall. Skyler's sure hands and low voice calmed the anxious animal as she examined his head and eyes closely for injury.

"Well, he looks okay, but we better keep an eye on him," Skyler told Jamie, who stood at her elbow. "How about rubbing him down for me and putting him in the last stall for tonight," she told the girl.

"Sky?" The girl hesitated. "All the other kids are afraid of Scott. We'll be glad if you guys throw him out of the program."

"That will be up to Kate." Skyler stared at her boots. "I shouldn't have handled Scott that roughly. I would never intentionally hurt one of you kids. You know that, don't you, James?"

"We all know that, Sky. Scott is so big and strong, there wasn't anything else you could do."

When the girl led the colt away, Skyler leaned her forehead against the wall of the wash stall and closed her eyes. She flinched when Jessica laid a hand on her shoulder.

"Hey, you okay?"

After a moment, Skyler turned. She didn't speak, but the haunted look in her eyes communicated more eloquently than words.

Jessica touched the blood oozing from the welt on her cheek. "That's a nasty cut. We better clean it up. Do you have something more than horse first aid stuff in the office?"

Skyler cleared her throat. "In my medicine cabinet upstairs."

"Come on. Let me take care of that for you." Jessica took Skyler's hand and guided her up the stairs. She sat her on the bed and went to find the supplies she needed in the bathroom. When she returned, Skyler's shoulders were slumped and her head bowed. Tears trickled down her tanned cheeks.

Jessica knelt before her and spoke softly as she wiped at a tear with her finger. "Hey, what's this, tough stuff?"

Skyler gave a hard shake of her head. "I never should have roughed him up like that. Scott has a lot of demons to deal with, and he can't control his temper tantrums yet. I'm supposed to be the one who stays in control. Instead, I give him the same rough treatment that put him in the program in the first place. Just like my father, I just can't seem to stop being a fuck-up."

It tore at Jessica's heart to see the strong trainer so emotionally fragile. She sat on the bed and gently grasped Skyler's hand. "You can't save them all. Scott needs more help than a few good role models and horses to play with. It has nothing to do with you failing him."

When Skyler didn't answer, Jessica reached for the medical supplies she had set on the bed. She gently cleaned the welt with a peroxide-soaked cotton ball, using her soft hands and low voice the same way Skyler did moments earlier, to gentle the injured colt.

"You are so good to these kids, Sky. Jamie and Charlie idolize you. You've helped so many. You shouldn't beat yourself up because one came along who needs professional counseling." She laid her hand on Skyler's damp cheek and gently turned the anguished face toward her. "You have such a big heart. I don't know why you spend so much time trying to convince people you're such a rascal."

Skyler raised her eyes to Jessica's and felt herself drowning in a sea of pale blue. "I am a rascal," she said with a small smile.

Jessica leaned close to touch her warm lips to Skyler's mouth. Skyler hesitated, fighting the confusion spinning in her head. "We can't do this," she said. "I can't do this."

"Yes, you can," came Jessica's soft, firm reply. "I believe in you, Skyler. Please. Take a chance on us."

Skyler wanted to take that chance. God, she needed Jessica. This was the one woman who seemed to ease her self-doubts and fill the empty places left by an abusive father and a lover's betrayal. "You're seeing Tory."

Jessica's eyes were pleading, her face flushed with desire. Her voice was husky. "Oh, Sky. It's you who makes my mouth go dry and my heart race, no matter how much I try to deny it. It's you, not Tory, that I want. I don't care if you don't want me tomorrow."

Skyler jumped up, nearly throwing Jessica onto the floor. "You deserve better, Jess. Kate knows it. Tory knows it. Hell, I know it."

Jessica stood and moved quickly so that she was toe-to-toe with Skyler. "You're wrong, Skyler Reese. You are dead wrong. *You* are what I need. You are what I want, no matter how hard you and everybody else try to change my mind. Am I wrong to think that you may feel the same way about me?"

She wasn't wrong. There was nothing Skyler needed, wanted, more than to feel Jessica's arms around her, holding her tight.

"Just tell me that you don't want me," Jessica said softly. "Tell me you don't dream about me at night like I dream about you. Tell me there is no part of your heart that wants to open up to me, and I'll leave you alone. No matter how much it hurts me, I'll leave you alone for good. We'll just be trainer and rider."

"I'm scared."

It was a whisper so soft, Jessica almost missed it. She reached up to cup Skyler's face in her warm, delicate hands. "Why, Sky? Why are you afraid of me?"

The dark eyes that met hers were enough to break her heart. She waited as Skyler worked to get the words to her lips. "I'm scared because you're not like the rest. I can't just sleep with you and move on. I'm scared because it will rip me apart if I let you in and then you move on."

Jessica drew Skyler's head down for a gentle kiss. It was a kiss of affection and promise. She stroked the still damp cheek, her eyes holding Skyler's. "That's good. Because I'm absolutely crazy about you," she whispered, guiding Skyler to the bed.

Jessica straddled Skyler's hips and pulled her into another kiss, a sweet kiss of longing and desire. Leaning back, Jessica pulled her shirt and bra off over her head, then slipped her hands under Skyler's shirt. Skyler arched up so the garment could be stripped from her, and Jessica sighed at the golden skin now exposed, the soft swell of breasts under the white sports bra. She laid her face against Skyler's warm chest and closed her eyes to focus on the heart beating wildly beneath her cheek.

Skyler trembled beneath her as Jessica began a journey to taste the smooth shoulders and the graceful curve of her neck. Her nails raked gently across the ridged abdomen, drawing more shivers.

"Oh God, Jess. I don't know about this."

"What don't you know, baby?"

"What if I fuck this up? What if I can't be what you need, like everybody says? What if wanting each other isn't enough?"

Jessica held Skyler's face in her hands and looked deep into her anxious eyes. "I thought we had this cleared up. Forget what the others think. I believe in you, Skyler. I believe in us. I've felt it since that day I froze at the downhill jump. You're so strong, and I felt so safe in your arms. We don't just want each other, Sky. We need each other."

Jessica planted small kisses along Skyler's jaw and lipped her sensitive earlobe. She pulled off the sports bra, removing the last barrier between their upper bodies. She leaned in and they both moaned as skin met skin, breast caressed soft breast, and nipples tightened.

"No barriers between us, Sky. Not our past, not what other people think. I want to be the one to touch you in places no one else is allowed," she said, placing a warm hand over the heart thumping hard in Skyler's chest. "I want to let you into the places I let no one else."

Skyler blocked out the warning sirens sounding in her head as her warm, tanned skin pressed against the pale, flushed skin of the woman she ached for. She hungrily sought Jessica's full lips, moaning her passion. Jessica cupped the soft swell of Skyler's breasts, squeezing slowly, taking delight in each touch. She moved away after a few exquisite moments, sliding down and pulling off Skyler's riding boots.

She reached for Skyler's belt, but paused before unbuckling it. "Bareback, Skyler. I want to feel all of you on all of me," she said in a husky voice. "I want to be so close that I can feel your thoughts, and you can hear mine."

They were naked in moments. Caught off balance by the younger woman's assertive seduction, Skyler gave in to sensation. The loss of control was dizzying, but she was helpless to stop it. Jessica's kisses grew more urgent, stoking a fire Skyler thought had been long dead inside her. A quick flip and their positions were reversed, but Skyler found she felt no more in control on top than when she'd been on her back.

She looked in awe at the blue-eyed, raven-haired beauty. "You are so beautiful. I can't believe how beautiful you are." She covered the smaller body with hers and worshipped it with soft, caressing kisses. She took each taut nipple into her mouth, one at and then the other, tasting and stroking with her tongue. Jessica's body arched to meet her while her gentle hands caressed Skyler's breasts.

Skyler slipped her arm underneath Jessica's arched back and stroked her firm buttocks, pressing Jessica's hips against her own. She nudged one hard thigh between Jessica's legs and groaned at the wet heat she found there. She jerked as Jessica's hand caressed her aching clit.

"Oh, Jess," Skyler breathed.

"Don't tease," Jessica begged as they moved against each other.

Skyler cradled Jessica in her arms and thought her heart

would burst at the sound of her pleading. "I just don't want to miss even one inch of you."

She slid down to taste the soft inside of Jessica's thigh. Nuzzling the dark curls, she inhaled her lover's musky scent. Her own desire was threatening to explode with every caress of her tongue across the throbbing sex that arched up to meet her lips. When she felt Jessica nearing climax, Skyler slowly dipped her fingers into Jessica's soft core.

Jessica gasped and stiffened. "Yes. Oh, Sky. Sky," she moaned as her orgasm washed over her.

Her body had barely stopped jerking with the aftershocks when Skyler moved up to latch on to a swollen nipple and buck her hips against Jessica's wetness. Reading her intent, Jessica brought her knees up and spread herself wide, fitting Skyler's slim hips between her legs and using her heels to guide Skyler's need closer. Skyler reached down to expose her hardened clit to Jessica's welcoming heat. Their hips moved together in a perfect, rhythmic dance, and in moments both cried out as release flooded their sweat-slick bodies.

They lay without speaking for a long time as they struggled to slow their breathing. Skyler rolled over on her back and pulled Jessica up to rest the dark head on her shoulder. Wrapping her arms around the slender body, she softly caressed Jessica's warm back. After a long moment, Skyler found her voice.

"Jess, I…"

"Just let it be, Sky. Let's just don't analyze this and let this go where it will. I don't want to hear any more doubts." Jessica fit her body closer, hugging her tightly. "Believe in us, Sky. I do."

Skyler stroked her hair. "I was just going to say that you make my mouth go dry and my heart beat fast, too."

Jessica's smile was brilliant. She slid her body along Skyler's to reach the lips that beckoned her. She captured Skyler's mouth and hungrily probed it with an insistent tongue. She began to blaze a slow trail of kisses and caresses downward as Skyler's legs trembled and her breathing rasped.

"God, Jess! I think I may be done for the moment."

"I'm sure you can hold up, stud," Jessica murmured before parting those strong thighs and sucking hard on the clit that pulsed between them.

CHAPTER ELEVEN

It was well after midnight when Jessica finally left Skyler's sleepy embrace and headed up to the house. She crept up the stairs so she wouldn't wake Kate and Charlie, but when she opened her bedroom door, there was a small boy sleeping in a tight ball on her bed. She took a quick shower, pulled on some soft flannel pajama pants and a clean T-shirt, and crawled into the bed beside him.

Charlie snuggled into her arms. "Where were you? I've been looking for you."

"I'm here now, Charlie. Did you have a bad dream or just feeling lonely?" She softly stroked the dark head.

The boy began to sniffle. "Kate said my uncle is coming to get me in the morning. I don't want to go. I want to stay here with you and Kate," he sobbed.

Poor Kate. She'd had a lot to deal with today. First Scott, then telling Charlie his uncle was coming to take him.

"Oh, Charlie. We both wish you could stay, too. But you need to give your uncle a chance. From what I hear, he really wants you to come live with him."

Charlie tightened his grip around Jessica's ribs as if he could stay by holding tighter. "I don't even know him. He and Mom would talk on the phone a lot, but he never came to see us. Mom said he lived really far away. What if he takes me really far away and I never see you again?"

"Honey, your mother must have trusted him very much to leave you in his care. Tell you what. I'll stick close to you all day, okay? If your Uncle Mark doesn't seem like a great guy, I'll personally tell him you are a horrible boy and cause lots of trouble so he should leave you here. How's that?"

Jessica hoped for a smile, but got only a sniffle and a trembling "Okay" from her young friend. She rubbed his back until she felt him relax and drift off the sleep. She closed her eyes, too, and fell into a deep, restful sleep laced with dreams of a certain blond trainer.

Jessica worked to keep the breakfast conversation lively, hoping to take Charlie's mind off his impending departure. But as they finished off huge stacks of pancakes topped with syrup and strawberries, Charlie grew quiet.

"We're expecting your uncle a little later, sometime after lunch," Kate said after taking a phone call. "He's already had the stuff from your mom's house shipped to his home in Atlanta. Do you have your clothes packed?"

"Yeah. I'm all packed," Charlie said glumly.

Jessica brightened. "Atlanta? Hey, Charlie. Remember I told you my mom lives there? I can come see you, if you like, when I go to visit her."

Charlie's face brightened. "That would be great."

"And you know what? How about we pack a picnic and take a trail ride this morning, since we have some extra time. We can ride up to Skyler's sunbathing spot and picnic there."

"Can Sky come with us?"

The vision of Skyler's nude body stretched out beneath her brought a warm flush to Jessica's cheeks. "Only if she promises to keep her clothes on," Jessica mumbled under her breath.

❖

Thirty minutes later, they were headed to Creek Barn with a scrumptious lunch packed in the saddlebags slung over their shoulders. Jessica wondered if Skyler would be sleeping in, since it had only been a few hours since she had left. But they found Skyler in the tack room, a small smile on her face as she worked the saddle leather. The smile broadened to a delighted grin when she saw them standing in the doorway.

"Hey, Sky," Charlie said excitedly, "we've got a picnic packed and we want you to go with us on a trail ride. Kate said we could."

Skyler's eyes traveled to Jessica. "A picnic? Well, if Kate said we could, I don't know how I can refuse that. You should have called me, though. I've already turned Trekker out. You'll have to go down to the pasture and bring him back up to the barn."

"Okay." Charlie grabbed a lead rope and ran toward the pasture.

Jessica smiled. "His uncle is coming to get him this afternoon. Kate thought it would be a good idea to keep his mind occupied until then." She paused. "Actually, I think Kate wanted some time alone, too. She's trying to hide it, but I can tell she's taking his leaving pretty hard."

Skyler walked over and placed a hand on the wall by Jessica's head. She leaned in close and said in a husky voice, "I need something to keep my mind occupied, too, so I'll stop playing last night over and over in my head."

"Last night isn't something I want you to forget, not even for a moment," Jessica whispered as Skyler's warm lips caressed her own.

Their kiss deepened to a passionate exchange, only to be curtailed by the sound of hooves nearing the barn. Jessica held Skyler's glazed stare a moment longer. *Maybe I'm breaking through that tough shell after all,* she thought.

❖

There was enough of a nip in the air to chase away the pesky deer flies that torment both horses and riders in the summer. Still, a cheerful sun shone from the deep blue, cloudless sky to warm their backs as they rode along the mountain trails littered with fallen leaves. They raced across the meadows, laughing and jumping logs and ditches small enough for Charlie to handle. When they reached the mountain trails, Jessica and Rampage led the way with Charlie and Trekker, Skyler and Con Air following. The happy warmth that radiated between them seemed to soothe the anxious youngster.

When they turned down the path to Skyler's ledge, they dismounted and Skyler loosened the horses' saddles and replaced their bridles with halters to make them more comfortable before tying them to nearby trees. Jessica cast a smug glance at her, and received a warm stare in return. Charlie didn't miss the exchange, and lowered his head as a light blush colored his cheeks. Jessica enlisted his help to spread a blanket on the smooth ledge, then unpacked their lunch. The sun shone warm on the exposed ledge, and Skyler began to remove the sweatshirt she wore over a short-sleeved polo shirt.

Charlie's face blanched when he looked up. "Jess. Sky…" he sputtered but could not put his thoughts into words.

Jessica was at a loss at first to understand his distress. "Oh," she said as realization dawned.

Skyler stopped while she still had one arm in her sweatshirt. "What?" she questioned as she looked at her companion's faces. "What's the matter?"

Jessica failed miserably in her efforts to look stern. "I think Charlie was hoping you would keep your clothes on this time. Skyler's mouth dropped open and Jessica gave up her effort to look serious. "Charlie was with me the day Scott showed us your sunbathing spot. I think he's afraid you're changing into your usual attire, or lack of it, for this location."

Charlie's face had turned a deep red. "I didn't look once I realized it was you, Sky," he mumbled.

Skyler's shock turned to amusement. She walked over and kneeled next to him, placing an arm around his shoulders. "I'm sure you didn't, Charlie. I was just taking my sweatshirt off because it was getting bit warm for me, but I want to explain something."

"Okay." Charlie's relief was apparent.

"Not that I would want people going around naked all the time," Skyler said, "but the human body is nothing to be ashamed of. Neither you nor I should be ashamed that you caught me sunbathing, because you were a real gentleman by not staring once you realized you had by accident imposed on my privacy. Your mom would be so proud of you for being thoughtful."

"Scott looked." Charlie grimaced.

"I'm sure he did. But you don't want to be like Scott, do you?"

Charlie shook his head vigorously.

"You're a handsome young man, Charlie, and, in a few years, you'll have plenty of girls interested in knowing you better."

He wrinkled his nose at the prediction.

"No. I'm telling you the truth. You'll be interested in them, too." Skyler chuckled. "When you find that happening, I want you to remember what a gentleman you were with me, and I want you to make me proud by treating those girls and their privacy with the same respect. Any guy can be a man when they reach a certain age, but not every guy is a gentleman. That's what will make you a real man, okay?"

The boy looked thoughtful. "Like Clint?"

Skyler smiled. "Exactly like Clint. He's a real gentleman."

Jessica's eyes filled as she watched the two. She loved the nurturing side that came out when Skyler was around the children.

"Hey, I don't know about you guys," she said, reaching into the saddlebags. "But ham sandwiches sure sound good to me."

Charlie's eyes lit up. "Yeah, I could eat two."

The lunch went by quickly and it was well past noon when Jessica looked at her watch and announced that it was time to head back. Charlie's face turned glum immediately.

"Hey, buddy, don't look that way," Jess said softly. "I have a good feeling about your uncle. You need to give him a chance. Your mom would have wanted that, don't you think?"

He nodded and attempted a small smile. "Okay, Jess."

"Okay, then. I bet the horses are getting tired of being tied up. Let's get everything together and head back to the center."

After repacking their saddlebags, they rode back slowly, each seemingly lost in thought. Skyler gave Charlie's shoulder a little squeeze after they dismounted.

Staring anxiously at the strange SUV parked in front of the house, he asked, "Is that him?"

"I guess," Skyler said.

They were tying the horses to the hitching posts in front of the barn, when Kate walked out of the barn trailed by a thirty-something, dark-haired man with the same brilliant blue eyes as Charlie.

"God, Charlie. Your uncle looks just like you…only older," Jessica said.

The young man knelt down and beckoned the boy. "Hey, Charlie. I'm your Uncle Mark. You probably don't remember me. I used to come visit you and your mom when you were little. Then I was out of the country because of my job. But your mom used to write long e-mails, telling me all about you. She sent lots of pictures." His eyes filled with tears. "I wish she had told me she was sick. I really miss her."

Mark held his arms and Charlie moved to him and began to sob into his shoulder. "I miss Mom so much, too."

They hugged tightly and Mark said, "I know you don't want to leave Kate, but the last time I talked to your mom, I promised her that you and I would take care of each other. It's what she wanted for both of us."

Charlie nodded, his tears slowing to sniffles.

"I'm going to be working in Atlanta nine months out of the year while you're in school, but I'll have to do some overseas traveling during the summer months. I thought you could spend summers here until you're old enough to travel with me."

Charlie's eyes grew wide and he asked Kate, "Can I?"

Kate held her arms out and he shyly walked into her bear hug. "Your uncle and I had a good talk. You can come every time he's away till you're tired of all this."

"I'll never get sick of being here," Charlie said solemnly. "I love it."

"And we love you," Kate said, wiping some tears.

At that very moment, a blood-curdling yowl came from the depths of the barn that sent them all rushing in to see what horse was standing on Peach's tail. Every hair stood out straight on the battle-scarred old tom as a chubby, black Labrador puppy jumped playfully around him.

"Look out there, fellow." Skyler laughed as she scooped the puppy up out of the reach of angry claws. "Peach probably isn't the best playmate for you, little guy."

Mark stepped forward and took the squirming puppy from her. "Oh, so that's where you got off to." He held the puppy up, facing Jessica and Skyler. "I'd introduce this little rascal to you, but he doesn't have a name yet. That's going to be up to Charlie because this is his new puppy."

"Wow! He's mine?" Charlie beamed as Mark handed the puppy to him. "Thanks, Uncle Mark. I'm going name him Rascal."

"That's a great name." Mark turned to the women as they watched the puppy joyfully lick at Charlie's face. "I don't know much about being a father, but I've had a lot of experience being a boy. I'm counting on that to get me and Charlie through without my sister here to supervise us."

"Why don't we go sit on the porch for a while so we can get to know each other?" Kate suggested.

"Skyler and I will take care of the horses," Jessica said. "Then I'll join you."

Jessica and Skyler made quick work of rubbing the horses down and turning them out in the paddocks to relax before they were brought in to the barn for the night. Their eyes met often, and they exchanged smiles as they went about their tasks in the barn. Skyler turned the last horse out and headed to the tack room to hang up the halter and lead rope in her hand. When she stepped through the doorway, Jessica reached out and grabbed Skyler's shirt, pulling her close.

"Seems like I've been waiting all day to kiss you again, and I just can't wait any longer." Burying her hand in Skyler's sun-streaked locks, she kissed her deeply.

Skyler pressed her body against Jessica's and they both moaned. When they finally broke the lip-lock, Skyler touched her forehead against Jessica's. "Think you could find your way back here later tonight?" she begged softly.

"I thought you didn't backtrack down trails you've already ridden," Jessica teased.

"I think this trail will need lots more exploration." Skyler's voice was also teasing, but her eyes were serious.

"Leave your door unlocked, stud. Maybe you'll get lucky."

This time it was Skyler who initiated a passionate kiss that made Jessica's knees go weak and her face flush with desire.

"I sure hope so," Skyler whispered.

❖

The house was quiet when Jessica slipped down the stairs after everyone had retired for the night. The cool night air and the fact that she hadn't injected her knee that day made her leg ache. The pain, though, was no match for her desire to be with Skyler again. She marched down the drive with a determined limp, her heart racing with the anticipation of lying next to Skyler's nude body.

She climbed the stairs to Skyler's apartment quietly and slowly opened the door. The apartment was dark except for flickering candlelight coming from the bathroom. "Skyler?" she called softly.

"In here, Jess," came Sky's low, husky voice.

When Jessica stepped into the doorway a slow smile spread across her face. Skyler was sitting chest deep in a whirlpool bathtub full of bubbles. The warm light of nearly twenty candles illuminated her sculpted features. She smiled at Jessica. "Join me?"

Jessica slowly began to strip off her clothes as Skyler's eyes followed every graceful movement. When she finally stood before Skyler completely naked in the flickering light, Skyler sighed. "God, Jess. You are so beautiful."

She held out her hand and Jessica took it in hers before stepping in the tub and sliding down to lay her body on top of Skyler's. They drank each other in. Skyler reached up to release Jessica's French braid and let the silky dark locks spread across her shoulders. They pressed their seeking mouths together.

"Let's go slow tonight," Skyler whispered. "I want to savor every moment with you."

"I'll bet you say that to all the girls?" Jessica teased.

Skyler stiffened. "No, actually."

"I was just flirting. There was nothing behind that remark," Jessica said with concern. "Baby, I'm so sorry. I didn't mean to upset you. You are too special to me."

Skyler's face was serious. "Do *you* say that to all the girls you've been with?"

Jessica gazed lovingly into her eyes. "No." She took a deep breath and decided to plunge forward. "I've never felt this way about anyone before." She stroked Skyler's cheek. "I know you've been hurt badly in the past and find it really hard to trust. So, I'm going to stick my neck out first and let you know exactly how I feel."

"Jess, you don't have to. I trust you."

She touched her fingers to Skyler's lips. "No, I do have to. Not telling you won't make it any less painful if you choose to turn away." She took a long breath and looked deeply into Skyler's eyes. "I'm in love with you, Skyler. You are always on my mind. I dream about you. When we are together, I feel complete, like I've finally stopped looking for something."

Skyler's eyes filled with tears. Jessica's heart fluttered as Skyler looked away for several long, tortuous moments, a mixture of feelings crossing her handsome face. When she finally looked back into Jessica's eyes, her voice was strained. "Jess. I've tried not to fall in love with you. Everybody told me it was wrong, that I'd mess it up. I think…thought I would mess it up, too. But scared as I am, I just can't help it. I can't think of anything but you. Nobody has made me feel that way since…well, for a very, very long time. I really didn't think I had it in me to be in love again."

Jessica leaned forward into a kiss, but her leg slipped in the tub and she grimaced as pain shot through her knee.

"What's the matter? Skyler said anxiously.

"I just hit my knee wrong. It'll be okay in a moment," Jessica said through clenched teeth.

Skyler took her shoulders and turned her around so she could straighten her legs out and rest her back against Skyler's chest. "Let's just relax a minute," she whispered in Jessica's ear, then ran some more hot water to warm the tub.

They relaxed back when the temperature was right again, their bodies sliding sensuously against each other.

The bare skin was too much for Skyler to resist, and she began nibbling the neck that lay exposed before her. Their bodies pulsed from the warm bath and building passion as they caressed and kissed various sensitive areas.

"I can't help myself, Jess. I just can't keep my hands off of you," Skyler purred.

"I think we need to continue this in the bed," Jessica gasped.

The night was a long marathon of slow, tender lovemaking, stroking hands, plunging fingers, exploring tongues, undulating bodies, breast against breast, and heart against heart as they reached ecstasy time and time again. Finally, they fell into an exhausted slumber, their hearts secure and their bodies sated.

Skyler shook her head to stop the ringing in her ears before she woke and realized it was her cell phone next to the bed. Shit! It was almost eight a.m.

She grabbed the phone and put it to her ear. "Hello?"

"Sky, you still asleep?" It was Kate on the other end. "Charlie and Mark are about to leave. I thought you might want to come say good-bye. You okay?" There was a pause. "Or are you just not alone?"

As Skyler tried to extricate herself from Jessica's warm embrace, she met with resistance. In her sleep Jessica snuggled closer, frowning.

"Uh, you're right, Kate. I do want to see Charlie off," Skyler said quickly, avoiding Kate's question. "Just give me ten minutes to get dressed."

"Wait. Have you seen Jess this morning?" Kate asked before she could hang up the phone. "I thought she was sleeping late but when I went up to wake her, the bed was already made."

Skyler shot a panicked look at Jessica, who blinked sleepily. "Maybe she's up at the gym."

Jessica grimaced and grabbed the phone. "I'm here with

Skyler, Kate. We'll be there as soon as we get dressed." She ended the call without waiting for a response.

Skyler covered her face with her hands and groaned.

"What? Are you ashamed for Kate to know about us?" Jessica demanded.

Skyler lowered her hands. "No! I'd just like to stay alive and employed. Kate warned me not to even think about putting my hands on you, and I promised her I wouldn't." Even before her explanation was finished, her eyes had already strayed and hands caressed the smooth curve of Jessica's hip. "As much as I respect her, I just couldn't keep that promise."

Jessica wiggled her eyebrows. "I happen to like the way you put your hands on me." She grinned. "Kate is a bit protective, but I can handle her…that is, if you're afraid of her," she teased.

Skyler jumped on top of Jessica and began tickling her. "My blood will be on your hands if she murders me or throws me off the farm."

"She's going to murder us both if we don't get cleaned up, dressed and up to the house in the next ten minutes." Jessica laughed, and on that note, they both jumped up and raced to the bathroom.

❖

"Skyler, I want see you in my office," Kate said as soon as they'd waved good-bye to Charlie and Mark.

Skyler started to follow, but Jessica grabbed her arm and stopped her. "No, Kate. I know this is about me, so you can say anything you have to say to Sky in front of me."

The big woman's normally cheerful face darkened. Few people had ever seen Kate angry, but Skyler had and she wasn't anxious to see it again.

"Okay," Kate said in a low voice. "Just what the hell do you two think you are doing?"

"Kate…" Skyler began.

"Don't 'Kate' me, Skyler. I made it perfectly clear that Jessica wasn't up for grabs. I trusted you to train her as a rider and condition her horse. You repaid me by violating that trust. Don't you have any control over yourself or was our friendship just not special enough for you to keep your promise?"

Skyler hung her head, but Jessica's eyes blazed as she stepped between them. "Kate Parker, you've been a second mother to me since I was a baby, but even my own mother hasn't had a say in my love interests since I started high school. As much as I value your opinion, my love life isn't your place to decide. And I really don't appreciate you talking to Skyler like I'm not even here or don't have a will of my own."

"This is about a promise Skyler made to me before you got here," Kate yelled. "It's about violating a trust between friends." She turned to Skyler. "Didn't I stand beside you when nobody else would give you a job? Haven't I looked the other way when you bedded half the female clients of this farm?"

Skyler dug the toe of her boot in the dirt as Kate's tirade continued.

"I don't intend to see you use Jess right under my nose like you do all the other women you sleep with."

Jessica's temper unfurled even further. Stepping within inches of Kate's face, she said, "If I want to sleep with Skyler, then I will. If you want me to leave the farm, I will. But I won't stop seeing Skyler."

"Just wait a minute here." Skyler grabbed Jessica's shoulders and pulled her away from Kate. "Now you guys are talking about me like *I'm* not here. I'm not going to be the one who comes between you. You mean too much to each other. You both mean too much to me."

"Looks like you thought of that too late, Skyler," Kate spat.

Skyler decided it was time to take her chances. Things couldn't go much worse than the way they were heading now. "You're wrong about this, Kate. I mean, you're not wrong about me breaking my promise to you. I deeply apologize for that. But

I won't apologize for being with Jess. This is different." A hot blush flooded her face. "I love...I'm *in* love with her."

"Love?" Kate scowled. "Give me a break."

Skyler stood her ground. "It's true, Kate. I never thought I could lose my heart again after Sarah, but Jess is different. If you hate me for this, then I'll be very sad to have lost my best friend." Skyler took Jessica's hand and pulled her in close. "But if you make me choose between our friendship and what I feel for Jess, I'll have to choose Jess."

Kate's brow knit together as she pressed her lips in a tight frown, considering Skyler's words as if really hearing them for the first time. "How can you know that? You couldn't have been sleeping together long. I would have known it. You can't know you're in love, just like that."

"That's where you are wrong again," Jessica said. "I mean, you're right that we haven't been sleeping together, but Sky and I have just spent months getting to know each other. I think that's what people should do before they form a lasting relationship, don't you?"

Kate turned a skeptical eye toward Skyler, but she seemed to be softening.

"Kate, I need...we need you to believe in us," Skyler begged.

Kate stared at her for a long time. "I never thought I'd hear those words coming out of your mouth again after Sarah tore your heart out, Sky." Then she raised her voice and jabbed her index finger in the air under Skyler's nose. "But if you hurt Jessica, I'm going to personally kick your butt from here to California. Is that clear?"

The new couple released simultaneous sighs of relief, and Skyler looked down at Jessica with unguarded adoration. "No chance of that. No chance of that at all."

CHAPTER TWELVE

Jessica was working on her last set on the thigh machine when she heard the gymnasium door open and close behind her. Her smile grew as quiet footsteps came closer. It was always hard to rise for her early workouts, but pulling herself away from Sky's warm embrace every morning was even tougher. She'd thought Sky would sleep longer for sure. *Couldn't stay away, huh? Maybe I'll get you naked in the whirlpool with me.*

She purposely pretended she didn't hear the stealthy steps until they were almost upon her.

"We've been apart way too long, lover," she said in a sultry voice. She smiled as she heard her stalker abruptly stop. She completed her last leg lift, but still didn't turn around. "And I'm glad you're here." She reached to point out a spot on the back of her neck. "I really need a kiss right there."

After she felt warm lips caress the back of her neck, she closed her eyes and turned her head to capture those same lips with her own. Her eyes flew open when she realized the mouth tasted familiar, but not like Skyler's.

"Wow, I should go out of town more weekends if that's the greeting I'm going to get when I return."

"Tory! I...I didn't know. What are you doing out here so early in the morning?"

The vet's grin began to fade and confusion washed over her face. "I got in late last night, but I just had an emergency call out this way so I thought I'd drop in. I knew you'd be up here starting your daily routine." She began to frown. "If you didn't know it was me, exactly who did you think it could be?"

Jessica's mind raced. She hadn't had time to think about how to tell Tory they could only be friends.

The tall vet stiffened at Jessica's hesitation. "I know we just had a few casual dates, but I thought you would have mentioned if you were seeing someone else, too."

At that moment, the gymnasium door swung open. Jessica rolled her eyes. Apparently her workout had become Grand Central Station. Skyler hesitated when she saw Tory.

"Tory just finished up an emergency out this way." Jessica knew her voice sounded strained.

Tory's green eyes turned angry as realization dawned. "Oh, I see. I'm gone only one weekend and the resident fox has been in the hen house." She started for the door.

"Tory, please wait," Jessica pleaded.

Tory stopped her retreat and paused for a moment before turning around. The hurt was evident in her eyes. "I'm sorry, Jess," she said stiffly. "But don't come looking for me when Skyler jumps to the next woman. I don't take her leftovers. It would keep me way too busy."

"Okay, I deserve that," Skyler said. "But, Tory, this is not like that."

"Are you telling me I'm mistaken, and you two aren't sleeping together?"

"No, but—"

"That's all I need to know." Tory strode out the door.

Skyler crossed the room and took Jessica in her arms. "That didn't go too well, did it?"

"It's not your fault." Jessica relaxed into her lover's embrace. "I should have told her."

"Don't worry, babe. Tory has a good head on her shoulders. After a while, she'll realize that we are really in love. She'll understand that this has nothing to do with her. Besides, she has women lining up. Someone will take your place."

"I didn't think I could be that easily replaced."

Skyler laughed at her pout. "Speaking as your lover, you, my delicious vixen, could never be replaced."

"Good answer," Jessica purred.

"But, speaking as your trainer, you have to get back to work and I have a barn full of horses looking for their breakfast."

"Slave driver," Jessica replied, tilting her head for another kiss.

At lunchtime, Jessica limped up the stairs to her bathroom to inject her knee before Rampage's afternoon gallops. The knee was swollen and bruised from the constant injections. But it was only a few months until Christmas, and, after the holidays, Rampage's workouts would begin to grow shorter so that he would peak at the March trials.

When her knee began to numb, she headed for the kitchen to make a sandwich. As she placed the makings on the kitchen island, she noticed Kate sitting alone on the patio. She had taken Charlie's leaving very hard, and seeing her and Skyler so happy together probably made her feel even more alone. Jessica frowned. She'd been pretty insensitive.

She grabbed a couple of sodas from the refrigerator and went to join Kate.

"You miss him pretty bad, huh," she said after a while.

Kate cleared her throat. Her blue eyes were watery. "Yeah, I guess so," she replied softly. "The kids come and go, but Charlie lived here for nearly a year while his mother was sick. It was nice to always have someone around to share the mornings and evenings with. Somebody around who needed me. I guess *I* needed him more than I realized."

"And now, when you need *me*, I'm spending all my time with Skyler," Jessica said softly.

Kate patted her on the knee. "You don't need to be worrying about me. Kate Parker has always taken care of herself. But I do hope you aren't making a mistake with Skyler. Even if she is sincere, it doesn't mean she is capable of being the woman you deserve." She gave Jessica a wan smile. "But don't listen to me. I just get a little blue when the house is empty. You should enjoy every moment of being in love while you can. There's nothing like that feeling."

"Have you ever really been in love, Kate?"

"Oh, yes. Infatuated several times. Deeply, seriously in love only once."

"What happened?"

Kate stared at her for a moment, then dropped her eyes to study the bricks of the patio. "She was worried that having two mommies would make her daughter the subject of ridicule."

Jessica's jaw dropped. "You mean…Mom? When you left, it was because of me?"

"Oh, honey. It wasn't anyone's fault. We both loved you too much to put anyone else first. I've never really loved another since her." Kate cocked her head and smiled again.

"Does she know that?" Jessica asked, turning this revelation over in her mind.

Kate shrugged. "It's water under the bridge, now. Promise me you won't say anything to her, Jess. I lost her as a lover years ago, and don't want to lose her as a friend because she doesn't feel the same way."

Jessica studied Kate, wondering at the years of longing she must have suffered. "Okay. I promise. I was going to ask Mom to come up for visit because I haven't seen her for months. I can't go see her because Rampage trains six days a week. Now, I don't know. I certainly don't want to have her come here if it is painful for you."

"Don't be ridiculous. Of course Laura can visit. I'd love to see her."

Jessica threw her arms around Kate's neck and held on tight. "Oh, Kate. You've been such an anchor in my life. Mother's not nearly as strong as you are." She laid her hands on Kate's tanned cheeks and gave her a smacking kiss on the mouth.

Kate's hearty laugh warmed her heart. "You better not let Skyler see you smooching on me. She always was the jealous type." She shooed Jessica toward the house. "Get out of here. I've got paperwork to do. You two can come up later for lasagna."

The sight of Skyler's drop-dead sexy smile temporarily erased Kate's request from Jessica's mind.

"Hey, gorgeous," Skyler purred. "How about if I saddle Con Air and we make Rampage's afternoon gallops an outing for both of us?"

"Only if you stop looking at me like that. I won't be able to concentrate enough to stay in the saddle."

They saddled the horses and headed for the maze of wide, dirt trails that wound around the paddocks and through the surrounding woods. Skyler carried a stopwatch and timed four- and five-minute slow canters with three-minute rests in between. The horses pranced and pulled at their bits, eager for something more vigorous.

The morning had brought the first icy breath of winter, a sharp change from the previous day's warm sun. Jessica's cheeks were pink from the cold, and her eyes glowed with the energy radiating from her steed.

"These guys really are geared up today," Skyler called to her. "Why don't we just let them get it out of their systems? Follow me and see if you can keep up."

Con Air lengthened his stride and veered to jump a paddock

fence. Rampage followed close on his heels. A zigzag race across the meadow took them over a stream and a large fallen tree trunk before they leapt the fence again and headed down a lane through the woods. When the path widened, Rampage edged next to the gray. Just as the bay was taking the lead, they broke out of the woods and Skyler turned Con Air sharply to the right. Not expecting the turn, Jessica and Rampage lost ground when they made a wide loop to alter their direction. The big stallion pounded the ground hard to catch Skyler and the gray. They were steadily gaining ground as they trailed Con Air over several fences. Glancing over her shoulder, Skyler hunkered down on Con Air. Man, that bay was some horse.

She eased the pace a little, and Jessica nudged Rampage into the lead. Skyler pulled Con Air back to give Rampage room to take the jump ahead, but stayed close enough to keep up the pressure of the contest. She saw Jessica's head lift a little in surprise. The water jump. Skyler had led them intentionally onto the cross-country course.

It took only that split second for Jessica to determine it was too late to abort the jump without risking injury. She leaned close to Rampage's neck and urged him forward with her hands and legs. Rampage responded immediately and sailed confidently over the jump and through the water. Piece of cake. Skyler and Con Air followed closely behind.

"We did it!" Jessica yelled as she pulled the big bay up. She turned an accusing glare on Skyler. "Very crafty, Ms. Reese." Rampage snorted in agreement. "How about I beat you back to the barn."

"How about we walk the horses back to let them cool down." Skyler smiled.

They walked the horses side by side for a while in companionable silence. Skyler reached over and took Jessica's hand.

Jessica soaked up the adoring gaze directed at her. "Have I told you how much I love you?" she asked.

"I never mind hearing it again," Skyler replied.

❖

The young horse shifted away uncomfortably as Skyler's dandy brush ran over his coat with the same tense speed as the thoughts racing through her head. "You're telling me that I have to meet your mother with no advance notice? Shit, Jess. I really don't have a good track record with in-laws."

Jessica snatched the brush from Skyler's hand.

"Skyler Reese, I never would have imagined you could be such a coward. First of all, my mom is going to love anybody I do, and secondly, I was just trying to find a way for her and Kate to quit dancing around each other and talk about how they feel. That's why I asked her to come."

"Do you really think Kate's ready for this?"

"She'll never be ready at the rate she's going, and neither will Mom. They've wasted years of their lives because they were too chicken-shit to face things together."

Skyler smiled at Jessica's stern posture, elbows out and hands on her slim hips. "You're beautiful when you're angry," she teased.

"Don't change the subject."

"Okay. You win. When is she getting here?"

"She just arrived. I'm going to go see her now and you're joining us for dinner."

"So I can at least get a shower and change into clean clothes? That's a relief."

A quick image of Skyler in the shower turned Jessica's gaze from angry to sexy. The corners of her mouth curled in a seductive smile. "Wear what you had on the night of the fund-raiser. I could hardly keep my hands off of you at that party." She trailed a finger down Skyler's shirt, tracing a path between her breasts and finally hooking her finger into Skyler's waistband to pull her closer. "Maybe I could use a shower, too."

After a quick glance to be sure they were alone, Skyler

followed Jessica's tug and kissed her lover deeply. "Race you upstairs," she whispered before lunging to get a head start.

❖

Laura Black was an older version of Jessica. She had the same dark hair, but peppered with gray and cropped in a short style more fitting her age. Her eyes were the same unusual blue as Jessica's.

"Hey, baby. How is your knee?"

"I'm doing fine," Jessica said. The numbness from her earlier injection was wearing off, but she could still walk like she'd never been injured.

"Kate seems worried, but you aren't even limping."

Jessica waved her hand in a dismissive gesture. "Kate and Skyler are just worry warts, Mom. I'm fine. The knee just looks a little bruised from the last steroid shots I got and they're freaking out over it."

"Well, that's good to know. Now, tell me about this Skyler I've been hearing about."

Jessica blushed. "Skyler's my trainer and, well…Mom, she's the love of my life."

Laura's eyebrows arched. "That's the first time I've heard you use that phrase when referring to a person rather than a horse. I was starting to worry." She glanced at Kate, who was sitting next to her on the couch with her eyes shining. "Is it true?"

Jessica grinned. Having Kate and her mom together really made her feel like she had a whole family again. She wished Kate hadn't made her promise not to say anything. Her mother hadn't lived with anyone else, man or woman, since Kate. Jessica was convinced she must still love her or she would have hooked up with someone else during all these years.

Kate raised her hands in a "hands off" gesture. "I'm definitely not getting in the middle of a mother-daughter thing. All I'll say is that I've known Skyler since she was a kid. She's the best trainer I've got and more committed to the youth equestrian program than anybody who works on this farm. And," she took a deep breath, "they both seem to think they're head over heels for each other. I feel like carrying a bucket of ice water around to throw on them a couple of times a day."

Jessica laughed. "Skyler's tough on the outside, but a real marshmallow when it comes to the kids." She walked behind the couch and leaned over to wrap her arms around her mom's shoulders. "She's also tall, blond, and incredibly sexy. You should see her in riding breeches."

"Quick, Kate. Get your bucket of ice water." Laura laughed, laying her hand on Kate's arm. "Seriously, Jess. Come around here and sit down. I want to talk to you."

"Oh God, Mom. This isn't the sex talk, is it? If it is, you're about ten years too late." Jessica caught a warning look from Kate and realized her mother was struggling with whatever she had to say. She sat on a chair opposite her and said more seriously, "You're okay, aren't you, Mom? You're not going to tell me you're sick or something, are you?"

Her mother gave her a weak grin. "No, honey, I'm just fine."

Jessica glanced at Kate again. "Are you going to tell me you've met someone, too?"

Laura gave Kate a quick, reassuring look. "No. It's nothing like that. It's just that...well, Jess, falling in love with another woman isn't an easy lifestyle. I know you've had relationships with both men and women. I'm concerned that something I've done has made you take this direction in your life."

Jessica let out the breath she was unconsciously holding. "Is that all?" She moved to take her mother's hands, squeezing them firmly. "Mom, you know as well as I do that being gay isn't a choice. My few relationships with men were really either close friendships or just experiments. You've given me every opportunity to choose men over women." She paused and glanced at Kate. "I'm afraid that you may have given up too much for my sake. All these years you've never lived with anyone since Kate."

The Parker heiress shifted uncomfortably in her chair and looked off into the distance, mumbling, "Let it go, Jess."

Don't worry, Kate, I'll stop short of telling her how you feel. Carefully, she said, "I'll always be grateful to you for bringing Kate into my life. You know how much I love her. She's been a wonderful second parent even though she has spoiled me rotten over the years."

Laura's eyes filled with tears. "I just had to know, Jess. I've always worried that you would be influenced by my life and find it as hard as I have."

"I'll tell you what I have learned from you, Mom. I've learned not to let what other people think keep me from being happy."

Laura looked up sharply.

"Mom, millions of heterosexual couples raise homosexual children, and the reverse is true, too. If you did anything to contribute to my sexual orientation, it was just passing along a gene that makes me love women. That doesn't upset me." Jessica waggled her finger at her mother. "But if I end up getting your high blood pressure gene, I'll surely be pissed about that. But I'm glad you brought this up. I want to say something you've needed to hear for a long time."

Her mother looked puzzled.

"Mom, your life has only been hard because you made it that way. I love you to death, but if you hadn't been so freaking paranoid about how things would affect me, you may have been able to have someone to share your life with other than me." She turned to a wide-eyed Kate. "Dinner at seven as usual?"

Speechless, Kate nodded.

"Good. I'm headed to the barn. Skyler and I will join you

later for dinner." She planted a quick kiss on her stunned mother's cheek and strode off to Creek Barn.

Kate and Laura stared after her.

"I just can't get used to her being a grown, opinionated woman instead of my little girl," Laura said.

"You and me both," Kate said uncomfortably.

The aroma of a roast with carrots and potatoes filled the room and made Jessica's stomach growl. Watching the two older women working together to prepare the meal, she wished she could have been a fly on the wall to hear what they said to each other after she left for the barn. She hadn't planned to trek all the way back, but she wanted to leave the house for a while to give them a chance to talk. They seemed to be doing fine.

Laura, as usual, looked elegant, even in casual clothing. She wore gray pants and a pale pink cashmere scoop-necked sweater. Kate wore a dark blue nylon running suit with a silk tank top under the jacket. As always, her sleeves were pushed up her strong forearms.

"Mom, Skyler's very nervous about meeting you, so please try to make her feel at ease," Jessica said. "I feel like a teenager waiting for my prom date to show up."

Laura smiled at Kate. "She makes it sound like I'd actually be something other than a gracious hostess."

Kate chuckled. "You do sort of have that steel magnolia face on tonight. You're going to scare my poor horse trainer to death." She turned to Jessica with a big grin. "Don't worry, Jess. I'll rein your mother in if I see Skyler start to panic and head for the hills."

"I can see you're both enjoying this immensely. If you don't behave, I'll make you sorry later," Jessica said with mock sternness.

She heard Skyler's knock at the front door, and shot one last warning glare at Kate and Laura before heading down the hall. Jesus, Skyler *was* nervous. She never knocked. She usually just stuck her head in the door and hollered.

Skyler stood on the porch, shifting from foot to foot, in the fading light. Jessica ran her eyes appreciatively over her lover's lean body. She made faded jeans look so sexy.

"Hey, good looking. If you don't already have a date for tonight, I'll bet I can find you one." Jessica paused as her appraisal reached Skyler's footwear. "Hey, where are the boots you wore at the party?"

Skyler looked down at the topsiders she'd chosen. "Come on, Jess. I don't want to appear too butch when I meet your mother for the first time."

Jessica wrapped her arms around the tall trainer. "Baby, there's nothing butch about you. You are way too beautiful."

Skyler tried to slip out of her embrace. "What if your mom sees us?"

"Skyler," Jessica said in an exasperated voice. "My mom is gay, too, you know. She won't find anything uncomfortable about us touching each other. And, besides, she already knows I'm crazy about you."

Skyler relaxed a little and hugged Jessica tight. "I like your outfit. What is that perfume you wearing?"

"Opium."

"It's never smelled that good on anybody else."

"You better not be smelling other women anymore," Jessica teased.

Skyler planted a quick kiss on her lips. "What other women? I only have eyes…uh, and a nose for you, dear."

"Good. I have a little present I picked up for you the other day."

"A present for me?"

"Actually, it's for me because I get to look at you when you wear it." Jessica pulled a gold chain from her pocket and fastened it around Skyler's neck. A small, 24-carat gold horse head charm hung from it. "That's why I asked you to wear that V-neck sweater. I knew you'd look stunning in it, and you do." Jessica stepped back to take in the fine gold chain draped over her lover's perfect collarbones.

"Well?" Skyler asked.

Jessica placed her mouth in the sexy hollow of her lover's shoulder, then continued along her graceful neck to tug gently at her soft earlobe.

Skyler blushed. "You've got to stop, Jess. It's tough enough to have to meet your mother for the first time. I don't need my legs to wobble when I walk into the house."

At that moment, Kate opened the door and stuck her head out. "Dinner's ready. Are you two going to stay out here all night, or have you worked up the courage to come in? Or do I need to get my bucket of ice water?"

Jessica laughed at Skyler's puzzled face. "Come on, tough stuff. My mom really doesn't bite."

Laura was in the dining room, putting the last of the food on the table. Jessica held tight to Skyler's left hand as she led her into the room. Kate brought up the rear.

"Mom, this is Skyler. Skyler, my mother, Laura."

"It's nice to meet you, Ms. Black." Skyler offered her free hand.

"Please, call me Laura." The older woman smiled warmly and took Skyler's hand in both of hers. "You know, this may be the first time we've been introduced, but I've seen you ride many times. In fact, Jessica and I were in the stands when you won that gold medal. You had quite a ride that day."

Skyler began to relax. Talking horses was familiar ground. "Con Man was quite a competitor."

"I've always been curious. What happens to horses like him when they're past their prime?"

"Stallions and mares are usually retired to breed."

"But your horse was a gelding, wasn't he?"

"Yeah. He didn't belong to me. The owners sold him to a fairly well-known writer. Now he lives on a Virginia farm where he only has to fox hunt once in a while. Most of his days are spent grazing in lush pastures with a warm stall to snooze in at night."

"Sky owns a full brother to Con Man now, Mom," Jessica said. "But he can't keep up with Rampage. You've got to see him jump."

"I'll see him jump tomorrow," Laura said.

"Enough horse talk," Kate commanded. "Let's eat and see if any of us know something about anything other than horses."

The conversation did move away from horses for a while, but not far. The four talked at length about the center's young equestrian program and the potential applicants Kate had asked Jessica and Skyler to help her interview. Jessica persuaded Skyler to explain her bareback lesson she gave to each group of kids, then thoroughly enjoyed retelling the picnic incident in which Charlie thought Skyler was disrobing.

"So, Laura, how long are you going to be able to visit?" Skyler asked.

"I don't really have a schedule." Laura glanced over at Kate. "I have a bit of news I haven't had a chance to tell Jessica yet. I'm in the process of selling my public relations business in Atlanta. The deal won't conclude until after the first of next year, but the buyer has already taken over management. I was thinking of traveling a bit."

"Really?" Jessica smiled. "It's about time you did something for yourself, Mom."

"So," Kate said slowly. "If you don't have an office to get back to, why don't you just stay here through the holidays?"

"Well, I had thought of that, but I didn't want to wear out my welcome."

"Honey, you are always welcome here, for as long as you like," Kate answered breathlessly.

"Okay, then," Laura said softly, her eyes never leaving Kate's.

"Excellent. It's settled." Jessica squeezed Skyler's hand painfully tight in her excitement. "We can Christmas shop together."

Skyler and Kate looked grateful that the shopping plans didn't seem to include them.

Finally, a yawn from Jessica reminded them all that the farm woke up early, about five a.m. The evening was no longer young. Skyler announced she should be heading out to the Creek Barn and Jessica stood with her.

"Walk me out?" Skyler asked.

"Walk you out? I'm going with you just like always."

Skyler blushed. "I just thought since your mom was here." Her voice trailed off and she glanced nervously at Kate for help.

"It's okay, Skyler," Laura interceded. "At twenty-six years of age, Jessica has been a consenting adult for a while now." Her eyes narrowed in mock sternness. "But before you carry my daughter off to your bed, I do want to know what your intentions are."

"Mom." Jessica gasped. "I can't believe you said that."

Skyler smiled. "That's an easy one, Laura. I intend to make your daughter as happy as I can for as long as she will have me. I'm crazy about her."

Then and there, Jessica fell in love all over again. God, she was really afraid her mom would scare her off. Well, that's one hurdle they'd made it over. She didn't even want to think about the ones down the road.

"In that case, you have my blessing," Laura said. "Now get out of here. You two are keeping us old ladies up way past our bedtime."

CHAPTER THIRTEEN

The holidays went by quickly with Laura staying until mid-January, when she returned to Atlanta to wrap up the sale of her business. She was back at Cherokee Falls six weeks later, just in time to travel with them to Southern Pines for the entire month of March. One of the last things to be taken care of was a final vet exam for Rampage. They were pulling out for North Carolina the next morning. Con Air would be coming along, too, so Skyler could accompany Jessica on Rampage's workouts. The trip would take about three hours and they planned to drive straight through to keep the time the horses would spend in the trailer to a minimum.

Skyler, Jessica, and Laura were standing in the hallway of the barn when Tory's truck pulled up next to the outdoor ring.

"Let me talk to her first," Jessica said. Tory had been sending associates out to the center ever since their uncomfortable parting, but Kate had persuaded her that the exam was too important for her to hand off. "I'll wave to you when she's ready for you to bring Rampage out to the ring," she told Skyler.

Tory was pulling instruments and syringes from the cabinets in the back of the truck when Jessica approached. She didn't acknowledge her right away. Jessica remained silent, waiting until she was ready to speak. After a cool greeting was finally offered, she asked, "Are you still angry with us?"

Tory let out a long sigh. "No, I guess not. I talked to Kate. She said you guys are serious. I guess it was fate, not Skyler's normal carousing after all." She gave Jessica a tepid smile. "I mean, I know we weren't sleeping together or anything. I'm just sorry it was Skyler that snagged you, not me."

"Can't we still be friends?"

Tory nodded and smiled. "Sure. I'd like that. I'll even give your damned trainer the benefit of the doubt, I guess. But I've got to warn you, I lied when I said I wouldn't take her leavings. If Sky ever walks away, I want to be the first person you call."

Jessica smiled. "You've got yourself a deal there, lady." She grabbed Tory in a quick hug.

"Hey!" Tory juggled the syringes in her hand. "You better be careful. I almost got a sample of your blood rather than Rampage's."

Jessica laughed. She was relieved they had mended their friendship. She really liked the amiable veterinarian. She waved the all clear for Skyler to bring Rampage to the ring. Laura trailed behind them.

"Hey, Sky," Tory drawled as Skyler led the stallion up to the truck. "You can drop that deer in the headlights look. Jess has talked me into putting my scalpels away."

"I'm really sorry about how everything happened," Skyler said. "But I'm not sorry about being with Jessica. She's the best thing that ever happened to me."

"Well, let's check this big guy out," Tory said as she walked around to his neck to draw some blood.

"He's already got a negative Coggins test. How come you are drawing blood?" Jessica asked.

"The Olympic folks have gotten so drug-test crazy with their athletes, Kate and I feel it wouldn't hurt to test his blood ourselves before he leaves, and right before and after he competes. It's our insurance in case the tests get mixed up or return a false positive. The Olympic vets will draw blood right before the trials begin and test random horses at the Sunday morning vet check before the show jumping concludes the event."

"Then you're coming to the trials?" Jessica asked hopefully.

Tory smiled. "Sure, I wouldn't miss it."

Skyler interrupted. "Hey, Tory. Do you have an extra bottle of Bute in your truck? Clint says he is getting low, and that old pony still founders on him every once in a while."

"Yeah, I think so, but you better take it now or I'll forget it later." Tory turned to Jessica. "Jess, can you look in that bottom right drawer and grab it? I need Sky to help me with the flexibility tests."

Jessica nodded and walked to the rear of the truck where a cabinet full of drawers held medical supplies and equipment, while the others headed inside the ring for the testing. "Did she say left or right?" She pulled a few drawers open and glanced through the tubes and syringes. Another drawer was filled with vaccines and a dozen vials of...*Carbocaine!*

Jessica glanced nervously at the group. They were all engrossed as Tory flexed and felt Rampage's legs. Jessica had never taken anything in her life. Well, there was that piece of bubble gum at the drug store when she was six years old. She had later tearfully confessed it to her mother and returned to pay for it.

But she was down to her last bottle of lidocaine and they would be in North Carolina for a whole month. There was a lot of money and months of hard work at stake here. She quickly palmed two of the vials and slipped them into the pocket of her jacket.

"Did you find it, Jess?" Tory called. "Be sure you get the one that isn't opened yet."

Jessica quickly pulled out the bottom right drawer and located an extra bottle of the big white anti-inflammatory pills. She held it up for Tory to see. "Got it right here."

Tory was meticulous and the exam lasted for more than an hour. She listened to Rampage's heart, his stomach, felt his legs, X-rayed his front feet and legs, and then completed a long series of tests in the ring to check for any sign of lameness.

"Well, I think I've never seen a horse in better shape," she said when she finally put her clipboard down. "The blood test will take a day or two, but since it's just for the record, it won't keep you from leaving for North Carolina tomorrow. I'll go develop the X-rays and call you this evening to let you know if they turned up anything we should be concerned about. But I don't expect to find anything."

"Thanks, Tory," Skyler said sincerely. "It makes me feel better knowing you're going to be with us in Southern Pines."

Tory smiled. They'd been friends too long to let Tory's disappointment come between them. "I know you two have worked very hard for this. I wish you both the best of luck at the trials...and personally."

Skyler gave her friend an affectionate hug. "Thanks, buddy."

❖

Tuesday morning was a great day for traveling. Mild temperatures and cloudless skies promised an easy trip. Skyler drove the farm's new Ford 350 truck that pulled the two-horse gooseneck show trailer. The front of the trailer was a camper complete with a small kitchen, half bath, and room to sleep four. They would get hotel rooms, of course, but there was always a field where the horse trailers could be parked to provide refuge during the long days of the competition. Those who didn't have trailers with campers would pitch open tents to lounge under while they waited their riders' turns.

Behind the camper were a tack compartment and padded stalls. Jessica rode with Skyler. Besides the fact that the two women seemed inseparable, Jessica was designated navigator for the trip. Kate and Laura followed in Jessica's Explorer, pulling a trailer filled with hay and feed. Skyler was always careful to carry their own feed so the horses wouldn't have any change in their diet.

Virginia's winter-bare hardwoods gave way to lush evergreen pines as they neared North Carolina's Sandhills area, named so because of the sandy soil that made it ideal equestrian footing.

Skyler expertly pulled the big rig onto the field where a few early arrivals like themselves were setting up. Kate and Laura had stopped at the training center to register and get their barn assignment while Skyler and Jessica walked the horses to let them stretch their legs and graze on the winter rye grass around the trailers.

"Wow, this place is everything they said it would be," Jessica said.

"I guess you're more used to soggy fields that end up being mud quagmires in the spring," Skyler said. "It is great down here. This is where Con Man and I trained. The sandy soil here dries out fast. That's what makes it so ideal for horses."

The Explorer pulled up next to them, and Laura climbed out of the passenger seat and stretched from the long ride while Kate issued orders. "Okay. The boys will be in that first barn over to your left. Here are their stall numbers. They said the stalls are already bedded. Laura can take Con Air and go with Jess to the barn. Skyler, you and I will unhook this U-Haul and load some feed and the tack trunks into the back of the Explorer and drive it up to the barn."

Accustomed to traveling, the horses settled quickly in their large stalls. This barn was only for geldings or stallions. Mares were housed separately. When Kate and Skyler joined them at the barn, a thin, grizzled man wearing a security uniform stood smiling at Jessica's side. She carried out the introductions, explaining, "Fred is the head security guy for this barn. Fred, this is my trainer, Skyler Reese, and my sponsor, Kate Parker."

The guard squinted at Skyler. "I know this young lady. How have you been, Sky?"

Skyler grinned at him. "Great, Fred. It makes me feel better to see you're still around. You're good, too, I hope?"

"Well, other than putting up with my arthritis, I can't complain." He went on to take down their phone numbers and explain the routine, pointing out that someone called Melvin watched over things at night. "We've both done time in the backstretch stables at Churchill Downs before we came here, so we know horses."

Slipping easily into his role as head groom, he pointed toward the stalls.

"Any special instructions need to be written on the clipboard on each horse's stall door. We walk the barn every hour, on the hour, to check on the horses. If we're not walking around out here, we're in that office right there. We got us a fancy security system now. It beeps every time anyone comes in any door so we know to stick our head out and see who's prowling around."

Kate nodded, satisfied the horses would be secure. "I think we'll just settle our boys in and go check into our hotel. We'll come back after supper to check on them before we turn in."

Jessica tugged at Skyler's arm. "Don't you think we need to tell them about Rampage?"

Skyler nodded. "Right. Why don't you write a warning on his stall clipboard." She turned back to the guard. "Fred, that bay stallion doesn't take kindly to strangers. In fact, he'll bite a plug out of just about anyone he doesn't know. The stable hands can muck the gray's stall, but we'll take care of Rampage. I don't want anyone hurt or the horse upset before the competition. Oh, and as always, I'll feed and water my own horses."

"Whatever you say, Sky. Hey, is that Con Man you've got there with you?"

"This is his brother. He's mine, but we're not competing. I'm here as a trainer, not a rider this time. Jess here is one of the best riders you'll see compete and that bay stallion is good enough he might have taken the gold from Con Man if they had competed against each other."

"Well, I sure wouldn't mind seeing someone different take the wind out of some of these bluebloods' sails." The old man scratched his chin. "Especially after the way they treated you."

"Don't sweat it, Fred. Things work out for the best. I really love what I'm doing now. I don't think I've ever been happier." She glanced at Jess.

"Glad to hear it. Get on, now. I'll see you after supper. If I'm not here, just introduce yourselves to Melvin."

After putting the tack trunks away and locking up the horse van and truck, they checked one more time on the boys. Con Air and Rampage were contentedly munching their hay. Laura laughed when she spotted the orange cat curled up in the corner of Rampage's stall. "I can't believe you brought that cat. Aren't you afraid he'll run away?"

"He always sticks close to Rampage," Jessica said. "I just hang the water lower so he can reach it, too, and he's fine. The whole stall is one big kitty box."

Laura smiled. "I guess I've seen stranger things, but I can't remember when."

The hotel, of course, was elegant since the small town was accustomed to hosting professional golfers and wealthy equestrians. They unpacked quickly and headed downstairs to the hotel restaurant. It had been a long day, but the conservation was pleasant. Before they left, Skyler ordered two double slices of bourbon cheesecake to go.

"You're not going to fit into those sexy riding breeches very long eating like that," Jessica teased.

"It's not for me, thank you very much. It happens to be Fred's favorite," Skyler said. "When I was hiring out as a rider, I sometimes had to supplement my income with a kitchen job at some of Southern Pines' finer restaurants. I would swipe a piece of bourbon cheesecake whenever I could for him. In return, he would tip me off when people were looking for a rider. He helped me through some lean times."

"You never forget friends who look out for you," Kate said, taking Laura's arm. "We're going to retire and leave you young people to go check on the horses."

Jessica smiled as she watched them head toward the elevators. She knew Kate often stayed up half the night and still rose at the crack of dawn. It was cute to see her cater to Laura's need for longer hours of rest.

"What?" Skyler asked, giving her a gentle nudge.

"Nothing." Jessica hooked arms with her lover. "I'm just glad to have all the important women in my life in one place."

"You know, you don't have to go back to the barn with me if you're too tired. I just want to check on the boys and give Fred his dessert," Skyler offered as they waited for the valet to bring the SUV.

"In case you haven't figured it out yet, I'm grafted to your side. You're going to need surgery to get rid of me."

"Good God, woman. You're going to make me wreck this vehicle." Skyler groaned, belting herself into the driver's seat.

Jessica leaned close to her ear and whispered, "I don't want you to wreck my truck, but I do plan to make you beg when we get back to our room." She smiled at the blush creeping up Skyler's neck. She enjoyed seeing her lover react to her touch.

Skyler's blush deepened. "You are one naughty girl. And I think I like that."

A thin face topped by a neat crew cut appeared when they arrived at the door of the barn office. "Hey, I heard the alarm system beep. I guess you are with the Parker crew?"

"That's them, Melvin." Fred's face appeared next and the two old men emerged from the office. "This is Skyler, the one I was telling you about. And this is Jessica. She's going to be riding that big stallion with the hands-off orders."

Jessica extended her hand. "Pleased to meet you, Melvin."

"That your orange cat?"

"Yes, but he shouldn't be any trouble. He'll stay in the stall with Rampage. For some reason the horse likes him, and behaves a lot better when that rough-looking old tom is around." She held up a can of 9-Lives tuna. "We brought his supper."

"Well, he's not exactly in the stall right now."

"He's not? Do you know where he is?"

Fred broke into a wide grin while Melvin explained. "Well, it didn't take long for him to figure his way out of that stall. He's in the office."

"I'm so sorry," Jessica hurriedly apologized. "I thought he would stay in the stall. I hope he hasn't been a bother."

"No trouble," Melvin deadpanned. "But I don't think he needs that can of cat food."

Fred began to chuckle, shaking his head. "Seems he dispatched two mice right away. He dragged them into the office for a trade."

"Since I had brought in a mess of catfish for mine and Fred's supper, we shared it with him," Melvin said. "He's watching the basketball game with us now."

Jessica laughed along with them as they peered into the office at the cat lounging on his back with his feet sticking up on either side of his bulging belly.

Skyler produced her gift. "Guess what I found on the hotel menu, Fred."

Fred's eyes lit up. "I'll be damned. That isn't a piece of bourbon cheesecake, is it?"

"Even better," Skyler grinned. "There are two pieces. But I wasn't sure if you'd still be around this late."

"Well, since both Melvin and I lost our wives some time ago, we kind of stick together. It's a comfortable life for two old grooms getting close to polishing their last saddles."

"I'm glad to know that. I remember when you lost your wife. I worried about you being lonely after that."

"How about you, Sky? You were pretty low when I saw you last."

"I'm absolutely great. You know me. I manage to land on my feet." Skyler placed the bag of cheesecake on the desk just inside the office. "It's getting late, and we're keeping you from your ballgame. We'll just make the horses comfortable and head back to the hotel."

"Sure, Sky. Thanks for the cheesecake, girl."

Skyler grabbed a muck bucket and pointed Jessica toward two muck rakes leaning against the wall. Jessica slid the door back on Rampage's stall while Skyler entered Con Air's, and they began to clean out any droppings so the horses could lie down comfortably.

"Well, one thing's for sure." Jessica laughed. "These guys sure do travel well. If you were worried about the trip bringing on a colic attack, you can relax. They're both making enough manure for a herd of horses. Does Con need more hay?"

"No, he's fine."

"Okay, I'll be right back," Jessica said over her shoulder as she headed out.

Skyler muttered to herself as she knelt down to feel Con Air's front legs. "You're not going to go lame on me, are you, buddy? You never were good at traveling. If you were, you'd be on the circuit right now." She patted the gelding affectionately. "You look okay, but I'm going to rub a little liniment on you for good measure."

She was kneeling beside the gelding and rubbing liniment into his front legs when a chillingly familiar voice drifted over the half door of the stall.

"If I didn't know better, I'd think that was Con Man you are rubbing down."

Skyler froze for a moment, then stood up. "Hello, Sarah."

The petite woman's light brown hair shone as she combed long, manicured fingernails through it, pushing the shoulder-length locks back from her face. Her hazel eyes drank in Skyler's tall form. "How've you been, Sky?" she asked softly.

"I've been just fine."

Melvin stuck his head out of the office door.

"It's okay, Melvin. It's just me," Sarah called out. He waved and disappeared back in to the office. She turned back to Skyler. "You here to ride?"

"No." Part of Skyler wanted to be a bitch. Sarah's betrayal still cut deep. But part of her said it didn't matter any longer. "I've been working as a trainer at Kate Parker's center since I left here."

"I know. Believe it or not, I've sort of kept up with you through friends. I was glad when Kate hired you."

"I wouldn't have imagined that you even cared," Skyler muttered.

"Okay. I deserved that." Sarah sighed.

Skyler gave her a sharp look. She hadn't expected...well, she didn't know what she expected Sarah to be like if they met again. They both fidgeted as an uncomfortable silence fell between them.

Sarah finally cleared her throat. "That the horse you're training?"

Skyler glanced at Con Air. "No. This is my personal horse. The horse I'm training for the trials is that bay stallion in the next stall."

Sarah walked over and read the clipboard on Rampage's stall. "I know this horse. Greg Knowles has been campaigning him. He's not bad, but he's inconsistent."

"Jessica Black is riding him now. She and Kate co-own him."

Sarah gave Skyler a sharp look. "Jessica Black? I thought that accident put her out of commission. Joe Sorenson mentioned it just the other day."

Skyler smiled. She'd counted on the Sorensons to tell

everyone about Jessica limping around on her cane. "For a while, yes. But she's back, and you better be looking over your shoulder for her if you're competing. They're more impressive than any team I've seen on the circuit in a long while."

Sarah stiffened. Before she could reply, Jessica strolled in with Rampage's full hay bag slung over her shoulder. She slowed her stride to size up the scene she seemed to be interrupting. Sarah looked her over carefully.

"Hi." Jessica stuck her hand out, and forced a gracious smile. "I'm Jessica Black."

Too schooled in polite manners to respond any other way, Sarah returned a stiff smile and gave her hand a weak shake. "Nice to make your acquaintance. I've seen you ride. I'm Sarah Tate. Well, it's Sarah Duke now, but I still use my maiden name on the circuit."

Jessica felt her face freeze for a split second. So this was the famous Sarah Berrington Tate. No wonder Skyler looked like her dinner hadn't agreed with her.

"I've seen you ride, too," Jessica said smoothly. "Are you here to compete?"

"I am. I didn't know you were back on the circuit. I'm surprised to see you recovered so soon."

She turned to Skyler and gave her a warm smile. "I'll see you around, Sky." She nodded at Jessica. "See you in the arena, Jessica."

Skyler didn't return the smile. "Are you ready to go?" she asked Jessica. Without waiting for her reply, she set off quickly in the opposite direction of Sarah's exit. Jessica quickly secured the hay bag, and then hurried to catch up. When she stepped through the barn's doorway and into the darkness, a long arm grabbed her. Skyler leaned against the side of the building and pulled her into a tight embrace. Her mouth hungrily sought Jessica's and her arms squeezed so hard, Jessica could hardly breathe.

"Sky, honey, are you okay?" she asked between short breaths.

Skyler relaxed her hold and buried her face in Jessica's neck. After a moment, she spoke without raising her head. "I knew it would be hard facing this crowd again, but I guess I didn't really know how it would feel."

Jessica was quiet, but her heart was racing. "Do you still have feelings for Sarah?"

"I don't know what I feel. A little sad, a lot angry, and at the same time somehow indifferent. Maybe I wanted her to look like she had suffered some, too. Like it had hurt her as bad as it hurt me. She tossed me away like a bad habit, though, when I stood between her and her father's money."

"She lost more than she gained," Jessica said, feeling Skyler's hot tears on her neck.

"Getting blacklisted on top of having my heart broken was just too much," Skyler said. "I felt like the worst piece of trash you can imagine. It felt just like when my father would beat me while he screamed about how worthless I was."

Jessica's heart ached for her. "Sky, you shouldn't need anybody to tell you what a great person you are, but I will." She took Skyler's face in her hands and looked deeply into her eyes. "You are the sexiest, most beautiful, most caring, wonderful lover a woman could have. I love to watch you work with the kids at the center. They all adore you. I adore you. Kate adores you. You have lots of real friends, and they're not from a crowd whose friendships go only as far as money or last names. Hell, Rampage even likes you, and he doesn't like anybody else but me and Peach."

This drew a small smile from Skyler.

"You don't have to be here if this is too painful," Jessica said softly. "You've done your job. Rampage and I can finish this."

Skyler brushed her lips with the softest of kisses. "I love you, Jess. I can face anything as long as you're next to me."

Jessica hugged her tight. "And that's where I'll always be, as long as you let me. Let's go, baby. We've had enough excitement for the day."

Skyler's kiss was slow and deep and tender, and filled with promise, reassuring them both that their bond was growing stronger every day.

Chapter Fourteen

The emotional bonding of the previous night had clicked something in place between Jessica and Skyler. They seemed to anchor each other, unconsciously finishing each other's sentences and tasks as they worked together to saddle the horses. There were sometimes long, comfortable silences because words were not necessary to feel their completeness.

Jessica felt Skyler had finally fully opened her heart to her. She had revealed two of her deepest hurts, her father and Sarah. Jessica considered that trust a precious gift. That's why it ate at her that she still withheld a terrible secret of her own. She was terrified Skyler would again feel betrayed if she discovered the true condition of her knee and what she was doing to still be able to ride. She knew she had to figure out how to tell her.

But the morning was crisp and sunny as she followed Skyler and Con Air down the wide, sandy paths, and Jessica pushed those despairing thoughts aside while Skyler carefully timed Rampage's gallops. The workout wound up with a long walk back to the barn to cool the horses down. The training facility had begun to teem with other riders, trainers, stable hands, and horses, but Skyler and Jessica didn't hide their affection for each other. Skyler insisted she didn't care who noticed. They'd already done their worst to her. Jessica thought she saw Sarah sitting with her trainer in the bleachers of the outdoor ring, watching another competitor practice over the show jumps. Her binoculars, however, had been trained on her and Skyler for the past few minutes. She studied them for a while longer before lowering the glasses and saying something to the man next to her.

After she walked away, leaving him there, he moved his binoculars to his eyes then dropped them with a jerk. He left the bleachers too, in the stride of a man who'd just seen something he didn't like. Jessica concluded he must have recognized Skyler on a horse that looked just like Con Man. Her heart raced suddenly. She hoped coming here was not going to create trouble. Jessica knew, despite Skyler's assurances, there were still people here who would stick a knife in her back.

Plenty of them were there to watch later that afternoon, when Jessica and Rampage floated into the dressage ring, relaxed and completely in sync. She took him fluidly through the elementary maneuvers usually required at a three-day event: medium trot, working trot, halt, salute, circle, half-pass, extended trot, circle—in a freestyle exhibition both horse and rider usually enjoyed. Others milling about outside the ring began to stop and lean against the rail to watch the superb stallion. Without even a glance to acknowledge the growing crowd of onlookers, Jessica asked Rampage to execute the more difficult movements required in at the higher levels of dressage, the piaffe and passage. The crowd was quiet, as though they were holding a collective breath.

Sitting next to Laura and Kate, Skyler said, "This *isn't* part of their training. She's just plain showing off now."

The corners of Jessica's mouth curled in a slight smile as Rampage smoothly transitioned into difficult flying changes, a skipping movement at a canter in which the horse changes his leading front leg every stride. Finally, after a flawless pirouette, the pair came to a halt in the center of the arena and saluted.

Jessica finally broke her stoic composure and a big grin spread across her face. The crowd smiled back and applauded their appreciation.

"Yeah, but can he jump?" one bystander called loudly.

Kate couldn't resist. "Jump? Hell, that's what he's really good at," she replied just as loudly.

Skyler shook her head and turned to Laura. "That daughter of yours, she's just incorrigible." But she could hear the pride and adoration in her own voice.

"Huh!" Laura sniffed, raising her chin in an arrogant gesture. "She's just showing the competition what they're going up against."

Jessica's heart soared with the applause as she and Rampage exited the ring. Waiting at the gate for their turn to practice was Sarah and her chestnut Thoroughbred mare. Sarah touched the end of her dressage whip to the bill of her riding helmet in a salute.

"He's magnificent," she said. "He never looked that good when Greg Knowles rode him."

"Thanks," Jessica replied with a gracious smile. "He and I just seem to click together."

A trace of envy tinged with sadness briefly altered Sarah's face. "You may be too hard of an act to follow," she said before trotting off into the arena.

While the emotional high of the day had kept Jessica's mind off the increasing ache in her knee, there was no mistaking that the most recent injection was quickly wearing off. Every step was becoming excruciating and she had to concentrate to keep the knee from giving way when she walked. It wasn't unusual for her limp to return after a day of riding, but Skyler noticed her gait as soon as she entered the barn.

"Hey, Miss Invincible, I think you should go back to the hotel and take care of that knee. I don't need the horse or you to go lame this close to the competition."

Jessica hesitated at being separated from her lover even a few hours, but she could see from the expression on Skyler's face there was no point in arguing.

"Go on now," Skyler urged. "I'll stay and take care of the horses. It will give me a chance to see who else is here to compete and catch up with my old buddy, Fred." She pulled her into Rampage's stall for privacy and gave her a long kiss. "I'll be back at the hotel by seven if you can make Kate wait that long for dinner. I've got the keys to the truck. You guys take the Explorer."

Jessica sighed and laid her head against Skyler's breast. "How can I rest without my favorite pillow?"

Skyler gave her a light slap on the rear. "You'll rest a lot better without me to tempt you into other things. Now go!"

❖

Back at the hotel, Jessica leaned back and closed her eyes in relief as the pain pill kicked in. The knee was badly swollen, so she climbed onto the bed, elevated her leg on a stack of pillows, and piled on several ice packs.

Laura knocked lightly on the bedroom door before entering. "Hey, sweetie. How's that leg?"

"It's fine, Mom. I guess I gave it quite a workout today, and it's swelling some. It will be fine."

"Let me look at that knee Skyler and Kate are so concerned about."

Jessica hunched protectively over her knee and shooed her mother away. "I just got comfortable with the ice packs in exactly the right place. You don't know how hard that is. I'll show it to you later."

Laura looked suspicious. "You're being evasive."

"You guys going somewhere?" Jessica asked, changing the subject.

"Well, I wanted to do a little shopping, but Kate's idea of

shopping is a visit to the golf pro shop. So, I guess we're going to the clubhouse for a drink. Kate says she wants to see who else is here. I really think that she just wants to go gloat after that display you and Rampage put on this afternoon."

Jessica grinned. "I'm happy I could contribute to her fun."

"Skyler's right. You are incorrigible."

After Kate and Laura left, Jessica was restless, having already napped earlier in the day. The hotel suite was too quiet. She iced her leg for nearly an hour, thumbed through a few magazines, then switched on the television. After an hour of flipping channels, she clicked it off. She missed her partner, damn it. She pulled on some loose sweatpants and called a cab to take her back to the equestrian center.

❖

Skyler had rubbed Rampage down and strolled the competitors' barns to see who else was showing up for the trials before joining Fred in the barn office to catch up on each other's lives. Fred was impressed as Skyler chatted on and on about the Young Equestrian Program.

"It sure sounds like you like it there," he told her.

"Things ever go sour for you here, Fred, you just call Kate or me. I can guarantee you a place on the farm if you ever want to move to Virginia," Skyler said earnestly.

Fred clapped her on the shoulder. "Thanks, Sky. I'm happy right here for now, but I'll always keep that in mind."

"Well, it's about time for me to feed the boys and think about heading back to the hotel. Kate's good nature wears thin when she's hungry. And when that happens, you *don't* want to be the one holding her up from eating dinner."

The old man followed Skyler into the barn's wide central hallway. "Skyler, I've got to ask you something." He shifted on his feet and stared at the dirt floor of the barn.

"Sure, Fred. Anything."

The old man seemed to struggle to form his question. Guessing at his reason, Skyler assured him, "Jess isn't like Sarah, Fred. She's the real deal, the best thing to ever happen to me."

He looked sharply down the barn hallway, as if checking to see if they were alone. "No, it's not that. It's just. Well, I've seen a lot of things when I worked the race track and…well, you're not doping that horse, are you?"

In equestrian sports, it was the horses, not riders, who were forbidden from using drugs to hide an injury or enhance performance. Skyler was incredulous at the suggestion. "Doping Rampage? Whatever for?"

"Well, you see, Melvin was emptying out the trash in the tack room and found a used syringe. He's insisting that nobody but you and your rider had been in there since he had emptied the trash earlier."

"You know me better than that," Skyler said. "I would never show a hurt horse. Rampage hasn't had a lame day since he came in my barn."

The old man straightened the slump in his shoulders. "That's exactly what I told him. He's just an old coot. Probably got mixed up and just thought he had emptied the trash earlier." He scratched his head. "Still, somebody is shooting up something around here. Keep your eyes open, okay?"

"Yeah, sure, Fred." Skyler's mind raced through the possibilities. She turned toward the horses' stalls. Surely not. Still, it couldn't hurt to be as cautious as possible. "Hey, if you have that syringe, maybe you should get the head of security to test it to see what was in it. I don't want to think this could happen, but maybe somebody is trying to sabotage the competition."

"Right you are. Melvin should have thought of that himself." He headed back to the office, mumbling to himself. "Old fart. Trying to say my friends were doping a horse. I should have busted his chops right then and there. He's going to owe them an apology when we find out what was in that syringe."

Skyler went immediately to the tack room to look around.

There were other horses in the barn already, but only a couple of trainers were storing their tack boxes in that room. She unlocked the boxes that had come from the center. The first trunk carried leg bandages and vet wrap, halters, brushes, and other things for the horses. The second trunk carried the riding habits, helmets, and boots Jessica would wear in the competition. Nothing seemed to be missing.

Skyler lifted a pouch from beneath one of the jackets. A bottle of Carbocaine slid out into her hand. She'd helped vet enough horses to know it was a numbing agent. Why would Jess have brought this along? Was there something wrong with Rampage that she was afraid to mention? Puzzled over what she'd found, she poured the horses' dinner into their feed pails and carefully checked each animal over. Maybe Jess's showing-off had attracted some unwanted attention. It took a lot of money to campaign one of these horses to the top. People harbored resentments. Or maybe it was about her. Maybe someone was trying to set her up.

"That's some pretty heavy thinking going on in there."

Skyler turned as Sarah slid the stall door back. She walked over to Rampage and ran an admiring hand over his sleek shoulder. "You were right. He and Jessica are pretty hot in the ring."

"Careful," Skyler warned. "He has a tendency to bite anyone he doesn't know, and he means business when he does."

But the stallion only snuffled Sarah's hand before he went back to his dinner.

"Well, how about that," Skyler said, rubbing the back of her neck. "That is definitely a first. He never takes to strangers."

"Maybe I remind him of Jessica." Sarah stared at the stallion so she didn't have to meet Skyler's eyes.

"You are alike in some ways, but very different in others," Skyler said.

Sarah stared at the floor, her expression bitter. "Different in the way that counts, I'm sure."

Skyler didn't know what to say. "We've both moved on."

"No, Sky. I have to say this. I can't tell you how sorry I am that I was a gutless debutante addicted to my father's money."

She swept watery hazel eyes up to Skyler. "Walking away from you was the worst decision of my life. I was just so scared. I could hardly live with how deeply I hurt you. What you don't know is how bad I hurt myself by losing you."

Skyler shifted uneasily. This wasn't a memory she wanted to revisit alone here with Sarah. She wished Jessica were with her. "It's not worth digging up old bones, Sarah."

"I need you to know that, as painful as it was, it made me grow up a lot." Sarah caressed Skyler's cheek. "As much as it hurts me to see you with somebody else, I'm so glad to see you are happy." Her sadness hung heavy over them as her eyes searched Skyler's. "You used to look at me the way you look at Jess. I can tell how much you care for her."

At that moment, Skyler realized her love for Jessica far surpassed what she'd once felt for Sarah.

Sarah's hand left Skyler's cheek and cupped the back of her neck. A tear trickled down her cheek as she planted a soft kiss on Skyler's lips. "Just be happy, Sky. You deserve that more than anyone else I know."

Skyler watched as Sarah turned and quietly left without looking back. "Good-bye, Sarah," she said softly to no one but herself.

She felt stunned by Sarah's visit. Stunned, but relieved. The hurt she'd carried around for so long could finally begin to heal. She realized that what had happened hadn't been a cold, calculated betrayal. It had been the action of a scared, immature young woman. That revelation seemed to erase the small, lurking insecurity that Jessica could one day do the same. The thought of her lover filled her with an urgency to wrap her arms around her and hold her close.

Skyler checked the water buckets. Satisfied the boys were bedded down for the night, she latched their stall doors and turned to leave. At the last moment, she remembered the vial and syringe she had set on a ledge outside the stalls. Picking them up, she studied them in her hand. Before she could take a step, her cell phone vibrated against her hip. She frowned as she glanced at the unfamiliar caller ID and flipped the phone open.

There was nothing but silence. "Hello?" she repeated.

"Sky?" Jamie's thin voice was plaintive. "You said to call you if…"

"Jamie, what's wrong? Are you okay?"

The girl began to sob. Skyler took a deep breath. Okay, one problem at a time. "Calm down, James, and tell me what's going on." Her concern grew urgent as the sobs continued. "Do you need somebody to come help you now? I'm not in town, but I can get Clint over there in just a few minutes."

"I'm not at home. It's so awful, I can't stand it," she wailed.

"Slow down, honey. Start at the beginning and tell me what's happened." She waited patiently as the sobs slowed to hiccups and sniffs. When the words finally came, they were so rushed she had to listen closely.

"Dad got a job driving a load to California, then another to Canada. He won't be back for weeks. He and Mom had a big fight just before he left because she just couldn't stand the thought of him being gone so long. Dad said he couldn't turn it down because the pay was so good." The girl's voice turned bitter and old beyond her young years. "He was hardly out of the driveway before she opened a fresh bottle. She drank for a while, and I hoped she would just go to bed. But she just got madder and madder. She said it was my fault because I was growing so fast I always needed clothes and stuff. Dad is always gone, she said, because he has to make enough money to pay for my stuff."

"You know that's not true," Skyler reassured her. "She just needs someone to blame. But finish telling me what happened."

Jamie's voice was strangled with tears. "She hurt me really

bad this time, Sky. She broke my arm. A neighbor called the police. They took me to the hospital and Mom's in jail."

Skyler choked down the fury that welled up at the news. But Jamie didn't need her anger right now. She needed safety. Skyler kept her voice calm. "Oh, James, I'm so sorry I wasn't there to stop her. Are you at the hospital now?"

"No. That was yesterday. Now they've taken me to some kind of orphanage or juvenile hall or something. They said they're going to put me in a foster home until my dad gets back. Please, Sky. Come and get me. I'm so scared."

"Don't you worry, Jamie. I'm on my way now. Will you be okay there tonight? I'm in North Carolina, about three hours away, but I'll be there first thing in the morning. I promise you, I'll do something about this."

"I didn't know anyone else to call," Jamie sniffed. "They can't get in touch with Dad while he's on the road. He only picks up messages during his rest stops. Mom is out of jail, but I can't go home until Dad gets back."

"You did the right thing calling me. Don't worry, kiddo. You just rest easy tonight. I'll be there in the morning. Kate and I will take care of everything."

"Okay, Sky."

Skyler ended the call and immediately phoned the hotel room, but got no answer. The next number she dialed was Kate's cell phone. She was relieved when she heard her friend's voice.

"Kate, thank God you had your phone on."

"Something wrong, Sky?" Kate's voice was overly loud and jovial. She'd downed several Manhattans as bragging rights had turned to friendly wagers with some old friends at the clubhouse.

"Damn. Where are you? I hope Laura hasn't been drinking as much as you sound like you have."

"Hey, I'm just having fun. We left Jess at the hotel. We're at the clubhouse, laying down a few wagers."

"How about letting me talk to Laura?"

She heard Kate hand off the phone to Laura, saying, "Spoilsport. She wants to talk to the sober one."

"Sky? Something wrong? Is Jess okay?" Laura was sober and concerned.

"I guess she's still at the hotel, but she must be asleep. She's not answering the phone. Listen, Laura. I've had an emergency come up back in Cherokee Falls. I've got to drive back tonight."

"What's wrong? Shouldn't Kate or Jess go with you?"

"No, Jess needs to stay here and stick to her training schedule. Kate needs to help her. I can't go into details right now, but when you get back to the hotel, I need Kate to call me with the phone number for her lawyer, George Brumley. She can call my cell phone. If I'm out of range, tell her to call my apartment and leave the information on my answering machine."

"Her lawyer? Are you in some kind of trouble, Skyler?"

"Not me, Laura. You just have to trust me." Skyler didn't know if she could say more because the Young Equestrian Program had strict confidentiality rules.

There was a short silence. "What do you want me to tell Jessica?"

"Tell her that I'll be back late tomorrow or the next day. She knows the schedule we've mapped out for Rampage. Just some slow trots and walking tomorrow morning and a little jumping tomorrow afternoon."

"I'll tell her."

What was that she heard in Laura's voice? Doubt? Irritation? "Laura…"

"Yes?"

"Tell Jess I love her. She can call my cell phone tonight after you guys get some dinner."

"I'll do that, Sky. And dinner's not a bad idea. I think Kate could use something to eat instead of another Manhattan."

❖

When the cab stopped at the gate of the equestrian center so the driver could talk to a security guard he knew, Jessica flagged him down. The sun had set quickly and clouds had moved in to make the night a very dark one. She sank back in the seat and asked the driver to take her to the Marriott. She was still shaking.

She'd been grinning at the thought of surprising her lover, as she'd neared the barn. Bright lights illuminated the interior. What she saw slowed her stride, then stopped her dead in her tracks. Sarah and Skyler were talking. Jessica watched Sarah caress Skyler's cheek, and Skyler didn't pull away. She saw the kiss, and Sarah's upset expression as she'd walked away. She hadn't jumped to conclusions. She knew Skyler's heart. There had to be a good explanation.

Jessica took a couple of deep breaths to settle the green-eyed monster that was threatening to rise up again. It wasn't the kiss that bothered her, but what came afterward when Skyler vanished for a few minutes, then appeared studying something in her hand. Jessica had recognized the vials immediately. *Oh, shit!* She wasn't ready for this. How could she explain without Skyler being hurt and furious? Her greatest fear was that the discovery would send Skyler back into Sarah's conveniently outstretched arms. She needed time to think about what to say when Skyler confronted her.

Her mind racing and gut churning in fear, she stared out the car window into the night. She needed to come clean before Skyler reached her own conclusions. But what if Skyler insisted that she withdraw from the competition rather than risk permanently injuring her knee? What if she felt like Jessica had betrayed her by violating the trust between them? *This isn't about her, this is about me! Hey, and what about her kissing Sarah?* She knew that Sarah had initiated the kiss. She also knew in her heart that Skyler didn't want Sarah, but, damn, love wasn't rational. It still irritated her and tugged at a tiny insecurity. The very thought of losing Skyler was like a jagged knife lodging in her chest. No, no. She wouldn't think about that. *She has to know I love her more than anything.* But not enough to be honest, the voice in her head reminded her.

Jessica didn't know what she would do if she lost Skyler. Sweat made her palms clammy. She wanted to tell the driver to hurry. When they finally pulled up at the hotel, she threw cash at him and limped frantically toward the elevators. But she hesitated as the doors opened. Kate and Laura were probably back in the suite by now, and she wasn't ready to face them. Her mother would know immediately that something was wrong and ask a million questions.

Only a few patrons were scattered among the small tables in the hotel's bar, so Jessica took a seat. A few drinks would calm her down, and having some time to think would help her decide what to say when Skyler returned.

Kate settled their dinner tab and was trudging across the lobby toward the elevators when Laura seized her arm. "Look."

They paused in front of the hotel bar where a very drunk Jessica was demonstrating for an amused bartender the advanced dressage movements she and Rampage had wowed the crowd with that afternoon.

Kate caught her as her attempt at a pirouette nearly landed her in the middle of some other hotel guests' table. "Whoa, your little celebration here makes mine look like a Sunday school class. Why don't we take you upstairs?"

Laura frowned at her daughter, and then turned to the female bartender. Laura's "gaydar" pinged loudly as she glared at the attractive young woman. "You know you could be sued for serving drinks to someone this inebriated."

The bartender shrugged. "She really didn't have that many

drinks. The last drink I poured for her was a virgin. Besides, I knew she was a hotel guest. I'm coming off duty in a few minutes and would have made sure she got up to her room okay."

I'll just bet you would have, Laura thought. "Well, thanks for looking out for her then."

"No problem," the bartender replied. "She probably just needs to eat something. She mentioned that she hadn't eaten dinner."

"Hey, where's Sky?" Jessica slurred as Kate helped her from the elevator to their hotel suite. "Wait, I know where she is. She's at the barn."

"No, she's not at the barn," Kate said patiently, moving Jess toward her bedroom.

Jessica clamped a hand over her mouth and groaned.

"Uh-oh. I've seen that look before." Kate quickly dragged her into the bathroom.

After a long session of bowing to the porcelain goddess, Laura and Kate put Jessica to bed. She was out cold seconds later.

"Geez. How can anybody who hasn't eaten throw up so much?" Kate said, wrinkling her nose as she turned out the light and closed the door to Jessica and Skyler's bedroom.

Laura frowned. "I wonder what this is all about? Jess normally isn't much of a drinker."

"I don't know. Maybe she took a pain pill for her knee. That could have magnified the affect of a few drinks. Things sure are getting crazy around here," Kate grumbled.

It was nearly midnight when the Virginia border came in sight and Skyler realized that Jess hadn't called. She was tired and worried and she really needed to hear her lover's voice. She felt around in the darkness of the truck cab for her phone. She'd set it in the double cup holder next to the cola she'd picked up at a drive-thru hours earlier. She flipped it open, but it did not light up. It felt sticky. She reached into the cup holder. It was full of cola. Great. Jess had probably been trying to call, but her phone had drowned.

Skyler wasn't anxious to stop anywhere this late at night since she was alone. Because the big truck had double diesel tanks, she didn't need to stop for fuel. Jess was probably asleep, anyway, and Skyler didn't want to disturb her rest; she would need to be fresh for her training tomorrow. *I'll just call her first thing in the morning.*

It was two-thirty a.m. when Skyler fell into her bed at the Creek Barn. The last thought that drifted through her mind before she slipped into an exhausted slumber was how empty the bed felt without Jessica next to her.

CHAPTER FIFTEEN

Sky?" Tory's voice was sleepy. "What are you doing back here? I thought you guys were in Southern Pines."

"One of the kids here at the center had a personal emergency. Hopefully, I'll be headed back this afternoon. Tory, are you aware of any injections Jess may be giving Rampage?"

"Injections?"

"One of the barn security guards found a used syringe in the tack room trash can. I did a little looking around and found a bottle of Carbocaine and some syringes in Jess's dressing trunk. I haven't had a chance to talk to her. Did she get that from you?"

"Carbocaine," Tory repeated. "Sky. My brain isn't awake yet. What time is it?"

"It's almost six." Tory was silent for so long Skyler wondered if she'd fallen back to sleep. "Tory?"

"I hope I'm wrong about this… How's Jess's knee been doing lately?"

"Well, it's bruised pretty badly and she's having to ice it constantly to keep the swelling down. She gets pissed if I make too big a deal about it, so I let it go because it doesn't seem to bother her too much. It just looks bad."

"I'm afraid I may be right, then. I'll bet my bottom dollar that she has been injecting that knee to deaden the pain. That's why it doesn't seem to bother her. She's probably slowly shredding that

ACL graft, and it's going to just rip in two at some point. She'll tear her whole knee out."

"Damn it. I knew I should have insisted she see a doctor. All we've been thinking about was getting her and Rampage ready for the trials."

"Don't blame yourself," Tory said. "Jess is an adult."

"But I do blame myself. Shit, I'm probably the only one she couldn't hide the bruising from. Maybe I just didn't want to see what was happening."

"Well, I may be to blame, too. I thought there were a few bottles of Carbocaine missing from my truck supplies, but the stuff is so cheap that nobody keeps close tabs on it. I figured I was just mistaken or one of the other vets borrowed some out of my truck. She may have helped herself to a few bottles. She must be injecting that knee two and three times a day to keep walking around on it."

"God, Tory. She's going to jump Rampage this afternoon."

"Call Kate," Tory said emphatically. "Tell her not to let her near the ring, or on that horse, until you and I can get down there. You don't need to give her any details, just tell her to wait for one of us."

"What if we're wrong? Jess will hate us."

Tory was silent for a long moment. "Okay. I'm going to shift my appointments to one of my associates. Did you say you were headed back today?"

"I'm hoping to, but I don't know how soon. It will be noon at the earliest. I may not be able to wrap things up here until tonight. Either way, it will be too late to stop her this afternoon."

"Okay. I'll leave this morning. If it takes three hours, I should be there by noon or one o'clock. I'll make her show me the knee before I accuse her of anything. I'm not a doctor, but I should be able to tell if she's injecting it with an anesthetic."

Skyler breathed a sigh of relief. "Thanks, Tory. Thanks for being such a good friend."

"You owe me."

"Anything I have is yours…except my girlfriend." Skyler chuckled.

Tory laughed, too. "See you in Southern Pines tonight."

❖

Susan Beck was at the door when their truck pulled into the driveway. A thin, pale woman, her face was haggard and her eyes red from crying. More tears streamed down her face when she saw Jamie's face and arm. She held the door as they filed in and gestured for them to sit in the living room, never meeting their eyes.

Carol, the center's social worker, made the introductions, then said, "Mrs. Beck, we need to talk about what's going to happen to Jamie until your husband returns."

"You must think I'm a monster," Susan muttered.

"Mrs. Beck, we don't think you are a monster. We just think you need some help," Skyler said. "Jamie is important to all of us at the equestrian center. She has been with us every afternoon for more than two years. We feel like she's part of our family, and we'd like to help if you'll let us."

"You aren't going to take my little girl away from me, are you?"

"Mrs. Beck, considering your bouts of depression that you self-medicate with alcohol, the state doesn't feel Jamie should be left with you until her father has returned," Carol said firmly.

Mrs. Beck looked timidly at Jamie. "Are you afraid of your own mother?"

After an encouraging nod from Skyler, Jamie stood up and went over to lay her head on her mother's shoulder. "I love you, Mom. But you hurt me when you drink. Skyler says you can't help it because you get so depressed when Dad isn't here."

The woman looked at Skyler and choked back a sob.

"Mrs. Beck," Skyler said softly. "All families have their problems. Jamie has told me how much she loves you and her dad, so Kate Parker has made some arrangements we hope you'll agree to."

The woman shifted uneasily in her chair, doubt darkening her face.

"Please, Mom, just listen to Skyler," Jamie pleaded.

Skyler set out the plan they'd arrived at with Kate's attorney, George Brumley. "We've made arrangements for you to be admitted to a private rehab facility. It's free of charge, paid for by the center's discretionary funds. While you're in the hospital, Jamie can stay at the center."

Mrs. Beck glanced nervously around the room. "I don't know what to do without your father here to help me decide."

"Please, Mom," Jamie pleaded softly. Tears began to run down her cheeks. "If you don't, they're going to put me in some foster home. Please let me stay with Sky and Kate at the farm."

"Mrs. Beck," Skyler pressed, "we've brought some papers you'll have to sign to satisfy the state. They give Kate temporary guardianship over Jamie until your husband returns or you are dismissed from the hospital. It's legally necessary for her to stay at the center."

The woman frowned and twisted a handkerchief she held in her hands. "A kid's a big responsibility. Why would you want to be responsible for someone else's kid?"

"Because the Parker family cared enough to help me out when I was a kid and now it's time for me to help Jamie. My mother wasn't worth saving and wouldn't take their help. But Jamie says you are a good mother. She wants you to get better."

Desperate sadness showed on Susan's face as she looked at her battered daughter. "Oh, baby. I can't believe I hurt you like that. I really can't remember any of it." She looked down at her hands again. "I'm so scared."

Jamie straightened her shoulders, obviously accustomed to

playing the adult in her father's absence. "I know this is what Dad would want you to do."

Carol also prodded. "Mrs. Beck, you and Jamie are very lucky that Kate Parker is offering this."

After a long moment, Susan looked up at Jamie, but spoke to the adults. "Give me the papers. I'll sign."

❖

"You better get up, missy, and get that hangover under control," Kate ordered. "We're expecting a visitor."

"A visitor?" Jessica carefully sat up and held her aching head in her hands, trying to recall the previous evening. She only remembered having two drinks. *Note to self: don't mix pain pills and alcohol ever again.* "Where's Sky?"

"She had an emergency and had to go back to Cherokee Falls last night. She'll be back later."

"What's the time?" Jessica fixed her gaze blearily on the radio alarm clock next to her bed. "Oh, my God. It's after twelve. I have to get to the barn. We're in the jump ring at four and Rampage has been standing in his stall all morning."

The hangover was making her queasy enough, but the sudden memory of Skyler staring at the syringe in her hand ratcheted her nausea up a notch and she quickly lurched out of bed and staggered to the bathroom. After she'd retched a few times, she collapsed over the counter, groaning in pain. Her knee was agonizing.

"I have to talk to Skyler," she called, but her room was empty. Kate had gone back into the other bedroom in the suite.

Panting, Jessica leaned against the doorway, beads of perspiration gathering across her forehead. At least she was alone. She went back into the bathroom, locked the door, and pulled a bottle of Carbocaine from her cosmetics bag. She had to inject her knee more often now. Once a day was not enough.

She'd just settled onto the bed and covered her rapidly numbing knee with ice packs when there was a light knock at the door. "It's open," she called.

To her astonishment Tory Greyson walked into the room. "Hey, Jess. How's it going?"

Jessica frowned. "What are you doing here?"

"That knee hurting you that much?" Tory asked, taking a seat on the edge of the bed. Before Jessica realized what Tory was after, the ice bags were pulled aside. "Christ. This looks bad. I may be a vet, but I'm not stupid. It doesn't take an orthopedic surgeon to see what kind of shape this is in."

She probed the bruised and swollen knee, but Jessica didn't flinch. "See? It doesn't hurt."

Tory wasn't buying it. "If you were a horse, I'd have to shoot you." She stood and went into the bathroom. A short while later, she returned holding up the evidence, a bottle of anesthetic and some syringes. "I don't guess it would hurt if you were keeping it numb with this."

Jessica didn't answer.

Tory tossed the bottles onto the bed. "The barn security guard found one of your syringes in the trash and asked Skyler if she was doping your horse."

"Oh, God." Jessica's stomach churned.

"Yes, that could get her officially banned from the circuit this time, and even Kate couldn't help her," Tory said crisply. "So, she started looking around. She found the Carbocaine in your tack trunk and called me to find out if we were treating Rampage for something. She thought you and I might be hiding a condition from her. It took me a bit to figure out what was really going on, but I did. And I told her what I thought."

Fear welled up in Jessica's throat and threatened to choke her. This wasn't how she'd wanted things to go. She wanted to confess, but Tory was a step ahead of her. Everything was spiraling out of her control, just like the moment lightning struck as she and Racer were clearing the water jump. This could not be happening again.

"She knows everything?" Jessica whispered.

"She didn't want to accuse you falsely. She wanted all the facts. She couldn't get here before tonight, and she was scared you'd blow that knee out jumping Rampage this afternoon. That's why I'm here. I came down to stop you."

"Are you going to tell Mom and Kate?"

"No, you're going to tell them," Tory said firmly. "Right before we load you up and take you to see a doctor this afternoon."

"No!"

"What do you mean, no, Jess? You don't have a choice. You can't keep abusing yourself."

Jessica's face was red with controlled fury. "I've come too far and worked too hard to back out now." She kept her voice low so Kate and Laura wouldn't overhear them from the next room. "I've been numbing this knee for months. There's no reason to think it won't hold out another week until the competition is over."

"Jess, this is madness," Tory argued. "Even if you make the team, this knee isn't going to hold out for you to train for the actual Olympics."

Jessica grabbed Tory by the collar. Her blue eyes were icy. "If you tell Kate, she'll pull Rampage from the competition. She can do that because she owns the majority interest in him. And, I swear, Tory, you do anything to stop me from competing and I will *never* speak to you again. *Ever.* It's not illegal for me to anesthetize my knee, so I'm not breaking any rules."

Tory was dumbfounded by Jessica's blunt ultimatum. After a moment, she threw her hands up. "Whatever. I tried. I'll just let you and Sky duke it out when she gets here. In the meantime, I'll hang close to pick you up when you rip through every ligament in that knee." She stalked to the door, before turning back for one last word. "You're making a bad decision here, Jess. I think Skyler is going to be very disappointed in you."

Jessica lay back on the pillows and sobbed after Tory left the room. Tory had no idea how her words had hit home.

❖

Jessica strode into the barn with grim determination. She stopped at Rampage's stall door and looked into his dark liquid eyes. She took several deep breaths, clearing her mind of anything but him. He didn't deserve to feel her pain. He needed to feel her confidence. *Deep breaths. Relax. Rampage needs to feel relaxed.*

She gave the stallion a soft smile. "Hey, buddy. Ready to do some jumping? I know you are. It's your favorite thing." She began a one-sided conversation meant to reassure herself as much as her mount. "We're going to sail over those jumps like we have wings. You and me, buddy. We're going to show them a dressage horse that knows how to jump."

A brooding Tory gave her a leg up, and walked beside them to the jumping arena. Kate and Laura were already sitting in the stands, watching as Sarah put her mare over the jumps. They weren't happy that she was riding, after hearing that Skyler was concerned, but they didn't know what was going on.

Jessica warmed Rampage up in a nearby outdoor ring while she waited their turn. She closed her eyes and absorbed the smooth, calming rhythm of the stallion moving through his gaits underneath her. His strength and control radiated through her. She concentrated on losing herself in the feeling. *We can do this, buddy. We're the best. We're going to fly!* She didn't look at Sarah as they passed each other at the arena entrance. She saw nothing but the jumps ahead and felt nothing but the twelve hundred pounds of muscle under her.

Relaxed and focused, Rampage sailed gracefully over the first jump. He was eager, and Jessica had to work to pace him over the course of seventeen jumps. The wall, the combination, and even the parallel oxer were no contest to the powerful horse. Another crowd began to gather. News of Rampage's performance on the previous day had spread fast. Sarah, still mounted, watched from the ring entrance.

Despite the anesthesia, pain radiated through Jessica's leg with each jump. They rounded the end of the arena to approach the tallest and most difficult of the obstacles, the vertical jump. Jessica blocked the pain from her mind and expertly guided Rampage's approach. *Be my hero and let's jump this one big, buddy!*

The stallion responded eagerly to the urging telegraphed through Jessica's hands. He gathered his body and, like a giant spring, rose upward and neatly tucked his feet to clear it with inches to spare. Jessica smiled as she felt them airborne. She shifted her weight to absorb the impact of their landing, but when she felt Rampage's front hooves hit the dirt, she also heard the popping of her knee. She pitched over the stallion's right shoulder and slammed to the ground, knocking the wind from her lungs. Her head was screaming at the pain in her leg, but she couldn't catch her breath to vocalize her agony.

Rampage came trotting back around, tossing his head and rolling his eyes wildly. He snorted uncertainly as Jessica writhed silently on the ground. Tory, Kate, and Laura, as well as a handful of onlookers, hurried into the arena. But Rampage circled his rider, bucking as they approached. Jessica began to catch her breath and moaned at the pain, clutching at her thigh. Her distress antagonized the stallion. He laid his ears back and shook his head at the people trying to get to his mistress.

"Whoa, Rampage," Tory crooned to him. "Settle down, boy, we just want to help." She approached slowly but when she reached for his reins, the stallion lunged at her with teeth bared. Tory barely dodged as he tore a long rip in the sleeve of her shirt. The other well-meaning people who had followed them in the arena retreated…all but Sarah.

"Let me try," she offered. "He let me close to him yesterday without trying to bite."

"At this point, I'll try anything," Tory said. "If you can't catch him, I'll have to dart him with a tranquilizer. I'd rather not have to wait that long to get Jess to the hospital."

Sarah nodded and moved slowly toward Rampage. The stallion snorted at her approach and laid his ears flat against his neck. "Hey, Rampage. Remember me? You liked me the other day," she said softly. "I just want to help Jessica. I know you think you're protecting her, but you need to let us help."

The stallion's ears came up and twitched forward at her voice. He looked puzzled and lowered his head to snuffle Jessica's head. Sarah moved slowly but confidently to his side. Rampage started to pull away when she reached for his bridle, but yielded when he felt her grasp on the reins. She led him some distance away from where Jessica lay moaning, and Tory, Kate and Laura rushed over.

"God." Tory gingerly felt her leg. "It feels like it's completely dislocated."

Somebody had called the paramedics, and Jessica bit off a scream as they splinted her leg and lifted her to the stretcher. "Where's Rampage?"

"He's right over there," Laura pointed.

Jessica tried to rise from the stretcher when she saw who was holding Rampage. The pain was a hot brand, a loud noise in her head, and she felt everything was slipping away from her... Skyler, the trials, Rampage. She wanted to strike out at something or someone. "I *don't* want her near my horse. Get him away from her," she insisted. *Does that bitch have to put her hands on everything that belongs to me?* She grabbed Tory's torn sleeve. "Get my horse away from her."

"I'll take care of Rampage for you, Jess," Tory said as she gently pushed Jessica back down to the stretcher. "These guys need to take you to the hospital. Don't worry about a thing."

Jessica lay back on the stretcher and closed her eyes as tears streamed down her cheeks.

Tory hesitated while she made a quick decision. "Kate, before you go, I need to tell you why Skyler asked you not to let her ride till I got here."

Kate's shoulders slumped as she listened. "I can't believe none of us picked up on what she was doing."

"Skyler blames herself," Tory said.

"No good can come from placing blame now. We all ignored our better judgment." Kate put her arm around Laura and kissed her cheek. "Come on. Let's go tell her we love her."

The lights of the emergency room were bright and Sarah squinted as she stepped in from the darkness of the parking lot. She spied Kate at one end of the emergency room waiting area, gesturing emphatically as she talked on her cell phone. Sarah leaned against the wall and listened to Kate's side of the conversation.

"Look, if he's the best orthopedic surgeon in the state, then I need him down here tonight." Kate gesticulated impatiently. "There's got to be something I could use to get him here. Does he like golf? Tell him that if he'll come down here, I'll give him my four tickets to the Masters golf tournament next month. Not only that, I can make sure he gets to play the course after the tournament as the guest of one of the members. That's right. Augusta National."

A huge smile broke across Kate's face. "Great. Since you guys are at Duke, he's only about an hour away. We won't let them do anything until he gets here. Yes, yes. I'll see if I can cut the red tape for him to use their operating room. What's his cell phone number?"

Sarah dug into her jacket pocket and handed Kate a felt-tipped pen. She used it to write the number on her own arm. As she ended the call, she turned back to Sarah. "You are here because…?"

"Shut up and give me your phone."

Kate had never been much good saying no to Sarah. She meekly obliged and listened to another woman who knew how to get what she wanted. Sarah even smiled sweetly as she spoke.

"Margaret? Hi. It's Sarah Duke." She exchanged the usual niceties before asking, "Is your handsome husband home? I've got sort of an emergency here that I need his help with. Thanks."

She tapped her foot and covered the phone, telling Kate, "Always go straight to the top." The smile appeared again. "Robert, how are you? Well, I've been better. Actually, I need your help. No, I'm fine, but a friend of mine has been rather seriously injured in a riding accident. Her orthopedic surgeon is on his way here, and he's probably going to need to do surgery in your hospital. His name…" She raised an eyebrow at Kate.

"Dr. Richard Struthers," Kate filled in.

"Did you catch that, Edward? So, you've heard of him? No offense to your doctors, but my friend's career may rest on this surgery and her injury has a complicated history. Thanks, I knew you would help. Give the kids a hug for me."

Kate tucked the phone into her pocket, impressed despite herself. "Thanks."

"It's the least I could do," Sarah said. "I know how much Jessica means to Skyler. I failed her as a lover, but I don't intend to fail her as a friend."

❖

Jessica blinked and frowned when her eyes shifted to Sarah standing in the doorway. Damned if this woman wasn't everywhere she turned. "What are you doing here?" Bitterness soaked her voice. "Come to gloat already?"

Kate had told her that Sarah moved a mountain of red tape

so Dr. Struthers could use this hospital's operating room, and she wanted a few minutes alone with her. Jessica wasn't impressed. She suspected an agenda.

Sarah sat down in the chair next to the bed. "I won't take much of your time. I know you are in a lot of pain, Jessica, but I really am just here to help."

Jessica glared at her. "I saw you kiss Skyler."

"What you saw wasn't what you think," Sarah said. "One of the security staff told me you left in a cab with a friend of his driving."

Did she have spies *everywhere*?

"What I saw was that you just can't stay out of my lover's life," Jessica threw at her.

"You listen to me, damn it. I went there to apologize to Skyler for being a spineless idiot and betraying her. What I did hurt both of us very much, but it made me grow up a lot. That kiss was a good-luck peck."

"You didn't look that happy when you left."

"Haven't you ever felt ashamed?" Sarah asked. "From what I hear you've made a few of your own mistakes."

"Yes, and I don't need you to remind me," Jessica said bitterly.

Sarah surprised her by laughing. "I can see why Sky loves you. You're as stubborn as those horses she loves to win over."

"Thanks. I think," Jessica said wearily. She wanted Skyler. Tears prickled and she swallowed a small sob.

"I just wanted you to know something," Sarah said. "I told Skyler I'm happily married to a wonderful man now and I'm really happy to see that she seems to have found the same thing with you. She deserves to be happy, and apparently you're the one who does that for her."

Sarah's declaration made it impossible to hold on to the anger that was keeping her fears at bay. Jessica blinked and wiped at the tears that were now streaming down her cheeks.

Sarah stood up. "Give Skyler a chance, Jess, and she'll stand by you through thick and thin. She's the strongest person and the purest heart I've ever known." She patted Jessica on the arm. "Right now, I need to get home or my husband will be wondering if I've run off with a stable hand…or a trainer."

"Sarah," Jessica choked out. "Thanks."

❖

"Miss, visitors must have a pass to come back here." A nurse hurried after Skyler. "If you will just wait at the admissions desk, we'll see if your friend is still in the ER and can have a visitor."

Skyler shook off the woman's hand, moving quickly from room to room, pulling doors open. "Jess? Jess? Where are you?" she shouted in the hallway.

Kate stepped out of a doorway in front of her, muttering, "Bull in a china shop."

She jumped back as Skyler burst into the room and rushed to Jessica's bedside. She looked Jessica over quickly and put her hand to her love's cheek, desperate with worry. "Jess, are you okay? Did they give you something for pain? What did the doctor say?"

Jessica reached up to gather her close. Clinging to her, she sobbed like her heart was breaking.

"Oh, baby. I'm so sorry I didn't realize you were doing this to yourself," Skyler said. "I should have seen it and stopped you."

Jessica sobbed even harder, and Skyler whispered words of reassurance as she kissed the tears from her face. After a while, Jessica's tears subsided, and Skyler handed her some tissues to blow her nose.

Jessica's red-rimmed blue eyes swept up. "I didn't mean to lie to you. I just didn't know how to tell you. And the longer I waited to tell you, the more afraid I was that you wouldn't love me anymore if you knew I wasn't being honest."

Skyler held Jessica close and kissed her deeply. "Oh, Jess.

I know you weren't trying to hurt me. I'm not going anywhere. You own me, heart and soul."

Jessica rested her head on Skyler's shoulder. "And you own my heart. I've been scared to death I might lose you."

"You're not getting rid of me that easy," Skyler gently joked. "You're stuck with me."

CHAPTER SIXTEEN

"Ms. Black...Jessica, I don't think you understand the full impact of your injury," Dr. Struthers said. "Although you should be able to walk, or golf, or maybe ride horses at a leisurely pace, you'll never be able to participate again in sports that require running or jumping...or jumping horses." In a gentle tone, he finished, "I'm afraid your professional riding career is over."

Jessica sagged back against the pillows, her eyes fixed on a distant spot somewhere beyond the people standing around her bed.

Skyler watched her pale face for a moment, and then asked, "Jess, are you okay?"

Jessica's eyes moved to Dr. Struthers. "Why can't you fix it?"

The surgeon returned to the X-ray he'd just discussed in detail. "Those ligaments were too weak to hold the femur and tibia bones in place, so when you continued to jump horses you pounded the ends of those bones into the lateral and medial meniscus."

"Cartilage?"

"Yes, the cartilage is the knee's shock absorbers." He used his pen to point to certain areas of the X-rays. "Once those were pounded flat, the ends of the bones were left to pound together, slipping and sliding in directions they shouldn't. At that point, you must have been injecting a great deal of local anesthetic into that knee to dull the pain."

He paused once more and drew a deep breath to deliver the verdict. "The impact of that final jump has done significant damage to the ends of your femur and tibia. There really is no other viable option here but total knee replacement."

Jessica closed her eyes a moment, struggling against the haze created in her head by the pain medicine. Finally she asked, "What's the recovery time?"

"We should do the surgery immediately…tonight. You'll have to stay in the hospital a few days, and then you'll go home with a walker or crutches. The total healing time really depends on your dedication to a regular physical therapy routine. Usually it takes three months, but most total knee replacement patients are elderly. Your young age and excellent physical condition should shorten that period."

"But even though my knee has been replaced, it won't be as good as new?"

"No," he said.

"I understand," Jessica said dully. With a long, sorrowful look at Skyler, she said, "Let's just get on with it."

The surgeon nodded. "They'll come get you in a few minutes to take you to the operating room. I'll see you upstairs."

After Dr. Struthers left the room, Skyler moved to sit on the bed, facing Jessica and holding both of her lover's delicate hands in her own larger ones. They stared at each other for a long moment until Jessica finally spoke. "See what you've gotten yourself into? Now you've got a crippled girlfriend and a useless rider when you were just about to make your name as a trainer."

Skyler smiled at her. "What I've got is the most beautiful woman in the world in love with me. Crippled? I thank God it was your knee, not your neck you busted. And, maybe now I won't have to endure long months away from you while you travel the world with the Olympic team. That was your dream, Jess, not mine. I'm very happy working for Kate and with the kids at the center. I'm ecstatically happy when I can crawl into bed at night and wrap my arms around you. I'm in heaven when I can wake up and the first thing I see are those baby blue eyes."

Jessica stared down at their entwined fingers. "You're just trying to make me feel better."

"I'm telling you the truth." Skyler looked into her eyes. "Winning an Olympic medal is all about spending the rest of your life looking back at what you once achieved. Being with *you* makes me look *forward* to what's in our future."

Jessica gathered the front of Skyler's shirt in her hand and pulled her down for a soft, lingering kiss. "I love you, Skyler Reese."

"And I love you. Don't you ever doubt that again."

"Hey, sleeping beauty," Skyler said softly, many hours later. "How are you feeling?"

Jessica blinked slowly. "You're all still here."

"We're leaving now," Laura said, stroking her daughter's hair.

Skyler had insisted the rest of them return to the hotel so Jamie could sleep in a proper bed instead of a chair in the waiting room, where she'd been ever since Skyler arrived hours earlier. Laura and Kate kissed Jessica good-bye and waited for Jamie to hug Skyler. The girl's injuries had been the second major shock of their day, but realizing that too much fuss would make her uncomfortable, they'd just smiled and made her feel welcome.

As they left the room, Jessica's eyes closed for a minute, then opened to focus on Skyler again. Her voice was hoarse, but clear. "Hey good lookin'. You haven't been chasing any nurses while I was out, have you?"

Skyler grinned, and dropped a soft kiss on Jessica's lips. "None that I could catch. Guess I better stick to the slow beautiful ones with a bum leg."

Jessica smiled, but keeping her eyes open was obviously a struggle. "Sleepy," she confessed.

"Then go to sleep, baby. I'll be right here when you wake up," Skyler said, stroking the dark head and delivering another quick kiss as Jessica lost the battle to stay awake.

❖

The weary group breathed a sigh of relief when they walked into the welcoming hotel suite. Kate settled Jamie in Skyler and Jessica's room, then fixed stiff toddies and delivered them to the balcony where Laura was staring into the darkness.

"Jess is going to be fine," she said as she handed Laura her drink. "Skyler won't take her eyes off her all night."

Laura took in a deep breath and let it out slowly. "I know. Jess is tough, and she has Skyler now. She'll figure things out and bounce back."

Kate stood behind Laura and wrapped her arms around her. "Feeling a little pushed aside?"

Laura leaned back against her solid frame. "Well, maybe a little. Our little girl is all grown up. But I was thinking about something else, Kate."

The love so evident between Skyler and Jessica had made Laura's heart ache. Watching her daughter cling to Skyler for strength and hearing Skyler's heartfelt confession of love played over and over in her mind. She remembered a time when she and Kate were bonded like that.

It had been preying on her mind that her excuse for being in North Carolina, to see Jess compete, had come to an end. Only a few days more and she'd be packing her bags to return home. Alone again. Much worse than just being alone, she would be without Kate. She finally admitted to herself that only Kate could fill the empty space in her. Not another lover, not a child…even as much as she loved Jessica. Time was running out to lay her cards on the table.

"I was thinking about how we make stupid decisions when we're young," she said. "Jess numbing her knee so she could keep training. And me sending you away all those years ago because of my insecurities."

Laura's eyes filled with tears. She laid her head back against Kate's shoulder and turned her face to look up into her hopeful eyes. "After all this time, I still love you, Kate Parker. This has been the happiest I've been since I let you walk out of my life. If I could go back and live those years all over again, I would live them *with* you instead of without you."

Kate caressed Laura's cheek, and bent to softly reacquaint herself with her one true love's lips. "And what do you want to do with the years ahead of us, baby," she murmured against Laura's warm mouth.

Laura turned to face her, offering a smoldering kiss that gave her answer. They were both shaky when they finally parted. Laura could feel Kate's heart pounding in her chest. Kate took her hand and stepped toward the door to the suite.

"Come to bed with me, Laura," she coaxed. "It's been way too long."

Laura turned shy, staring at her hand in Kate's. "Kate, I'm not twenty years old anymore. This isn't the body you remember."

Kate chuckled softly as she drew Laura again into a warm embrace. "You think I look the same?" Her eyes twinkled as she cocked her head. "You do remember how, don't you?"

"Why don't you try me?" Laura's mischievous look was the one Kate often recalled on lonely evenings. It always melted her. "Let's see how many of your hot spots I remember."

❖

The sight of Sarah in Jessica's hospital room stopped Skyler cold. The two women smiled at her, enjoying her discomfort at having them both in the same room together.

"Hi, Sarah." Skyler strode over to take Jessica's hand and give her a light kiss. "Where's Laura?"

"I sent her back to the hotel to spend some time with Kate," Jessica replied smugly. "I don't suppose the Parker heiress filled you in on what's going on."

"What's going on?" When Skyler returned to the hotel a few hours earlier to shower and change her clothes, Kate had been in an unusually good mood. But she hadn't shared any news. "Is it about Jamie?"

Sarah and Jessica exchanged conspiratorial smiles. Surprisingly, Sarah was the one to speak up. "It seems that the sparks flying off you and Jess have ignited the old flame between Kate and Laura."

Skyler's eyebrows shot up. "No kidding. And I thought that old dog didn't hunt anymore."

Jessica laughed. "Mom and Kate aren't that old, you know. Mom is only fifty-two and Kate just turned fifty-six. We'll be that old before you know it. Look at me. I'm already using a walker."

Skyler turned amused eyes at her love. "That must be some good pain medicine they put you on. You certainly seem to be in a good mood."

"Mom says the pain medicine is making me bossy, and you say it's making me happy. I wish you guys would make up your minds." Jessica grew solemn. "Truthfully, I don't think the impact of everything has really hit me yet. It may not, until I see Rampage jumping without me on his back. I'm not sure how I'll feel then."

Skyler watched a stream of emotions run across Jessica's somber face. She sat down on the bed next to her and slipped an arm around her shoulders. "That's not going to happen unless you want it to."

Jessica picked at a string on the bed sheets. "Sky, Sarah came here today with an offer to buy Rampage."

"Jess, you want to sell Rampage? I thought you were planning to stand him at stud."

"After he retires," Jessica said. "In the meantime it's not fair to keep him out of the competition just because I've been stupid. Even if I waited until the next Olympics, I still wouldn't be able to jump him. You heard Dr. Struthers. My career is history."

"My mare is good, but she can't touch that stallion," Sarah said. "You were right, Sky. I think he could even have beaten Con Man."

Jessica cleared her throat, and said hoarsely, "I'm not going to sell Rampage. What I've agreed is that Sarah try him during the next week. If they click together, she'll ride him in the competition rather than her mare."

"A week?" Skyler argued. "We spent months pairing you two up. You expect her to do that in just a week? You know how particular he is."

Jessica held up a hand to silence her protests. "I think she can do it. For some reason only Rampage knows, he seems to trust her. After I fell, Sarah was the only person he would let approach him. He was standing over me, biting and kicking, but he let her catch him."

Skyler frowned as she mulled over what Jessica was saying.

"So," she continued, "if Sarah decides after a week to ride Rampage, and they win a place on the Olympic team, I've agreed to lease him to her until after the Olympics. After that, he will come back to Cherokee Falls to stand at stud. If she wins a medal on him, I've agreed to a bonus that will entitle her to three free breedings to Rampage. This is all contingent on Kate's agreement, too, of course."

Skyler shifted uneasily, looking for reasons this would not be a good idea. She was having trouble finding any.

"Sky, if Rampage and I make it on the Olympic team, I would

want to hire you as a consulting trainer," Sarah said, sweetening the deal even more. "I mean, I know you don't want to be away from Cherokee Falls a lot, but you've obviously figured out what this horse needs. You could map out a training regimen for the team's trainer to follow."

Skyler stared down at Jessica's hand encased in her own. "It's not that," she muttered. "It's just—"

"What, babe?" Jessica asked. "Just go ahead and spit it out. Sarah and I have been honest with each other. If you don't want to work with Sarah, then we won't do this. You and I are partners in everything. It's not a deal unless we're both comfortable with it."

Skyler looked deep into the eyes that seemed to mirror her soul these days. "I'm surprised you would pick Sarah to take your place on Rampage." She knew how the thought of another rider on her stallion seared Jessica. "You don't have to do this for me."

"I'm doing this for all of us, hon. Sarah is as good as any top rider on the circuit, and she's the only one Rampage apparently has chosen. If she can take him to the Olympics, his stud fees will rocket with his reputation. You know that's money in our pockets." Jessica gave Skyler a soft kiss. "I'm also doing this for Rampage. He's worked damn hard for this competition, and he deserves his moment in the spotlight."

Skyler thought for a moment about Jessica's words. Maybe she needed to see Rampage go on to win, so all of their hard work wouldn't be for nothing. "Well, it looks like you guys have it all figured out. What's next?"

Jessica's eyes misted. "Hand me my bag over there on the shelf, please." After Skyler passed her the bag she retrieved a dog-eared copy of *Black Beauty*. "He likes you to read to him after his supper, especially when he's nervous."

Sarah looked truly touched as she accepted the book. "I'll be sure and read to him every night."

"Thanks." Jessica smiled, tucking away the emotion that

threatened to bring more tears. She was tired of being in pain and tired of crying. She wanted to move on to the next jump. "Now, get me out of this hospital. We have a lot of work to do with Sarah and Rampage to get them on the same page for the competition."

CHAPTER SEVENTEEN

R ampage nickered at Sarah as she approached.
"You shameless slut," Jessica teased the big bay. "I'm in the hospital only a few days and you've already been courting another woman."

Sarah offered her hand for the stallion to sniff. She smiled at Jessica. "I noticed that you wear Opium perfume. I put just a little on this morning so maybe it would seem familiar to him."

Skyler watched as Jessica smiled back. *I wonder how she's really going to feel when she sees Sarah on her mount.*

Peach picked that moment to stroll out of the feed room, boldly threading his way between Rampage's legs. The fat orange tomcat stood on his hind legs to touch noses with the big bay before running over to the barn office and neatly hooking the edge of the door with his claws to pull it open and let himself in.

"Who was that?" Sarah laughed.

"That, Sarah, is the rest of Rampage's baggage," Skyler said. "I didn't believe it at first either, but it's amazing the calming effect that battle-scarred tom has when Rampage is nervous or pissed."

"The cat comes with him?" Sarah looked doubtful.

"Trust me. You do not want to take that horse without taking the cat along, too," Jessica said.

"Okay, ladies. Let's head to the practice arena and see if this fellow will work for Sarah." Skyler gave Sarah a leg up and walked slowly along with Jessica as she hobbled on her crutches. Jamie, always at Skyler's heels, trailed along, absorbing everything they were saying about horses.

Rampage's ears worked back and forth as he kept turning a puzzled face in Jessica's direction. When they reached the arena, an amused Skyler stood by as Jessica rattled off Rampage's likes and dislikes to Sarah.

"Hey, who's the trainer here?" Skyler kidded. "Am I getting competition now?"

Jessica turned an adoring gaze on her lover. "Nobody is competition for you, sweetie." She shifted her crutches and gave Sky a one-armed hug. "You're the best."

Jessica settled into a canvas chair and spent the next hour watching Sarah and Rampage, and calling out instructions from the sidelines. Skyler stood in the center of the arena watching and advising. There were only a few hitches at misread communications, but the last run-through went off flawlessly.

"Jess, he's a dream." Sarah's face shone as they walked back to the stables. "I've ridden a lot of high-dollar horses, but never one so smooth. He makes you feel like a mere guest on his back while he performs."

Jessica grinned. "You can see, then, why I can't bear to sell him. I'm just hoping he's as good a stud as he is a showman."

Skyler was so proud. Jessica never ceased to amaze her. Anybody else would be sitting around feeling sorry for herself, but Jessica was finding another way to do what she loved. Skyler smiled as she listened to the two women discussing Rampage's finer points. Signaling Jamie, she said, "Come on. We have work to do."

Jamie had quickly become adept in handling a muck rake with her one good arm. Letting her help made her feel like part of their team, but Skyler was mindful of the girl's still healing injuries. She limited how much Jamie tried to do.

"Uh, Sky?" Jamie was quiet as they ran rakes through the wood chips on the stallion's stall floor to cull out the balls of manure. "Isn't Sarah an old girlfriend of yours?"

"Yes, why do you ask?"

"I'm going to be thirteen next month," Jamie said, tossing her wheat-colored hair back from her face. "And I do know a few things."

"Such as," Skyler prompted.

"I have an aunt who's gay. She and her girlfriend come and visit Mom sometimes. I like them. Mom knows about you, too, you know. She doesn't mind."

Skyler smiled. "I'm glad you told me. I won't worry then that she'll change her mind about you staying with us."

Jamie grinned. "I'm used to being around my aunt and her girlfriend. It doesn't freak me out to see you guys kissing or anything. My aunt kisses her girlfriend in front of me all the time."

Skyler blushed and her rake slowed as she mentally slapped herself. With everything happening, she realized they hadn't been very discreet around Jamie.

"I'll keep that in mind, kiddo."

Jamie stared down at the stall bedding as she raked the same spot for the third time. "Anyway, you and Sarah used to go together, right?"

Skyler smiled at the old high school phrase for dating. "Yeah, but that was a long time ago."

"Still, I think I would be jealous, if I was Jess." Jamie looked up and raised a rather adult eyebrow at Skyler. "I would worry that you might still like Sarah some."

Skyler wanted to laugh hilariously at the slender twelve-year-old's rendition of Kate's "I'll kick your ass" look. But she knew Jamie was serious. The fact that Jamie was being protective of Jessica made Skyler oddly proud of the kid.

"You know what? Jess never has to worry about *that*," Skyler assured her. "She means more to me that anything in this world. I'm not going to screw this up."

"That's good." Jamie went back to her raking.

Skyler thought about her struggle to trust her heart to other people. She knew a lot of her reluctance stemmed from the low self-esteem instilled by her abusive father. She prayed they'd addressed Jamie's home situation before it damaged her, too.

"You know, my dad told me so many times that I was worthless, I guess I grew up believing that I didn't deserve to be loved," she said softly.

Jamie kept raking, her head down, but she nodded. Yes, she knew.

"I guess that's why I dated so many women. I just didn't believe any of them could really love me, so I wouldn't let myself love anyone back," she confessed. "Jess helped me realize that I do deserve to be loved. And I love her, with every breath I take."

When Jamie looked up, her eyes were bright. "She is kind of special, isn't she?"

"Really special." Skyler smiled.

❖

"Uh-oh. Here comes trouble," Skyler muttered, yanked from her pleasant daydreams by the approach of a short wiry man with a wavy mane of white hair, dark piercing eyes, and a face made leathery by too many years on the golf course—Willard Lexington Tate. At Tate's elbow was Sarah's trainer, Jason Wright, and lagging reluctantly behind was Matthew Richard Duke, her husband.

Tate glared at Skyler, and she met him with a level stare. *I'm not afraid of you, old man. You can't hurt me anymore.* She smiled with satisfaction to see him straightening his shoulders to try and match her height.

"I heard they had let some trash back on the circuit," he remarked with a sneer.

"Hello, Mr. Tate. It's good to see you again, too," Skyler said in a cool voice.

The man gave a condescending snort. "I'll get to the point, Ms. Reese. I hear from several sources that you've been hanging around my daughter again. Starving you out didn't keep you away, so I'm offering a different approach." He pulled his checkbook from his pocket and flipped it open.

"Hey, Sarah, Daddy is here to see you," Skyler called into the office. She turned back to Will Tate. "You may have bought your own daughter before, but I've never been for sale, you bastard."

Sarah, Kate and Jessica stepped out of the office. Skyler felt Jessica's hand on her back, offering support, as Sarah moved between Skyler and her father.

"So, Jason. I see you wasted no time bringing Daddy out here to rat me out." She shook her head and clicked her tongue. Her voice was cold and her manner nonchalant. "And you dragged poor Matt with you."

Sarah's husband Matt shrugged apologetically.

"Don't get in my way, Sarah," Tate growled.

"Why not, Daddy? You've meddled in my life enough. It's time to put a few things on the table. I'm not involved with Skyler again. What I am doing is leasing this stallion from Jess. He makes the high-dollar mare you picked out for me look like a mule in the arena. I'm riding Rampage in the trials. I just signed the lease papers. Jessica and Skyler are acting as my trainers." Sarah turned on her former trainer. "As for you, you're fired. You aren't half the trainer Skyler is. You're nothing but a watchdog for my father."

"Your daddy pays my fee, not you," Jason sneered.

"Well then, I suggest you find somebody else to ride his mare so he'll have a reason to keep signing your paycheck," she replied.

"You ride that stallion in the trials with that queer trainer following you around, and I'll disinherit you in a minute," Tate spat, pulling his usual trump card.

"Won't work this time, Daddy. I'm not that scared little girl you intimidated before. You see, I took the money Grandmother left me and made a killing in stocks a while back. I would guess it surprises you that a girl has a brain, but I'll be very comfortable on my own money, not to mention my husband's estate. Isn't that right, honey?"

Matt, six-foot-two and sandy-haired, lounged against the wall. He seemed to be enjoying the show. "Right you are, babe."

"Shut up, faggot," Tate shouted at him. Seeing he was outnumbered, he began to tuck his checkbook in his pocket. "Come on, Jason."

"Don't put that checkbook away so fast," Sarah warned. "Kate and I anticipated your interference, and we've been doing a little background work."

Kate, who had been watching silently from the outskirts of the group, folded her arms over her chest and gave Tate a challenging stare.

"I want you to open that checkbook and write out a check to the Cherokee Falls Youth Equestrian Program for fifty thousand dollars," Sarah told him.

"And why would I do that?"

"Because if you don't, Kate's lawyer will file a slander suit against you for maligning the character of Skyler Reese and, by association, the Cherokee Falls Equestrian Center."

"George Brumley says we have a very good case against you." Kate's voice was quiet, yet deadly with controlled anger. "We've obtained signed affidavits showing that you blackmailed several people into blacklisting Skyler."

Tate's eyes flicked nervously. "You're bluffing."

"Try me, Will. Just remember, you aren't dealing with a young, penniless rider now. You're dealing with me."

Tate's face reddened. The Parker name and estate dwarfed his own. "What do you call this? You're blackmailing me."

Kate grinned. "Nope. It's not blackmail, Will. We see the donation as an apology. One that is long overdue."

Snorting his disgust, he angrily scribbled out a check and thrust it toward Kate.

"Thank you. We'll send you a receipt for your tax deduction," Kate said politely.

"Blackmailed by my own daughter." He glared at Sarah. "I don't even know you. In fact, you aren't my daughter," he snarled.

Sarah stared at him. He seemed much smaller and older to her now. "Oh, but I am your daughter, Daddy. I learned every underhanded move I know from watching you operate."

Tate's face blanched. Without another word, he strode out of the barn with Jason on his heels.

Matt laid a supportive hand on Sarah's shoulder. "I've never seen this side of you, babe. I think I like it."

Sarah gave him an affectionate smile. "Come here, you." She hugged the man. "I hope you know this is just a horse deal with friends here. I really should have talked to you first to make sure you were okay with what I have planned."

"Hey, I've got old girlfriends in my past, too," he said, waggling his eyebrows at Skyler.

Sarah smiled up at him. "Ladies, this is my wonderful husband, Matt. Good looking, great in bed, and has money, too. What more could a woman want?"

Matt blushed at his wife's teasing. "So, is this stallion as good as the rumor mill says he is?"

"He's even better," Jessica bragged.

❖

As if to live up to his owner's words, Rampage ran away with Friday's dressage competition. Smooth and confident, he turned in a flawless performance that quickly intimidated the lesser riders in the competition and had the veteran competitors looking over their shoulders.

Saturday was the real test. Endurance/cross country. This all-day competition was designed to test a horse's speed, endurance, and jumping ability. On the cross-country course horses and riders had to be bold and smart. The course was about four miles long and was ridden at a good gallop. The obstacles could be very difficult—jumping uphill, jumping over solid obstacles, jumping downhill, jumping several series of fences and—Jessica's bane— jumping over a solid obstacle into a knee-deep pool of water on the other side. Riders were permitted to walk the course before the competition, but the horses were seeing it for the first time. This made good communication essential for a winning run.

Dark clouds hung overhead, threatening rain, but also bringing a welcome breeze. Kate rented a large SUV and had already picked an advantageous viewing spot atop a hill overlooking the steeplechase and cross-country courses. She also produced binoculars for everyone.

Sarah was focused and quiet as Rampage pranced, picking up on his rider's anticipation. His workouts over the past week had been light and he was bursting with pent-up energy. She smiled. "I thought I was supposed to be the one with a case of nerves."

"Don't worry. Once you get him started and give him a job to do, he'll settle down," Jessica said. But Jessica didn't feel quite as confident as her words. She fidgeted as she leaned on her crutches.

"I swear, Jess. I've never seen anyone pace on crutches, but you're doing a good job of it," Skyler said with a warning look. "Hold still. Rampage is picking up on your nerves."

Jessica stilled her body for a moment, then limped off toward the others waiting at the truck.

"You need to cut her some slack, Sky," Sarah said. "I know

it would be hard for me to train all year, and then watch someone else ride my horse in the trials."

"It's not just that, I don't think," Skyler replied. "There's something else bothering her. She'll chew on it for a while before she spits it out and tells me her real problem. She's sort of like this boy." She patted the bay's shoulder. "You have to coax her, not force her."

Skyler checked Sarah's saddle and stirrups, murmuring to sooth the tense horse. She squeezed Sarah's knee. "Ride well and be safe. Trust Rampage. He's a hell of a horse."

Skyler joined the others at the SUV and stood behind Jessica, arms wrapped around her. "What's on your mind, babe?" she coaxed. "That was supposed to be you down there on Rampage. Is it harder than you thought, watching Sarah take your ride?"

Jessica looked worriedly at the clouds threatening overhead. She squeezed her lover's embrace even tighter. "It's just the clouds and wind. I've just got a bad feeling. It's like déjà vu or something."

Skyler's mind raced back to Jessica's accident on Racer. "Don't even think it. That was a freak accident. This is a different day, a different situation." She could feel Jessica tremble in her arms. "Hey, trust me and Rampage, okay?"

Jessica leaned her body into Skyler's. She did feel warm and secure in her tall lover's arms. She wanted to trust that everything would be fine.

They moved to join Kate, Laura, and Jamie, who were seated in lawn chairs and intently following Sarah and Rampage as they began their first phase. The stallion was a coiled spring, straining to be let loose. His brisk trot ate up the ground before him and the pair turned in a time more than a minute shorter than the nearest competitor.

Skyler frowned. "She needs to hold him in. She's coming out too fast and won't have anything left for the cross-country."

"They're okay," Jessica disagreed softly. "He's got more

stamina than any horse I've ridden. If she holds him in too much, he'll sulk and fight her. They'll lose their rhythm."

Entering the steeplechase phase, Sarah gave in a little more to the eager bay. The hilltop group could hear the crowd seated in the stands below murmur in admiration as the horse and rider sailed over the course. The judges were checking their watches and shaking their heads.

As they began the third phase, a slow trot and walking to cool down, Jessica and Skyler hopped in the SUV so they could meet Sarah at the veterinary check. Sarah was breathing hard from the adrenaline rush when she hopped down from the saddle.

"You're taking him too fast," Skyler scolded. "I don't know if he'll have enough left for the cross-country."

"Are you kidding? I'm having a hell of a time holding him in. He acts like he hasn't even taken his edge off yet."

Jessica moved closer. "Then he's going to be tough over the cross-country. He loves to jump and tends to get more and more excited as you go farther along the course. You have to use the little distractions I showed you to keep his attention on you and not just the next series of jumps."

Sarah nodded and sipped from the sports drink Jessica handed her. Skyler led Rampage through the vet check, walking him the full ten minutes to calm him yet keep his momentum.

"Don't look so worried," Sarah said when she was back in the saddle. "It's in the bag."

Skyler shook her head at Sarah's bravado and stepped back as she turned Rampage toward the cross-country.

When Jessica and Skyler returned to the hilltop, the clouds had grown heavier. The coming storm still was too far away to hear the thunder, but sheets of lightning were visible in the distance. Jessica peered up at the darkening sky and clung to Skyler's hand with a death grip.

Skyler muttered under her breath as she watched Sarah wind Rampage through the course. "Too fast, Sarah. You're losing control over him. Slow him down."

Jessica pulled a stopwatch from her pocket and returned her binoculars to her eyes. She clicked the watch as Sarah left the chevrons and headed toward a double ski jump. Rampage rushed the first jump, and Sarah struggled to slow him for the more dramatic drop on the second jump. Rampage shook his head at her pressure, but sailed over the second jump while maintaining perfect balance.

"He's giving her a really hard time," Jessica said, "but she's hanging in there with him."

The wind picked up, swaying the trees as Jessica tracked her binoculars ahead of the horse and rider. Christ, the water jump. Rampage continued to shake his head as Sarah worked to slow him down. Rain began to pelt down and thunder rumbled as they approached the jump. Oh, God. It was happening again.

"No!" Jessica screamed as Rampage slipped when he launched his body over the jump. Flipping sideways, he landed heavily on his side in the water. Sarah was pitched clear of the horse. They all stood frozen, heedless of the rain pelting them.

"This can't be happening again," Jessica moaned before turning and limping as fast as her crutches could carry her toward the truck.

Skyler caught her and held her tight in her arms. "Jess, baby, hold on a minute," she pleaded.

They all held their breath as Sarah rolled, then sprang to her feet. Rampage also struggled up and shook the water from his coat like a big dog before looking for his rider.

"They're both up and okay," Kate called out.

Sarah quickly led him to a spot where she was standing uphill from the horse and launched herself back into the saddle. A quick pat on the stallion's neck and the two were off again. Everyone breathed a collective sigh of relief. Skyler watched the big bay's progress closely for lameness. The downpour was brief and already had subsided to a sprinkle.

Jessica sniffled, her face still buried in Skyler's shoulder.

"Jess, baby, look. They're okay. Sarah is finishing the

course." Skyler rubbed her lover's back with one hand while she held her binoculars with the other.

"I can't look," Jessica mumbled. "You watch for me."

Skyler placed a soft kiss on her forehead and gave her a running report of Rampage's progress. "They're over the solid wall, taking the hedges with room to spare. Sarah really is pushing it to make up their lost time. God, Jess, Rampage is flying. That's it. They're home free."

Jessica sniffed, clinging to her. "I'm sorry. I just keep hearing Racer scream and seeing that bone sticking out of his leg. I can't even describe how bad my own leg hurt. It's probably a good thing that I can't jump horses anymore. I think that accident will haunt me forever."

Skyler brushed Jessica's dark locks back from her face. "And I will always be here to help chase that bad memory away. We'll replace it with lots of good memories," Skyler promised. "Come on. Let's go see Rampage and Sarah."

Sarah's face glowed as she recounted the incredible recovery at the water jump. "Damn that rain," she griped. "We would have been in first place if we hadn't slipped on those wet rocks."

They all turned as Matt trotted into the barn. "Well, all the scores are in. That fall really cost you, Sarah, but you are still only a tenth of a point behind third place."

"Nature of the game, my dear," Kate drawled. "The good news is that you are in fine striking distance. A clean performance in the show jumping and you should be back among the top three leaders."

"Let's celebrate," Matt crowed. The top three were assured places on the Olympic team.

The women all smiled at his enthusiasm.

"Not so fast," Skyler said. "Tomorrow is the biggest test.

We have to make sure Rampage doesn't stock up after today's workout and be too stiff to jump well tomorrow."

"That's why they show jump on the last day, hon," Sarah explained to her enthusiastic husband. "The cross-country actually has more difficult jumps, but the test is to see if your horse is in good enough shape to complete the cross-country and still be limber enough to do precision jumping the next day."

"I'm going to be earning my pay tonight," Skyler said. "We need to walk him and rub his legs down every four hours to keep him from getting stiff."

Kate grinned. "We've got several hours before he needs another rubdown. Let's all go somewhere to eat. Then, we'll split the shifts." She reeled off the assignments, leaving her own name off the list. She needed her sleep.

"What about you, horse co-owner?" Laura teased.

Kate straightened up to her full height. "Because I'm the senior member, meaning I'm too old to be rubbing down horses," Kate whispered in Laura's ear. "And it's not a horse I want to be rubbing my hands on tonight."

Kate's comment had been too softly spoken for the others to hear, but Jessica didn't miss her mother's blush. "I'm not sure I like this, Kate. You're planning to snuggle in with my mother while you send my bed warmer into the cold night to rub a horse down?"

"Don't forget, dear, I pay her salary." Kate winked at Skyler. "After all these years, I've finally found a good use for the Parker millions."

"Sky, a little help here?" Jessica requested as she heard Skyler spit out her toothpaste and rinse her mouth in the next room. "My knee is too sore to bend enough to get my pants the rest of the way off."

Skyler strode into the room, wiping her mouth on a thick white hand towel. The sight before her made her legs feel weak. She eyed the dark-haired beauty lying on the bed with her chest bare and her jeans pulled halfway down her hips. The half-lidded, blue eyes twinkled at her under long dark eyelashes.

Oh, yeah. This was an ambush, all right.

Mustering her sexiest smile, she leaned down to kiss her lover's full lips. "I guess if I get to undress you each night, there are some definite advantages to this whole knee surgery thing." Skyler burned a hot trail of kisses down Jessica's taut stomach, down her thighs, and down her calves as she tugged her lover's jeans the rest of the way off. She stopped to kiss the bandaged knee on her journey back up, then nuzzled Jessica's soft breasts.

"Oh, sweetie. I missed your touch so much these past few nights," Jessica moaned.

Skyler lifted her head from the nipple she was teasing. "I didn't think you were up for making love, with everything that has happened. It seems very selfish for me to ask, but I just can't keep my hands off of you any longer."

"You know, my knee may be hurt, but the other parts of me are working fine." Jessica smiled as she discarded the T-shirt Skyler had planned to sleep in. The underwear came off next.

Jessica rolled onto her side, laying her injured leg straight and bending her other leg to balance herself. She pulled Skyler down to the bed and pressed her over onto her back. "Please let me," she urged softly as Skyler moved to regain her dominant position.

Her lover had lost a lot in the past week, Skyler realized, control of her career, control of her horse. And there was nothing she would deny those beautiful eyes now darkened with lust and longing. So, in answer to her love's request, Skyler settled back and took the smaller hand in her long fingers, leading it to the moist blond curls between her legs. Jessica leaned over to kiss, lick, then suck at Skyler's neck and the breasts that arched up to receive her mouth. She dipped her fingers into the dripping, hot folds and slowly stoked the fire of Skyler's sex.

"I want to feel you inside me," Skyler moaned.

Jessica plunged two fingers into the hot canal, but withdrew as she sensed Skyler's climax building.

"Please, Jess," Skyler begged for release.

"Not yet, babe," Jessica purred. "Flip over for me." She ran her hands, then her lips over Skyler's graceful neck and smoothly muscled back. She rested her cheek on Skyler's warm, taut buttock before teasing the sensitive flesh with a series of nips and kisses. She reached between her lover's legs again and entered her again with her thumb, while her fingers stroked the hard clit as she thrust with a steady stroke. Skyler moaned and the sound increased Jessica's own ache to a throb.

"Oh, baby, don't stop!" Skyler gasped out.

"Let me slide under you," Jessica demanded, pushing Skyler onto her knees.

It only took a split second for Skyler to see the advantage of this new position. She straddled Jessica's head, and then buried her face in the raven curls to draw Jessica's stiff clitoris into her warm mouth.

They stroked and sucked and cried out together as their pleasure peaked and hard orgasms washed over them. A light sheen of sweat covered their bodies as they clung to each other and kissed away the sweet nectar of each other's climax. Skyler lay lightly upon Jessica, resting most of her weight still on her knees and elbows. Jessica stroked the back of Skyler's muscled thighs. She loved the musky smell of her lover and the ownership she felt over this incredibly sexy woman.

Skyler gathered Jessica's entire body in her arms to rest her on the disarray of pillows. "I love you, Jess," she whispered reverently. Pulling the blanket up over them, she settled back with Jessica's dark head resting in the well of her shoulder.

Jessica stretched a protective arm across Skyler's waist and drew her good leg up across Skyler's. The heat of her lover's body warmed her through to the core of her very soul. "I love *you*, Sky. So much," she murmured.

Chapter Eighteen

Saturday's clouds had long since blown out to the North Carolina coast, leaving a crisp blue sky overhead. Jessica watched nervously as Skyler tacked Rampage up for the final competition. "Shorten that strap on the martingale," she instructed. "Maybe the saddle should slide up another inch."

Skyler stopped and turned slowly to her backseat driver. "Jess, how many years have I been saddling horses?"

"I know. It's a little harder than I thought it would be to watch someone else ride him, especially in the show jumping. I don't know why the show jumping is different, maybe because it's my favorite." Tears filled Jessica's eyes. "I wanted so badly to be taking him in that ring myself."

Skyler pulled her into a protective embrace. "I know, baby. But this is a very selfless thing you're doing. You've made me and everybody else in our little family very proud."

Jamie came running, breathless, into the barn. "Rampage is next on deck!"

Skyler unhooked Rampage from the crossties and led the stallion forward.

Sarah straightened her red riding jacket and brushed the barn dust from her polished boots. "Leg up?" she requested when she was ready.

Matt stepped forward quickly. "I'll do it. I'm learning a

few things around this place." He lifted his wife into the saddle. "Break a leg?"

Skyler snorted, and then whispered something in his ear. He grinned.

"Ride well and be safe," he offered to his smiling wife.

Sarah steered Rampage to the warm-up area to loosen his muscles.

Waiting for them at the entrance to the arena, Kate gave her a quick lay-of-the-land. "This is a tough course, Sarah. The leader pulled two faults, slow time and one rail down. His horse wasn't in a very good mood and fought him a lot. The woman second in the standings is the only one so far to make a clean run, and the woman holding third dropped a rail on the vertical jump. Run it clean and you've got a spot on the team."

Sarah adjusted the chinstrap on her helmet. Her smile was gone, replaced by an expression of intense focus. *Like a bronco rider getting ready to signal for an open gate,* Kate thought.

Rampage snorted and shifted his feet as they waited.

"Okay, love," Sarah crooned to the ears that flicked back and forth at the sound of her voice. "This is it. This is what you and Jess have been working for. You're the best, and we're going to show them that."

When Skyler and Kate joined the others in the Parker box at the indoor arena, Jessica pulled Skyler down into the chair and clung to her arm. Skyler winked at Jamie, who was sitting next to Tory, almost bouncing at the excitement of the moment. Laura sat between Kate and Matt, clutching each of their hands as they watched the officials replace a rail knocked down by the last rider.

Sarah was up next.

Getting the go-ahead from the judges, she turned Rampage in a large circle before trotting him into the ring and activating the electric eye of the timer. He cantered with the relaxed ease of a Sunday stroll. The crowd held its collective breath as he sailed over the first jump, neatly tucking his feet and landing softly on the other side.

This course had seventeen jumps. Just sixteen more to go. They sailed over the oxers. The triple bar was barely a ripple in their pace. And they cleared the wall jump without even a slight hesitation.

"Look at their time," Jessica breathed. "They're on a perfect pace."

The crowd tensed again as the pair approached the combination, but Rampage made the shift to shorten his stride between the closely placed fences with little effort. The television cameras followed their progress as the announcer quickly shuffled through his papers to find the background commentary on this emerging star.

Sarah urged the big bay to quicken his pace as he approached the vertical jump. Standing five feet and six inches high, it was one of the most difficult for a horse to jump. Rampage's muscles bulged as he gathered to launch himself over the top rail. He neatly tucked his feet and cleared it with at least three inches to spare. A hushed murmur rippled across the crowd, all well schooled in the need to remain quiet until the competitor finished the course.

Two difficult jumps left to go.

The water jump on a show course was tough because horse and rider must clear the water on the other side of the jump rather than land in it. This course's water jump had been placed between two vertical jumps, so the competitor had to leap vertically, then horizontally over the water, then vertically once more. This final series of jumps was where most competitors were racking up their faults.

Sarah leaned forward expertly over Rampage's neck, encouraging him to stretch out over the water jump rather than jump more vertically. The stallion landed clean, neatly clearing the water.

The television announcer narrated quietly into his microphone. "One last jump, and the crowd is holding its breath. This is an amazing stallion that Sarah Tate is riding today. An advanced dressage horse who loves to jump according to his trainer, former gold medalist Skyler Reese. A clean round ensures Tate a place on the Olympic team… They're up. Look at that horse jump. Wait, his back foot touched that top rail. It's vibrating…No, it's not going to fall!"

The crowd's applause was deafening in the indoor arena. The Parker box was jubilant.

"We did it." Jessica couldn't stop crying. With one dream shattered, she'd awakened to another. And, strangely, everything felt right, as if it were meant to be.

Skyler grinned as she wiped away the tears of joy that ran down Jessica's cheeks. They kissed and waved at Sarah.

Jamie was the only one with the presence of mind to jump from the box and run to greet Sarah and Rampage as they exited the arena.

The rest was a blur. The television crew gathered Kate, Skyler, Jessica, and Sarah together for a final interview, threading together a storybook tale from Jessica's injury problems to Sarah's last-minute substitution. Cameras followed Rampage to a small outdoor paddock where he was unsaddled and rubbed down before being turned loose to prance and shake his head for an admiring crowd.

Sarah was still beaming and singing Rampage's praises when the group gathered at her house later that evening for a celebratory cookout. She chatted endlessly about which mares she would select to breed to the bay stallion after the Olympics while Matt barbecued his famous ribs over a slow fire.

It didn't seem to bother him that he was the only male present at the party, and the women had long since decided they definitely liked the easy-going man. He sipped his beer and explained to Jamie the secrets of barbecuing ribs while letting her flip them for him.

Jessica sat with her injured leg propped in Skyler's lap. Always enjoying any contact with her beautiful lover, Skyler absently performed a gentle massage along Jessica's thigh and calf.

They all joined in the laughter as Kate recounted her visit to the showground's clubhouse right after the trials' conclusion. "I've got at least ten checks in my pocket for the Youth Equestrian Program," she chortled. "That will teach those bluebloods to bet against Kate Parker."

"Bluebloods? What do you think *you* are, Ms. Parker?" Laura teased.

"My daddy swore there must have been a blue collar in my mother's bloodlines to produce a loud-mouthed tomboy daughter like me." Kate laughed. "Mother said it was from his side of the family marrying too close." Her story was nowhere close to the truth. Both of her parents had adored Kate and lavished her with love.

After filling themselves with beer and ribs, the group was tired and pleasantly reflective. It was Jessica who put a voice to all of their thoughts. "So where do we go from here?"

Sarah smiled at Matt. "Well, I can tell you that my life for the next few years is well mapped." She slid her hand into his and laced their fingers together. "After Rampage and I win a gold medal, Matt and I are going to concentrate on starting a family. We love kids, and having Jamie around this week has made us realize our biological clocks are ticking. When I'm pregnant, I hope to be taking care of a top mare or two carrying a Rampage baby."

Skyler held Sarah's gaze for a moment. "I think you guys will be excellent parents," she said. "I'm very happy for you, Sarah." Jessica squeezed her arm to let her know she had said just the right thing.

Taking the opening in the conversation, Kate cleared her throat.

"Well, I guess this is as good a time as any to tell you guys what Laura and I are planning."

"You and Mom?" Jessica frowned slightly.

"That's right," replied Laura, reaching for Kate's hand and pulling it into her lap. "We've stupidly wasted too many years apart and have quite a bit of catching up to do." Adoration shone from her eyes as she gave Kate a slight nod to go ahead and reveal their plans.

"We both want to do a little traveling," Kate said. "Up until recent years, Laura has been busy raising a daughter and running a public relations firm. And I've been running an equestrian center. It's time we did something for ourselves."

"What about the center?" Skyler asked, incredulous that Kate would be leaving Cherokee Falls.

"Well, what I'd like to do is turn the operation of the farm over to you two. Jess can be the farm manager, and you can run the Youth Equestrian Program," Kate explained. "I know you have some ideas for expanding the program to more kids. You guys could move into my house. Do what you want to with it. It will be Jess's house anyway when I'm not around anymore." She raised a hand to forestall Jessica's protest.

"When we come back from Europe, we may settle in a house at the beach," Laura said.

"We'd just spend several months a year at Cherokee Falls," Kate added. "I don't mean to put you on the spot. Talk it over and tell me what you think later, if you want."

"There's nothing to discuss," Skyler said after checking in with Jessica. "There's nothing else we'd rather do."

Kate whooped. "Then it's settled." She gave Laura a big kiss. "We're packing our bags for Italy, sweetie."

Jamie jumped up and gave Jessica and Skyler each a hug. "That's so cool, you guys."

"What about you, Jamie?" Matt teased. "Who was that cute stable boy I saw hanging around you yesterday?"

"Ugh. That was Tommy. I like horses, not boys." Jamie wrinkled her nose.

"That will change soon enough." Skyler laughed. "In the meantime, I've got plans for you, Jamie. You're going to be the next professional rider I train to represent Cherokee Falls. I'm thinking the Junior Olympics would be a good goal."

The girl's eyes shone. "Really, Sky? Really? I'll work hard every day."

"Really, Jamie. It was Jess's idea. She likes your riding form, and thinks she can make an event rider out of you."

"This is the best night of my life!" Jamie exclaimed.

Skyler entwined her fingers with Jessica's and gazed affectionately into her lover's shining eyes. "I think there are going to be a lot of best nights waiting for all of us."

About the Author

Jackson Leigh grew up barefoot and happy, swimming in farm ponds and riding rude ponies in rural south Georgia. Her love of reading was nurtured early on by her grandmother, who patiently taught her to work *New York Times* crossword puzzles in the daily paper, and by her mother, who stretched the slim family budget to bring home grocery-store copies of Trixie Belden mysteries and Bobbsey Twins adventures that Jackson would sit up all night reading. It was her passion for writing that led her quite accidentally to a career in journalism, and North Carolina, where she now feeds nightly off the adrenaline rush of breaking news and close deadlines. She shares her life with her wonderful partner, a very wise Jack Russell terrier, and "the cat" that made herself at home when Jackson and the JRT weren't watchful.

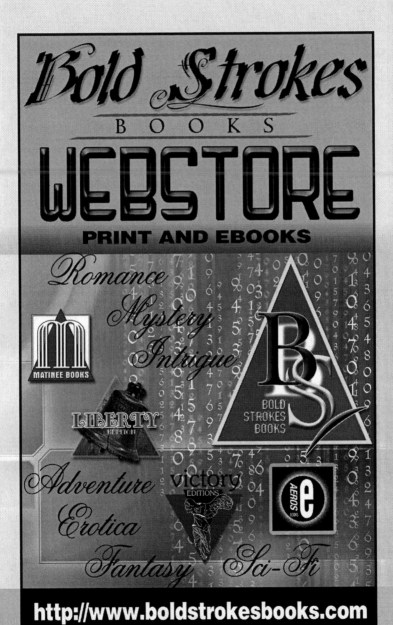